LAST FLIGHT

A NOVEL

LAST FLIGHT

By Tom Chase

to Denis —
In appreciation of your taking the
time to peruse — and I hope
enjoy — my little book.

Tom Chase
August, 2003

PETER E. RANDALL PUBLISHER
Portsmouth, New Hampshire
2003

© 2003 by Tom Chase
Printed in the United States of America

Cover design: Grace Peirce
Cover photo composite: Peter E. Randall, Grace Peirce
Text design: Deidre Randall

Peter E. Randall Publisher
Box 4726, Portsmouth, NH 03802
www.PERPublisher.com

Distributed by University Press of New England
        Hanover and London

ISBN: 1-931807-13-2

        Library of Congress Control Number:
                2003092043

"I have lifted my plane . . . for a thousand flights and I have never felt her wheels glide from the earth without knowing the uncertainty and the exhilaration of firstborn adventure."

—Beryl Markham, *West with the Night*

To Lorie, for her encouragement, patience, and gentle humor.

Acknowledgments

I wish to thank the astronomer John Gianforte for providing a wealth of information on the night sky, and my son Mark for supplying details about modern navigation systems. I also wish to acknowledge the contributions of pilots, both civilian and military, and other crew members who constantly take to the air, and whose daily courage and professionalism receive scant recognition.

I also wish to acknowledge the generous assistance of Peter Randall, Deidre Randall, Grace Peirce, Doris Troy, and Lory Pratt, in preparing this novel for publication.

CHAPTER ONE

PREPARATIONS

Rob Robertson slowly roused from his hour-long nap. He felt oddly unnerved; he'd been sleeping deeply, and it took a few moments to return to reality, to realize he'd had a troubling dream. Usually his dreams faded quickly, but as he dozed the nightmarish scene persisted. He was standing before a broad, cluttered desk in a richly paneled office. A thin, sallow-faced man with a dark goatee and beaked nose reclined in a leather-upholstered swivel chair, his polished black shoes propped on the desk. Behind him, a large television screen showed a city's jagged skyline where, in the distance, orange flames and black smoke billowed angrily from twin skyscrapers.

The man had glared at him, then snarled, "Out'a here, flyboy!" He bore the unmistakable voice and visage of Frank Yeganeh, one of the richest men in America, the tyrannical owner of Trans Globe Airlines. Rob, speechless, pointed at the horrific televised scene, but the screechy voice continued. "You hard of hearing? You're finished. Kaput!" Yeganeh leaned forward, extended a bony finger to jab a button that set off a jangling alarm. "You're too goddamned old!"

The steady jingle of the windup alarm clock jerked Rob awake. Gradually assimilating the comfortable familiarity of his bedroom, softly illuminated by the golden rays of the afternoon sun slanting through curtained windows, and with a sigh of relief, he realized that only a dream had sullied his customary snooze before embarking on a long overnight flight. A dream, except that no person—especially an airline pilot—could ever forget that tragic day just two months ago. His eyes focused on the clock. The hands indicated four in the afternoon; the alarm continued its insistent ringing.

Alongside the bed, a big furry dog lay curled on the braided rug. She raised her head, eyed Rob, who had still not budged, and barked a gentle *woof*.

"Just testing your hearing, Nell," Rob retorted as he switched off the alarm, then reached down to scratch the dog's head. Her thick, coppery-colored coat blended to a grizzled white around the eyes and muzzle, lending a wise and matronly look appropriate to her advanced age. "Darn! Maybe a man *is* over the hill when he dreams about his boss instead of some beautiful lady—okay, or golden retriever." He patted her again, yawned, stretched his arms. "But I still have to work the red-eye tonight, one last time."

In four hours the veteran pilot would settle into the cockpit of a giant Starliner aircraft to command Trans Globe Flight 810 from Boston to Paris. The return flight, following a twenty-seven-hour layover in the French capital, would be his last Atlantic crossing before mandatory retirement at age sixty.

Rob tossed back the quilt of muted blue and brown squares, said affectionately, "You sure take up a lot of space, Nell," then swung his legs wide to reach an unoccupied corner of the rug. He might have more easily slipped out the other side of the bed, but that had been Jane's side, and his routine had not changed since the accident that had taken her life.

Wearing the blue boxer shorts he'd slept in, he fluffed the pillow, smoothed the covers, then retrieved his black, soft-sided suitcase from the closet and set it on the bed.

The suitcase had a built-in frame with a retractable handle and small wheels. For years Rob had resisted buying this type of luggage, thinking it somehow looked unprofessional for an airline captain to stride through the terminal pulling these so-called wheelies. But finally he'd examined one, discovered it was remarkably light yet plenty sturdy, had useful compartments, and even had straps for attaching his heavy flight kit so that it could ride along, too. After he'd used it for a few weeks, his lower back, naggingly troublesome for years, improved dramatically.

Rob picked up the remote control and thumbed the power button to activate a small television perched atop the maple dresser. Alongside it rested an opaline vase, his gift to Jane, and an olive drab model airplane, an uncle's boyhood gift to him. He selected the Weather Channel, concerned about an unseasonably late hurricane, given the designation "Pauline." Earlier in the week, the powerful storm had brushed the Leeward Islands in the Caribbean before swinging northeasterly, away from the Florida coastline.

A comely, dark-haired woman appeared on the screen and announced that, according to the National Hurricane Center, Pauline's winds had decreased to less than seventy-five miles per hour, meaning the hurricane had been officially downgraded to a tropical storm. A satellite photo showed Pauline's present location, hundreds of miles east of the Carolinas, and gradually losing energy over the colder ocean. Rob studied the image intently for several seconds as the woman projected the storm's likely path. New England would be spared its heavy rains and strong winds, she explained, but the downgraded storm would threaten the Canadian Maritimes in two days. Rob was relieved that Pauline was still too far south to affect tonight's flight, and would pass too far east to cause problems at home while he was away. However, if the storm behaved as predicted, the return flight on Sunday might require a lengthy, circuitous route. "No need to worry about that now, Nell. One day at a time in this business, right?"

Keeping an eye on the television while moving quickly in an oft-repeated routine, Rob packed the usual things: three sets of clean socks and underwear, and a white uniform shirt, unstarched but neatly pressed, for the return flight. For the layover he added a button-down shirt, necktie, slacks, and his favorite tweed sport coat. In European cities, particularly Paris, most people dressed neatly, and Rob respected that convention. He remembered strolling through the Luxembourg Gardens on a summer afternoon and noticing a raucous group of high school-age girls, sloppily dressed in stained baggy sweatshirts and ragged jeans. Loud voices confirmed their nationality—American.

One of the suitcase's small zippered pockets contained the Berlitz *French for Travelers,* a well-thumbed Michelin map of Paris, and a half-read paperback copy of Neville Shute's *The Rainbow and the Rose,* holdovers from his previous trip. "If there's one thing I've learned," he mumbled aloud, "it's how to pack a suitcase. Maybe I should give lessons." The dog twitched an ear, then returned to her peaceful slumber. She seemed to understand what the packing meant.

After a deluge of commercials, the meteorologist returned to the screen to summarize the international weather. "Europe will be lovely tomorrow," she said, pointing out a dome of high pressure centered over Belgium while noting the mild temperatures. And perfect for one last jog along the Seine, Rob decided, switching off the TV, then stuffing running shoes, shorts, athletic socks, a pale blue T-shirt (bearing the legend DOWNHOME 10K), and a lightweight running suit into a separate compartment of the suitcase.

"This is it, Nell, my final trip for old Trans Globe." He silently reminisced . . . *thirty-seven years of flying airplanes . . . a lifetime of association with fellow pilots . . . the congenial company of flight attendants . . . being responsible for the lives of hundreds of thousands of people . . . and in a couple of days it'll be over, just like that*—he snapped his fingers, bringing another twitch of Nellie's ear—*because I'll be too damned old!* He remembered the dream and thought, yes, maybe Yeganeh was right.

"Yep, Nell, over to Paris tonight and home on Sunday, and I'm done. Bet you'll like that." Her tail flicked in apparent agreement. "Where'd the years go? Just think, in three days I'll be sixty." He winced, knowing precisely what that meant—he'd be officially obsolete. By federal law, on that day he would no longer be permitted to do the thing he did best: to fly as the captain of a jet airliner. Decades ago, the Federal Aviation Administration had decreed that he, like all other pilots, must surrender his cherished ATP, his Airline Transport Pilot license, upon reaching that age.

When the so-called age-sixty rule first became federal law, Rob—a Trans Globe "new hire" at the time—had welcomed the idea. Airline advancement, and choice of flights, was based on seniority. This rule would hasten the retirement of Trans Globe's most senior fliers, he had reasoned, and ensure that he would keep moving up, in pay and prestige, from flight engineer to first officer and, eventually, to captain. But now, this instant, he didn't feel ready to be put out to pasture like some aged draft horse, to be unceremoniously shoved off the top rung of the seniority ladder it had taken more than three decades to scale. Admittedly, he needed reading glasses for the diabolically fine print on navigation charts. Sure, there had been some top-range hearing loss from being exposed to jet engine noise all his grown life. And . . . "Ah, heck, Nell. Maybe they're right. Maybe I *am* too old for this job."

Rob looked closer to fifty than nearly sixty, despite a mat of chalk white chest hair. An erect bearing and broad shoulders capping a surprisingly youthful body made him seem taller than his medium height, and his waistline had enlarged only three—all right, four—inches since college days. Sandy gray, thin-on-top hair and an unruly fringe of silvery sideburns framed a cockpit- and farm-tanned face. Crow's-feet wrinkles in the corners of his eyes attested to twenty-seven thousand hours—more than three years of his life—spent aloft.

The ring of the telephone on the bedside table interrupted his reverie. "Hello," he said, truly hoping it was not Crew Scheduling calling to say that his flight had been canceled.

"Rob. It's Harriet Brown. I've just been chatting with Chief Knowles and he said you told him you're leaving the fire department because you were, well, at that age, which just doesn't seem possible to me and that you told him you had to retire from flying, too, and I just can't believe it because you still look so, well, so . . ."

Rob took advantage of her rare loss for words. "Yep, it's true." Harriet, fifty-something, widowed several years, was the longtime assistant town clerk. She knew everyone, and everything that happened, in the tiny township of Deerwood, New Hampshire. Rupert Knowles was the staunch, taciturn chief of the twelve-man Deerwood Volunteer Fire Department—and unofficial men's club, according to some residents. "Oddly enough, both our fire department and the Federal Aviation Administration require that one quit at age sixty. Heck, I'm too old to be climbing ladders to rescue damsels in distress, and besides, I've done my civic duty."

"Well, I don't know what they'll do without you and . . ."

"They'll do just fine," Rob insisted, not sure if she meant the airline or the fire department. In any event, there were very few incidents in Deerwood. Most call outs were for motor vehicle mishaps, chimney fires caused by creosote buildup from wood-burning stoves, and malfunctioning alarm systems in some of those pretentious new homes in town. He could recall only one actual house fire, the old Crawford place, which had burned to the ground. "Can't talk right now. I'm getting ready to head for the airport."

"Where are you flying to? Someplace romantic, I bet."

"Well, Paris, but . . ."

"With all those pretty young stewardesses? I'm so jealous!"

"Harriet, most flight attendants nowadays are married and have families." Rob winced, realizing she might interpret his remark as a sign of encouragement. He never knew quite what to say to Harriet. She had been his high school sweetheart, briefly, and he still liked her in a genial, small-town way. She was attractive despite her bountiful charms, but he had no intention of . . .

"Couldn't you take me along, Rob? Don't they give you free passes? I could be ready in an hour. I'd just love to have *you* show me Paris, and don't forget, I can be lots of fun." She giggled louder than necessary. "Bet you remember my senior prom." Quickly changing her tone, she added in mock self-admonishment, "Oh my goodness, I shouldn't say such things!"

"Passes are for family members only, Harriet. Sorry. You'd need a ticket, and a passport, and a French visa—no, not a visa."

"Well, we really should get together. I know! I'll throw a party— a nice retirement party for you, and we'll have it at my big, old, empty house, and I'll invite all the firemen and the historical society, oh, and the quilting . . ."

"Really, I can't talk right now."

"Oh, Rob. You're always just leaving for someplace. All right, keep playing hard to get, but you can't mourn forever, and none of us is getting any younger. Bye-bye."

"You're right about that," Rob muttered to himself as he set down the telephone. He glanced at the dog, wondering if her age-related infirmities provided an inkling of what lay in store for him. "What's that formula, Nell? One dog year equals seven for people? Hmm. . . . Seven times fourteen makes you about eighty-four. By golly, you've earned the right to take life easy."

In the adjoining bathroom Rob shaved, reminded by the mirror image of the age spots on his hands, then stepped into the shower. As the hot water rained down, he contemplated how life would be lonelier without the companionship of airline friends. No one had filled the void, the lingering emptiness, and he certainly was not getting any younger. He loved this old house and farm, but maybe he should turn over everything to the Corrados, the couple who'd been in his employ for so long, and move to the Sun Belt like so many other retirees.

He thought about Jane. Rob, an only child and a late-in-life surprise for his parents, had met her the summer before his senior year in college when he'd worked as a waiter at an upscale restaurant on Cape Cod, where her wealthy parents had a summer home. Following a mostly long-distance courtship, they'd married two weeks after he finished Air Force pilot training. Upon completing five years of military service—the last twelve long months in Vietnam—he had immediately been hired by Trans Globe, at the time one of the world's premier airlines. He'd been assigned to the Boston domicile, and as soon as they could afford it they had bought a house on Massachusetts's fashionable North Shore. Soon Jane had become pregnant; he pictured her grown large with child, recalled how they had anticipated the momentous day. And the bitter disappointment that followed.

However, after Rob's father died, and with the homestead too much for his mother to manage alone, Rob and Jane had sold their suburban home and moved into the old farmhouse.

But the homestead life was not for Jane. She'd grown restless in the quiet village, and yearned for the bustle of the suburbs. "Surely, dear," she accosted a startled Rob before resuming her membership in the Rolling Hills Golf and Tennis Club, "you don't expect me to sit around and braid rugs with the town gossips all day."

At first Jane had played only golf, but later tennis became her favorite pastime. She took lessons from the pro, and although her self-described "pleasingly plump" physique caused her to be a bit slow on the court, she compensated by hitting the ball quite hard and accurately. And often. There were various leagues and ladders, and occasional weekend tournaments. In winter and during inclement weather, bridge replaced golf, and tennis switched to the indoor courts. Rolling Hills was an active place.

And those were busy years for the airlines. Trans Globe had expanded dramatically, and Rob quickly advanced from flight engineer to first officer, and from 727s to 707s. In only six years he'd been awarded a JFK captain bid.

Why, he wondered, reaching for the soap, in these fifteen years since her death, had he avoided women? He'd met any number of attractive flight attendants with whom he'd shared cockpit laughs and layover dinners, certainly, and several who had shown interest, but he resisted becoming involved. Was he afraid? Admit it, he told himself. And he saw his prospects growing slimmer.

But wouldn't life be richer with a woman—no, not Harriet—in his life? Someone special, someone to fill the emptiness, to share the future with, someone like . . . And he recalled, yet again, a layover in Athens, years ago . . . Visiting the Acropolis with a slender young flight attendant who frolicked nimbly over those ancient marble steps, her long, flaxen hair shimmering in the bright sunshine . . .

Sixty! Why had he put off thinking about retirement? What about this farm? It had been a subsistence farm for his parents. They had grown hay and vegetables, kept a cow and a few chickens, cut firewood, led a nearly self-sufficient existence here. Rob had grown up in this house, as a boy had performed the multifarious country chores.

The Corrados came soon after he and Jane had moved back to this old homestead—Isabella to care for Rob's mother in her final years and to relieve Jane of the household duties, Alejo as a part-time "hired man" to assist with the farm. Rob purchased the bungalow next door and had it renovated into a pleasant home for the Cuban family.

Alejo, a sinewy, industrious man, also drove the Deerwood school bus. In summer, and on weekends during spring and fall, he operated a small fishing boat out of nearby Chester Harbor. Their daughter, Carmina, attended community college; son Pedro, a high school student, cared for Nellie whenever Rob was away.

Rob wanted to continue the farm life, but to accommodate his busy flying schedule, he settled on being a "gentleman farmer," with Christmas trees his specialty. Christmas trees would not require extensive, day-to-day attention, but should provide some useful supplemental income for a then low-seniority airline pilot, a job constantly subject to work and pay stoppages because of employee strikes or furloughs wrought by economic downturns. He and Alejo planted and nurtured thousands of balsam and Fraser fir seedlings in the dormant hayfields.

Rob had envisioned a blissful, bucolic existence. Deerwood was small, uncluttered, a place where one might imagine oneself in the nineteenth century rather than the twenty-first. To him, both the old house and the physical work in the fields provided a soothing respite from the demanding routine of airline flying. But it had surprised and disappointed him that Jane found life less idyllic in the somnolent community. Once she blurted out, "This town—and half the people in it—bores me to tears," and similarly disparaging comments often escaped her lips.

Realizing that he was dawdling, Rob stepped out of the shower and quickly toweled off. As he dressed he chuckled at how little the pilots' uniforms had changed in his thirty-two years with Trans Globe. Materials had improved, coat lapels and neckties had alternately widened and narrowed as changing fashions dictated, and trouser cuffs and pleats had come and quickly gone, thank goodness, but the black color and single-breasted jacket style endured, along with the simple gold-braid stripes at the end of each sleeve to denote cockpit status: four stripes for captain; first officer, three; flight engineer, two. He donned a short-sleeved shirt with little shoulder straps to which he'd attached black epaulets, also bearing four gold stripes. He slipped a mechanical pencil and ballpoint pen into a slot in the flap above the left breast pocket; the other contained a Pocket Reference Card with technical data for the Starliner aircraft such as fuel tank capacities, operating weights, and engine limits. On the back of the card Rob had listed telephone numbers of operations offices and other departments at several Trans Globe stations.

Rob headed for the kitchen, followed by the dog, whose arthritic hips slowed her pace. He opened the refrigerator, grimly eyed its contents, settled on a small bowl of leftover macaroni and cheese, and heated it in the microwave. Nellie plunked down beside his chair, within easy reach for pats and dog treats.

He finished eating and quickly washed the few dishes, set them in the rack to dry, and called, "Come on, Nell, time to head next door." Rob led her outside, adjusting to her slowed gait as they walked the fifty yards across both lawns. He tapped on the Corrados' door.

"Come in," a woman's voice called. Rob held open the door for Nellie to enter the porch. Knowing the drill, the dog hobbled up the steps and circled her favorite rug before settling down on it.

Isabella, a gentle woman in her mid-forties, short and round with playful brown eyes, black hair, and skin like oiled mahogany, greeted Rob. Her long, loose-fitting cotton dress blazed with tropical colors.

Rob said, "Hi, Isabella. I just came to bring Nellie over."

"Come in, come in." Isabella motioned for him to follow her into the kitchen. "You like soup, *Capitán?*" Isabella asked, setting a bowl of hot soup and a mug of coffee on the table. When Rob was in uniform, headed for a flight, she invariably addressed him as *Capitán.*

Rob replied, "I just . . ." but the soup smelled irresistible. "You needn't have, but thanks." He sat down and sipped the coffee. "I just watched the Weather Channel—they say that hurricane's not headed this way."

"I no worry 'bout that—I feel in my bones when hurricane come."

"But the sea could get pretty rough; I hope Alejo won't take his boat out this weekend."

"I tell him." She paused. "So, tonight you fly 'cross ocean, *verdad?*"

"Yep. Be home day after tomorrow—Sunday afternoon. Around five." He lifted a spoonful of the spicy soup to his mouth. "Umm, this is good."

"Just vegetables and chicken with my sofrito seasoning. Then you fly 'way no more, *verdad?*"

"Yep, my very last trip. On Monday I officially retire."

"I am glad. Is too . . . What is word like *peligroso?*"

"You mean dangerous? Oh, not really." He knew full well that flying involved certain risks—especially now, with the constant threat of terrorism—but had long ago accepted risk as part of the bargain. Still, it seemed unlike Isabella to express such concern.

"Maybe this time you meet nice lady. You should, *Capitán*. You too long alone."

"In Paris? Hmm. . . . I suppose it's theoretically possible," Rob replied, chuckling as he remembered the lovely vision while he had showered, "but the chances are pretty slim. My French is lousy. No, it should be the usual exciting layover—I'll grab a few hours' sleep at the hotel, then go for a run, maybe play tourist later, and in the evening look for a good restaurant with some of the crew and hit the sack early. Same old routine. Not very romantic."

"No, I see pretty lady. Someone you know already. Don't be discouraged; you still young man. Yes, I leave nice dinner in your fridge, maybe my paella. Okay?"

He shrugged. "If you insist, but really . . ."

That settled, she changed the subject. "Pedro be home soon from *futbol* practice to take care of doggie." She shook her head. "I no understand this *futbol américano*. Not like in Cuba." Suddenly a frown clouded her brown face. "Alejo, he worry. He say, 'Will Rob need us if he no fly plane? If he no go away no more?' "

Rob jumped to his feet. "Need you? Goodness, haven't I said anything? I'm sorry. I've been so darned worried about retiring I haven't thought . . . ," he stammered, embarrassed by this oversight. "Heck, yes. Please stay on. I'll still need you both, and Pedro. That won't change." He patted the front of his shirt. "Well, maybe one thing. You won't have to iron these shirts anymore."

Her mood quickly brightened. "Good. I clean house tomorrow."

"Well, okay, if you think it needs it. Oh, and remind Alejo that on Tuesday we need to finish shearing those trees in the north field and then I'd like to start harvesting."

"I tell him. Christmas almost here."

Rob finished the soup and coffee, and thanked her again. They bade farewell. "We take good care of doggie," she said.

"Thanks, Isabella."

On the porch, Rob squatted down near eye level with Nellie, and gently stroked her head. "Good-bye, girl. Pedro will be here soon."

As Rob started across the lawn, Isabella called out, "I have paella all ready—just heat in micro." She held her hand over her heart. "I have a feeling, *Capitán*."

Back in his home, Rob briskly prepared to leave for the flight. He brushed his teeth—all his own except for a capped, slightly darker front tooth, the consequence of a high school football game, back before helmets had fancy faceguards—and made a couple of sweeps with a comb, more from habit than necessity. He carefully knotted but did not tighten his black necktie, and checked his wallet's cache of both dollars and francs. He ensured that the metal captain's wings were securely fastened to his uniform jacket and his union pin to the lapel, and that an inside pocket held his passport. He tucked the jacket and his captain's hat under his arm, grabbed the handle of his suitcase, and stepped out the back door.

In the manner of pilots everywhere, Rob paused to scan the skies. Honking one another encouragement, a gaggle of Canada geese—fifty or more—passed low overhead in near-perfect V-formation, heading southwesterly to warmer climes. Miles higher, barely audible but aimed in the same direction, a 747 etched sharp white contrails across the cloudless azure sky. "A fine day for flying," Rob said aloud, striding across the yard to the open shed attached to the side of the century-old red barn. A rake, shovel, hoe, and other implements hung in neat array on the far wall. Under the shed roof, aligned side by side, reposed a dust-caked, mid-sized John Deere tractor, a flatbed trailer with stake sides, various tractor attachments, and a riding lawn mower. Also Rob's forest green two-year-old Ford pickup and a pristine, burgundy '85 BMW 320i—Jane's car, and he suddenly pictured her blowing a kiss as she sped away for a tennis date at the club.

In another month he'd store this car in the barn for the long New Hampshire winter, safely away from the corrosive effects of snow, ice, and road salt, in favor of the sturdy pickup, but tonight the Beamer would make one last run to the airport.

Earlier in the day Rob had checked the car's tire pressure and various fluid levels—it burned a little oil, an inevitable legacy, perhaps, of Jane's vigorous driving style. He placed his hat and folded jacket on the passenger seat and hoisted his suitcase onto the floor in back of the driver's seat, slid behind the wheel, and fastened his seatbelt and shoulder harness. The engine fired up on the first try, and he began the hour-and-a-half drive to Boston's Logan International Airport.

CHAPTER TWO

PREFLIGHT

Rob accelerated the little BMW briskly through its gears. Its odometer registered 103,913 miles, but he maintained the car in topnotch condition. Once on the state highway, he inserted a cassette into the tape deck. A nasal male voice began, "Your passport, please, sir." A woman's voice followed with *"Votre passeport, s'il vous plaît, monsieur."* There was a pause during which Rob repeated the phrase, his Yankee twang no match for the woman's polished accent. "Here are my suitcases," the tape continued, *"Voici mes valises . . ."*

Approaching Boston, the increasingly hectic traffic reminded Rob of the standing airline joke about the most dangerous part of flying being the trip to and from the airport. His drive invariably began quite pleasantly, but as the congestion thickened near the bustling metropolis, there seemed to be a corresponding breakdown in courtesy, even human decency. He wondered sometimes if civilization was crumbling into complete and utter chaos. Then he'd remember peaceful Deerwood.

As the traffic grew heavier, Rob especially appreciated the BMW's nimbleness, responsive steering, and powerful brakes. The German car had been Jane's idea. He recalled the day she'd said, "We need a sporty car. Honestly, Rob, I feel like an old lady driving that clunky Ford to the club."

"Clunky? The Ford?" Rob rather liked their Ford Fairlane sedan. It had been very reliable, and besides, he'd always driven Fords—Jim Cynewski, his college roommate, owned the dealership over in Stansbury. "What would you want instead?" he'd asked.

"Marilyn Dunsmore has the most gorgeous Mercedes—silvery green." She rubbed her hand on his arm. "You're a *captain* now. Shouldn't we have a decent car, something appropriate to our status?"

"A Mercedes?" True, they could afford one, barely, but Rob was thinking that such an expensive, luxurious car would seem ostentatious in a community like Deerwood. Of course, he also wanted to please his wife.

"Don't you realize what an awful drive it is to the club? Over an hour each way?"

"Sure, but . . ."

"It's so embarrassing to park next to all those nicer cars."

Rob considered suggesting a Thunderbird, but knew she wouldn't like it. The early versions were sporty enough, but now they were huge, and much heavier. He thought for a moment. "Would you settle for a BMW? Not a big one, something like the 320i?"

"You're a dear," she'd replied, lightly kissing his cheek. "Burgundy would be lovely."

Rob had understood, of course. He was away from home, flying, half of every month. He wondered now why he hadn't sought to please Jane sooner with that car. Things might have been different.

A motorist's blaring horn—not directed at him, he hoped—made Rob realize that the tape had ended while his thoughts strayed. He ejected the cassette, which switched on the radio, and pressed the fourth of five buttons, each set to an FM station featuring classical music, arranged geographically, north to south, from the Maine PBS station to WCRB in Massachusetts. He appreciated having such choices, recalling layovers in several large, booming American cities with no classical music stations at all.

The announcer, caught in mid-sentence, said, " . . . emergency meeting of the U.N. Security Council, the Libyan ambassador called the incident a deliberate act of aggression. However, a spokes-woman at the Pentagon stated that the aircraft carrier *Farragut* was cruising in international waters in the Mediterranean Sea when it tracked an unidentified aircraft on a threatening course, and took defensive action. Once again the top story: Earlier today a Navy fighter plane reportedly shot down a Libyan Airways Skybus. There appear to be no survivors."

Rob felt a tingling at the back of his neck. He deliberately relaxed his grip on the steering wheel, but could not dismiss a vision of the fearful commotion inside the Skybus's cockpit as the pilots con-fronted the sudden emergency. He imagined the terror gripping the passengers as the plane began its steep plunge toward the sea. He knew also that deadly reprisals had followed similar events; some-times other airliners had been the quarry. Would planeloads of inno-cent people be the pawns in another round of merciless revenge? Would there be no end to this diabolical recipe for disaster, this steamy broth of religious fanaticism, wounded national pride, and vengeance? "This job isn't getting any easier," Rob muttered to him-self. "Maybe I should be glad it's my last trip for old Trans Globe."

It wasn't the first time a lone airliner had been destroyed over international waters for venturing too close to a Navy task force, Rob recalled. During the Gulf War a missile downed an Iranian A-300 over the Persian Gulf. Of course, since September 11 no potential threat could be ignored. Still, Rob wondered why the Mediterranean had become an *American* sea. Several times in recent years, on flights from Paris to Cairo or Tel Aviv, he'd observed U.S. Navy flotillas, easily identified by the formidable presence of a gigantic, canted-deck aircraft carrier.

The announcer continued, "Tropical storm Pauline is presently located five hundred miles east of Cape Hatteras, North Carolina, while continuing to move northeasterly. The storm is packing winds of sixty-five miles per hour but is forecast to remain well clear of the eastern seaboard, although heavy surf and strong riptides can be expected from Cape Hatteras to Eastport, Maine, for the next forty-eight hours. Now, some soothing music for our harried commuters, Mozart's Piano Sonata in C major, K.330, with Victor Kolinski and the Stuttgart Chamber Ensemble."

The harmonious notes seemed as sharp and crystal-clear as icicles on a bright winter morning.

At six twenty-five, Rob swung past a sign reading TRANS GLOBE AIRLINES, EMPLOYEE PARKING ONLY.

He located a vacant space, parked the BMW, climbed out, and stretched his arms wide. He tightened his necktie, donned his jacket and hat, checked that the car's lights and other switches were off and the windows closed before locking the door, then paused to look around. The sun had just set, pulling a brilliant red sunset behind it. Across the Inner Harbor, the skyscrapers of downtown Boston, their lights blinking awake like the stars now beginning to appear overhead, stood silhouetted against the glowing horizon. Carried by the breeze, an invisible cloud of exhaust fumes drifted by, the kerosene-like smell so utterly familiar that he barely noticed it. To the east, landing lights from arriving aircraft, strung out at equidistant intervals on the final approach path, hung like a sparkling necklace in the crisp air, while the deafening roar of departing jetliners shattered the space around him and shook the ground beneath his feet.

The realization that this four-decade chapter in the book of his life would soon end shook him as well, and for several moments he stood motionless, consumed by the scene. Then, remembering that he had a job to do, he strode to the crew bus waiting area, towing his suitcase by the handle.

The bus, a converted utility van, was painted white and embellished with Trans Globe Airlines' logo and distinctive triple red stripes. The door swung open as Rob approached. "Evening, John," he greeted the driver, a thickset man with graying hair who, Rob realized, had been with the airline as long as he could remember. "Don't tell me you're stuck on the night shift?"

"'Fraid so, Rob. Things sure have gone to hell around here with all this downsizing."

"That's for sure," Rob agreed, settling into one of the bench seats. "How'd the Bruins do last night?"

"Great! Beat the Devils in overtime." John was an avid sports fan. "They're heading for the playoffs this year." He had made the run to the terminal so many times he seemed to drive on autopilot, with his head swiveled toward Rob. "And how 'bout those Patriots? They started out terrible but now they're five and four. I was discouraged when the Sox had their September swoon, but now there's something to look forward to."

"You know what they say about the Sox, John—wait till next year."

"Yeah, maybe. So what d'ya think about that Arab airliner?"

"Sounds like a bad case of mistaken identity and an itchy trigger finger—usually a fatal combination."

"I don't know what to believe. Say, what's this I hear about you retiring?"

"Yep, it's true. Tonight's my last trip. Eight-ten to Charles de Gaulle, back on Sunday."

"You mean if that son-of-a-bitch Yeganeh didn't sell the route during your days off!"

Five chaotic years previously, with its stock hovering at an all-time low, corporate raider Frank Yeganeh had leveraged a junk-bond buyout of Trans Globe Airlines. *The Wall Street Ledger* had lauded his business acumen, editorializing that the "sum" of Trans Globe's many "parts"—routes, aircraft, gates and landing slots at major airports, ground equipment, the new reservation system—was worth considerably more than the "whole" of its stock. Since his takeover, Yeganeh had sold many of these parts and pocketed the profits. Rob never understood why Yeganeh was lionized by the press for his ruthless tactics. Most employees, and especially those former employees cast aside in the downsizing, hated his guts.

"Don't tell me he's found something else to hawk," Rob said.

"Heard a rumor today that he sold our parking lot to the Airport Authority. No more free parking starting next month. Christ, they say it'll cost us fifty bucks a month to park here after they take it over. You sure picked a good time to call it quits."

"Had no choice, John—I turn sixty on Monday."

"What'll you do with yourself?"

"I haven't made any plans. Some traveling, maybe."

"Sure envy you, Rob. Me, when I'm done with this job I'll be at Fenway every game—that's if I can afford it."

The crew bus shuttled between the employees' parking lot and the departure level of the passenger terminal. As they approached the waiting area, John stuck out his hand and said, "I'll be off Sunday, but I sure hope you have a good last trip and a great retirement."

"Thanks, John, and thanks for the lift."

Several uniformed Trans Globe employees waited to board the bus as Rob stepped off. Because Boston was the smallest of the airline's crew domiciles, he was acquainted with most of the crew members based here. He called, "Hello, Carol, hi, June," to two flight attendants he'd flown with the previous month, and just hi to another whose name he didn't recall. "How's the family, Win?" he asked a tall, dapper captain sporting a narrow mustache, and with dyed-black hair beneath his cap, cocked at a jaunty angle. Win Rundell, who some said paid alimony to three ex-wives, still hadn't forgiven Rob for his role in the pay cuts after Yeganeh bought the airline, and barely nodded in reply.

Another pilot, a blond bear of a man whose sleeves bore a first officer's three stripes, gripped Rob's hand in his mitt-sized paw. "Rob, you're retiring?"

"I have no choice, Olaf, I turn sixty on Monday. By the way, congratulations. Didn't I see your name on the list of new captains?"

"Ya, and it's thanks to you, Rob. You saved my job. I'll never forget that day."

Rob remembered that day too, ten or eleven years ago. As a check captain—authorized by the Federal Aviation Agency and the company to give proficiency checks to other pilots—Rob had been temporarily assigned to Trans Globe's JFK training center. One morning he'd been scheduled to check-ride a young copilot named Olaf Svenson. Several line captains had complained that Svenson was rough on the controls and difficult to understand because of his accent, and making matters worse, on his last trip he'd landed hard during a stormy night in Atlanta. A note in the flight folder from Brad Hollingbrooke, now one of Yeganeh's top henchmen but at that time in charge of training, tersely ordered, "Terminate this dumb Swede."

Rob knew that finding Svenson's airmanship lacking shouldn't be difficult. A mean-spirited check captain could nitpick Lindbergh himself into busting a check ride. But during the climbout, Rob immediately discerned Olaf's problem—his prodigious strength, which caused him unconsciously to overcontrol the airplane. Then, as he became exasperated, his accent grew heavier. "Relax, Olaf. I've got it," Rob had said, taking over the controls. "Let me give you a little flying lesson."

"There *are* moments when you have to manhandle an airplane," Rob had explained, "and you must always be decisive in your flying, but most of the time you can be gentle. You're not rowing a boat. Try using just your fingertips on the control wheel—pretend you're holding the woman you love." After spending several minutes demonstrating smooth turns and nearly imperceptible power changes, they entered the traffic pattern. Rob executed the first landing to demonstrate the proper technique, then said, "Okay, Olaf, your turn, and don't worry if it's not perfect."

At the end of the two-hour flight, which included a dozen landings, Rob had torn up the note, patted Olaf on the back, and grinned. "Now you're flying like a Trans Globe pilot," he'd said. "I'm sending you back to the line." And that had marked the end of Svenson's problems.

As the crew members boarded the crew bus, Olaf said, "See you on Sunday. I hear Sparky's planning a little reception." Other voices called out, "Good luck, Rob" and "We're going to miss you."

The words echoed in Rob's head as he stepped into the terminal. Passing Trans Globe's brightly lit check-in counter, he observed that a sizable crowd had gathered for tonight's flights. Air travel had not returned to normal, but people were overcoming their fears as the hijacking threat diminished. The air of excitement made him think of Harriet's phone call. Maybe someday he *should* invite her to . . . No! That would be dangerous. Deerwood was too small a town. He'd feel committed. Forty-two years ago he had dated her during his senior year in high school when she was a slender sophomore. It had been a circumspect relationship; in those innocent days, certain taboos were not lightly violated. However, two years later, after he'd gone off to college, she'd invited him to her senior prom, and afterward he'd parked his father's elderly sedan on a quiet, moonlit lane. Emboldened, or enraptured perhaps, by her strapless gown and evocative perfume, he'd passionately kissed her neck. Suddenly she'd reached behind her back and tugged at her zipper, allowing the dress to fall away and exposing her small, round, creamy white breasts. Afterward, he was never sure who had lured whom into that first sexual experience. Scared, embarrassed, shy, or some combination of all three, he had piously avoided any further entanglement with Harriet.

"Hey, buddy, which one of these damn line's for Chicago?" an exasperated-looking man bellowed while blocking Rob's path.

"What? Oh, let's see," Rob responded, peering past the milling throng to the signs above the ticket counter. "That line's for first class, sir, this is for coach if you already have a ticket, and that one," Rob waved toward the end of the counter, "is for purchasing tickets."

The man grunted unintelligibly in reply. Rob squeezed past two dozen middle-aged women with heavily made-up faces beneath frosted, beehive hairdos, all displaying large pink buttons (THE SINGING SQUARES) on ample bosoms, and wearing—he'd read the line somewhere—"polyester pantsuits in colors not known in nature." One of the women murmured, louder than necessary, "I'll bet he's our captain, Mabel. Isn't he adorable?" Rob's ears turned a shade redder.

Long lines of people and their luggage wove back from the security checkpoint. No cursory checks tonight, Rob was pleased to see. While young, M-16-toting soldiers in camouflage battle dress stood nearby, gray-uniformed personnel combed through handbags, scrutinized each bag as the conveyor belt bore an assortment of carry-ons past the X-ray machine, and monitored each person passing through the metal detector. Occasionally a passenger would be asked to step aside to be examined more thoroughly with sensitive wands. Although crew members in uniform were permitted to proceed to the head of the line, Rob patiently waited his turn. He had plenty of time. Pilots were required to report for duty one hour before departure; tonight, as usual, he had allowed himself an additional hour. Traffic snarls (fairly often), a broken fan belt (once, five years ago), or other problems could easily devour that extra time. Passengers demanded punctuality; being delayed because of a tardy crew member would not win fans.

A ponderous, red-faced man preceding him in line swung around and loudly declared, "Ah reckon our boys showed them rag-heads who's boss, right, Captain?" He reeked of beer and tobacco, and wore a baseball cap bearing the Dallas Cowboys' emblem and a silver-and-blue warm-up jacket that strained to contain the vast perimeter of his belly.

Before Rob could respond, a tiny, bespectacled, gray-haired woman behind him rapped on his arm and said, "You won't fly me right into that terrible hurricane, will you, dearie?"

"No, ma'am," Rob replied, and inquired about her destination. She was off to Minneapolis, she said, to visit her three darling little grandchildren—Henry, William, and Susan. Rob determined that she was booked on a competing airline, and assured her that her pilots would not go anywhere near a hurricane.

Rob had long understood that crew members in uniform were fair game for nervous passengers, but with a twinge of regret he realized that in a couple of days no one would ever again ask him such questions, expecting informed answers that only airline captains were supposedly privy to. He would never again be the fatherly figure allaying concerns, no longer permitted to wear, proudly, this uniform. In a couple of days he'd be just another face in the crowd.

Rob politely accepted the same intense scrutiny that each passenger received from the security staff. He knew that many pilots, using the enigmatic logic that "no pilot had ever hijacked his own airplane," bitterly opposed being inspected, but Rob approved of the system, despite its limitations. He knew that firearms and other lethal devices that had no place on a commercial airplane were almost always detected and confiscated.

He continued down the broad concourse past the gate areas of other airlines, then stopped at a metal door guarded by a combination lock and a sign that read TRANS GLOBE AIRLINES EMPLOYEES ONLY.

He punched in a five-digit code, swung open the door, parked his suitcase in the designated storage area, and descended on the stairs to the ground level. The stairway opened onto a wide corridor whose beige walls were decorated with framed black-and-white and color photographs, some rather faded, of the various aircraft that

Trans Globe had operated since its founding in 1927: Northrup Alphas, Ford Trimotors, Douglas DC-3s, the graceful Lockheed Constellations with which the airline had inaugurated trans-Atlantic service, and Boeing 707s, Trans Globe's first jets. Other photographs depicted many of the original corps of pilots, men who had flown before the Laws of Aeronautics had been discovered, and the first flight attendants, called stewardesses in earlier times—the men and women whose skill and courage had enabled Trans Globe to survive and prosper during aviation's perilous gestation years. Rob had flown with several of these revered aviators when he was a brand-new copilot and they were the seasoned veterans. He felt a quiet pride in having helped carry on Trans Globe's hallowed traditions, in being a member of this unique fraternity of airmen. Yes, he would miss the special camaraderie of the men and women who fly.

Farther down the corridor Rob entered the employees' men's room. Standing at the urinal, he glanced at the still faintly visible, misspelled graffiti on the wall, likely the handiwork of some disenchanted baggage handler: CAPTIN ROBERTSON = YEGENER'S WHORE. Those cruel words had somehow survived innumerable scrubbings; similarly pithy aphorisms defiled the walls of company lavatories at other Trans Globe stations. Rob remembered the blow to his self-esteem, the feeling of betrayal, when he'd first seen his name attached to such a bitter message.

After Jane's death, he had become active—sought refuge, perhaps—in union affairs, serving on the Membership and, later, the Safety Committee. When Yeganeh took control of the airline, Rob was asked by the chairman of the Trans Globe Pilots Association to serve on a so-called Transition Team, along with representatives from the mechanics, flight attendants, and other crafts, which would seek accommodation with this new management.

Because of the economic downturn at the time, Trans Globe had been mired in financial difficulty. In fact, many employees saw Yeganeh as the white knight come to rescue this damsel of an airline in distress. An undefinable combination of dread, euphoria, and relief permeated the air.

The first meeting between Yeganeh, accompanied by a cordon of nattily attired Wall Street lawyers, and the Transition Team, held at

Yeganeh's plush offices in Manhattan, had been fairly cordial. The unions quickly okayed "temporary" salary reductions of twenty percent and minor changes in the working agreements, making the airline "more competitive." Yeganeh would dispose of a "few surplus airplanes," he said, and relinquish some "unproductive" routes. Furloughs would be held to a minimum. Both sides seemed satisfied.

Rob had come to that meeting in uniform, directly from a flight. When the meeting concluded, Yeganeh had jumped up, grinning fiendishly, donned Rob's captain's hat, and pranced around the room singing, in a voice straight from a scratchy old 78 rpm record, "Come fly with me, come fly away . . ."

Six months later, Yeganeh had called another meeting. He demanded an additional fifteen percent pay cut or he would sell more airplanes, abandon additional routes, and lay off more workers. "There's thousands of clowns out there that'll take your jobs for half the pay, with pleasure," he'd ranted. "I can fill your shoes in two weeks, every damn one!"

The inexperience of the union representatives had cost them dearly. In negotiations with the previous management, union goals had been simply to maintain parity in pay, benefits, and working conditions with the other major airlines. But compared to Yeganeh's slick shysters, the Transition Team members were hapless amateurs, flounders thrown to the sharks.

The lawyers had graphs and charts. And the company books. The Transition Team saw no choice but again to accede to his demands. It didn't matter. Yeganeh failed to honor his own agreement. Rob recognized too late that Yeganeh's only plan was to systematically dismantle the airline for his own profit. Dedicated employees had become mere chattels of the emperor. Thousands more were furloughed; staffing fell from twenty-six thousand employees to less than fifteen thousand. Pilots, mechanics, flight attendants, reservation agents—no class or craft proved immune. Perhaps there was nothing the Transition Team could have done to change the outcome, but Rob still anguished over its failure to reach a humane agreement.

Meanwhile, Yeganeh had peddled away a third of the fleet and cast off international routes that Trans Globe pilots had pioneered. After five years of Yeganeh's reign, the once proud airline retained service to only a handful of foreign destinations, and its domestic structure had shrunk by half. Trans Globe Airline's glorious, seventy-five-year heritage, its significant contributions to aviation, its unparalleled record of thousands of Atlantic crossings without the loss of a single passenger, had been squandered.

Rob knew he had been betrayed by Yeganeh, but many fellow employees, men like Win Rundell, blamed him and the other union negotiators for caving in. That explained the graffiti; being scorned by longtime acquaintances was harder to swallow.

It'll soon be over, Rob thought. In a few days I'll be just a memory around here, like one of those fading pictures on the wall.

After washing his hands and rinsing his face with cold water, Rob continued down the corridor and entered a room marked PILOTS' MAIL ROOM. At one of three FLACCS (Flight and Cabin Crew Scheduling) computer stations, he typed in a five-letter code, then the numbers 1-1-6-2-6, his employee identification number. This brief action electronically notified Crew Scheduling, Payroll, and other departments that he was on duty and prepared to operate his flight pairing. He typed in another code, which directed the printer to produce a document showing the details of his trip tonight. When the printer finished its frenzied action, he tore off the sheet. It read:

FLIGHT PAIRING #2001-5728 (ALL TIMES LOCAL)

DATE	FLT#	DEPART	ARRIVE	FLT HRS	LAYOVER
16 NOV	810	BOS 0830PM	CDG 0815AM	6:45	27:50 HRS
18 NOV	811	CDG 1205PM	BOS 0300PM	7:55	

SKD FLT HRS = 14:40   TRIP HRS = 54:10

POS	EMP#	NAME	SENIORITY#
CAP	11626	ROBERTSON, F. C.	0213
F/O	24583	CURTIS, C. C.	2074

Rob didn't recognize the first officer's name. It should not matter. Trans Globe's training emphasized crew coordination;

theoretically, it made no difference which copilot occupied a Starliner's right seat. Still, Rob preferred flying with someone he knew. Dave Conley had been his first officer the past two months, but, Rob recalled, Dave had mentioned having two weeks' vacation coming. Rob typed in another code that produced a list of the cabin crew. He neatly folded both lists and slipped them into his shirt pocket. He tossed his hat on the table, draped his jacket over a chair, retrieved his flight kit from the storage rack, and sauntered to the metal filing cabinet that served as the pilots' mailbox. Bending low to open the bottom drawer, he made his usual wish that his name had been higher on the alphabetical pecking order, found his folder, and removed the contents.

He sat at a table to review the material. A note from the chief pilot read, "Rob—F/O Curtis needs initial overwater qualification check. Sorry to bother you with this on last trip—Hank." The note was stapled to a form that Rob, still a check captain, would later fill out to certify that Curtis had satisfactorily completed his trans-Atlantic checkout. This simply meant that, in addition to commanding the flight, Rob would give Curtis operational training on the eastbound flight and a proficiency check on the return. Routine stuff. Fine, Rob thought. Curtis will be fresh out of international procedures ground school; he'll probably teach me a thing or two.

His folder also held two thick manila envelopes, one containing the weekly revisions to airport approach charts, airway maps, and other aviation data for North America, the other for Europe and the Middle East. If anything was the bane of a pilot's existence, it had to be this tiresome chore of revising manuals. Rob imagined a major bureaucracy somewhere that did nothing but look for ways to modify aeronautical charts. In addition, revisions to the Starliner Operating Manual and to Federal Aviation Regulations occasionally added to the stack.

He was delighted to discover two dozen humorous "farewell" cards from pilots, flight attendants, and office staff; these he set aside to peruse during the Paris layover. Then he methodically inserted each revised page into his manuals, carefully examining any that pertained to the operation of tonight's flight—such as one for the airport in Halifax, Nova Scotia, close to the usual route and a handy place to land should a problem develop. He recognized the scant likelihood of needing data for Atlanta, Athens, Algiers, or most other airports whose charts and diagrams filled his thick manuals, but just in case, every page would be meticulously correct.

CHAPTER THREE

SOMEONE FROM THE PAST

One hour and fifteen minutes before scheduled departure time, Rob, at his usual brisk gait, headed down the long corridor to the Operations Room, the nerve center for Trans Globe's Boston flights. Hourly weather reports, Notices to Airmen (NOTAMs), and other aeronautical information was posted along the wall opposite the long vinyl counter. Surface analysis weather charts and winds aloft diagrams were thumbtacked to a large bulletin board. In one corner, a printer clattered relentlessly. Along the outer wall, thick windows afforded a view of the floodlit ramp area, where, like minions attending their stately queen, baggage carts, commissary trucks, and other vehicles huddled close to a huge, shiny Starliner passenger jet nosed into Gate 19.

Three middle-aged mechanics wearing standard blue coveralls stood near the coffeepot, which was simmering on a small table at the end of the counter. "Evening, gents," Rob said. "Got a good airplane for eight-ten?"

One of the mechanics replied, "Sure do, Captain. She's ready and waiting." He gestured toward the windows.

Rob noticed a hand-lettered sign propped on the counter. CAPT. ROB ROBERTSON: HAVE A *GREAT* LAST TRIP, it read.

Sparky Miller, the operations agent, a thin, wiry man with short-cropped, salt-and-pepper hair that stood straight up, reached across the counter, grabbed Rob's hand, and pumped it vigorously. "Rob, you old bastard. So we're finally getting rid of you."

"Yep, and I hear you're next," Rob said. Sparky, whose face was permanently creased with smile wrinkles, had more years with Trans Globe than any other employee Rob knew. While still a teen, he had served as a radio operator in the Royal Canadian Air Force during the Cold War, flying antisubmarine patrols from Newfoundland over the North Atlantic, and had been hired by the airline soon after his hitch ended. Trans Globe had acquired routes to Europe, and the cantankerous, crystal-controlled radios then in use on trans-Atlantic Constellation flights required a radio operator's expertise. But in the late fifties, when better radios came along, the radio operators were dismissed. Sparky next had trained to become a navigator, only to find a decade later that "black boxes" replaced the navigators. Fortunately, operations agents were still required. "That's *if* they'll let you retire, Sparky," Rob added. "This outfit couldn't run without you."

"Not so, but thanks. Still have a couple of months to go. Wish it was today. My union's saying that Yeganeh wants to 'renegotiate' what's left of our retirement package, which means a little more blood to go with the pound of flesh he already took. Listen, you short-timer, you'd better get back here on time Sunday. I even volunteered to work that day!" He rotated the sign to reveal its back side, which read: FAREWELL ROB—FLIGHT OPS WISHES YOU HAPPY LANDINGS IN RETIREMENT.

"We're planning a little party," Sparky continued. "Just some of your old friends, Boston troops, mostly. My goodness," he declared, waving a slip of paper, "there's even a message here saying that arse-kisser Hollingbrooke from New York will be here to meet your flight." His staccato laugh resonated like Morse code.

After Yeganeh had taken control of the airline, Brad Hollingbrooke broke ranks with the pilots and inveigled the airline's tyrannical new owner into making him his right-hand man. Hollingbrooke had cunningly switched to management's side of the table and was now smugly ensconced as Trans Globe's vice president for flight operations. "Can't imagine why," Rob jested. "Do you suppose he's coming here to carry off my flight kit?"

Traditionally, when a Trans Globe captain taxied his airplane to the gate, parked the brakes, and shut down the engines for the final time before retirement, the chief pilot—or his assistant, at least— would be waiting in the jetway. After the passengers deplaned, he would come to the cockpit, give the usual congratulations, and respectfully tote the captain's flight kit back to ops. However, Rob could recall no instance when the VP for flight operations had performed this cordial, gracious gesture. "I wouldn't dare miss my party," Rob continued, "but not because of Hollingbrooke. You know, Sparky, for the last thirty-two years my goal has been to give my passengers a smooth, on-time ride, stay out of trouble, and keep such a low profile that when my turn came to retire, nobody in management would even notice I was gone."

Sparky said, "When my day comes, I'm heading straight for my favorite fishing spot in Newfoundland. Say, how about a cup of coffee? Made some fresh a few minutes ago."

"I'm buying," Rob replied. He dropped a dollar bill into the till box, filled Sparky's proffered mug, handed it back to him over the counter, and half-filled a paper cup for himself.

"Have you seen the news?" Sparky asked, jabbing a finger toward a small television set perched on a shelf above the printer. The screen showed an aerial view of what appeared to be human bodies, seat cushions, and an assortment of flotsam bobbing in an undulating, blue-green sea. The familiar voice of the evening news anchorman droned, " . . . shown earlier today on Euronet Television. A Navy F-14 reportedly fired a missile at a Libyan Airways Skybus over the Mediterranean Sea. The plane went down seventy-five miles northwest of Benghazi at approximately 4:30 P.M. Western Europe time." The screen displayed a simplified map of the North African coastline with a line of dashes extending from the Libyan city into the Gulf of Sidra, ending in a red X at the impact point. "No survivors have been located. The airliner carried two hundred and twenty-seven passengers and a crew of twelve." The TV image changed to canned footage of an unnamed aircraft carrier cruising at sea, then switched to close-up shots of Tomcat fighters being catapulted off the deck. Next the screen filled with irrelevant scenes of jumbo jets parked on the ramp at Dulles International Airport. The announcer continued, "Libyan authorities claim the airliner was carrying pilgrims returning from the *hajj* to Mecca and had stopped in Benghazi to refuel before going on to Algiers. The U.S. government has not issued an apology. There are unconfirmed reports that Hamas and other terrorist groups have vowed revenge."

As the broadcast switched to domestic news, Rob said, "Didn't Ramadan begin yesterday? I can believe the Muslim world is angry." He shook his head, then turned to the operations agent. "I sure don't like the looks of that, Sparky, but I guess we'd better see about getting all those nice folks who pay our salaries over to Paree tonight. What've you got for us?" By force of habit, Rob used the collective terms *we* and *us* although he was aware that the first officer had not yet materialized to assist in the flight planning.

Sparky quipped, "Plenty of paperwork, that's for sure." He had neatly arranged Flight 810's documents on the counter: weather reports, forecasts, and NOTAMs for every major airport in the northeastern United States, Canada's Maritime Provinces, Greenland, Iceland, the Azores, and western Europe. There were three copies of the computer-generated flight plan, charts showing the winds, cloud levels, and areas of possible turbulence at various altitudes, and a surface analysis chart depicting the fronts, highs, and lows of several weather systems.

Rob examined the latter chart first. The data, less than an hour old, placed the eye of tropical storm Pauline at 34° 15′ north latitude and 66° 30′ west longitude, about 150 nautical miles northwest of Bermuda—well south of the usual paths of the many flights, including Trans Globe 810, intending to span the North Atlantic tonight.

But there were other considerations. Rob recalled that, a few years ago, the notion of flying a two-engine passenger jet like the Starliner across the Atlantic would have been laughed at. With the advent of the jet age, three decades earlier, the airlines operated four-engine equipment such as the American-made 707 and DC-8, the British VC-10, or Russia's IL-62 on overwater flights. Later, wide-bodied 747s and three-engine L-1011s and DC-10s came into use.

Now, with far more powerful, dependable, and fuel-efficient engines like the Starliner's mighty Vickerys—twin-engine overwater operations had become feasible.

Still, Rob knew, occasionally—even on modern aircraft—an engine failed. Sitting in the darkened cockpit in the middle of the night, halfway across that cold, black ocean, he had often wondered if his passengers also considered that possibility.

Like all commercial twin-engine aircraft, the Starliner could be flown on one engine just fine, though not as high, of course, and not as fast. And all Trans Globe pilots were well trained in engine-out procedures. Every six months, Rob, like his contemporaries, faced a career-threatening check ride in the earthbound simulator, required to demonstrate his proficiency in handling every conceivable emergency circumstance: engine cuts during takeoff, low-visibility approaches on one engine, emergency descents dictated by the loss of cabin pressurization. And like other pilots, Rob strove to avoid such trials in the real world.

"Sparky, what do we have for alternates tonight?" he asked.

If an engine failed in flight, federal aviation regulations authorized a three- or four-engine aircraft to continue to its destination on the remaining engines, whereas a two-engine airliner must immediately divert to the "nearest suitable airport"—one whose runways and meteorological conditions would permit an approach and landing. For long overwater flights, the FAA required that "twins" such as the Starliner remain within 825 nautical miles of suitable alternate airports, that being the no-wind distance the aircraft could theoretically fly in two hours on one engine, assuming the other engine failed while at cruise altitude, followed by a "drift down" to optimum single-engine altitude. This "two-hour rule" made twin-engine Extended Operations (ETOPS) feasible, as the only "suitable airports" between North America and Europe are distantly located in Greenland, Iceland, and the Azores.

Prior to ETOPS certification, the Starliner's Vickery engines had been required to demonstrate a high level of reliability. Should his flight divert to an alternate because of engine failure, Rob knew that—again, theoretically—the probability of a second engine failure within those two hours was on the order of once per million hours of operation; however, he would not choose to wager two hundred lives, including his own, on the validity of that theory.

Of course, corporate and military twin- and even single-engine aircraft routinely cross oceans without these restrictions, but they don't haul fare-paying passengers.

"Goose, Kef, and Shannon," Sparky replied, the abridged nicknames denoting Goose Bay, Labrador; Keflavik, Iceland; and Shannon, Ireland, "and they're all good."

"Maybe the weather gods know it's my last trip," Rob joked. Tonight, only scattered low clouds spread from the Maritime Provinces to Scotland, and England and France would be clear. A perfect night for flying. As he examined the weather reports and forecasts, Rob hoped that someday, maybe in time for the next generation of pilots, the world would agree on a universal weather language. In the United States, ceilings were reported in feet, visibility in miles, barometric pressure in inches of mercury, temperature in degrees Fahrenheit. Most other countries used the metric system: meters, kilometers, millibars, and Celsius measurements.

Rob next examined the flight plan. Trans Globe's flight-planning computer, jokingly called Hal after the omniscient one in the movie *2001*, searched for the most favorable altitudes and winds within the available route structure. Tonight Hal had selected a route passing over St. John, New Brunswick, over Goose Bay, track "V" across the Atlantic, then past Dublin, Ireland, southwestern England, and across the English Channel to France.

Many passengers might not realize that most Atlantic crossings proceeded so far north, Rob thought. However, a world globe would show that this "great circle route," with minor adjustments to take advantage of the optimum winds and to accommodate air traffic, renders the shortest distance from the northeastern United States to Europe. It worked as well for Charles Lindbergh in 1927 as it does for the airlines of today.

Sparky asked, "You happy with that fuel load, Rob?"

Rob sipped his coffee as he rechecked the flight plan. "Let's see, the release gives us eighty-three thousand three hundred pounds. Hal says we'll burn seventy-five three and have eight thousand reserve over de Gaulle—just enough to be legal. Guess I'm getting old, Sparky, but I like a little extra. Last trip we had a long taxi delay, didn't get our altitude, then Oceanic sent us on the longest track. Burned nearly three thousand pounds more than expected. Make it eighty-six grand for takeoff—we're okay on weight."

"You got it," Sparky replied, and immediately notified the refueling personnel over the intercom.

Rob glanced at the clock on the wall, then at his watch. Both showed fifty-five minutes to departure time. He glanced around the room, stepped out into the corridor, looked both ways, walked quickly back to the pilot's mailroom, checked inside, then returned to operations. "Has anybody seen my first officer?" he asked. He pulled the crew pairing sheet from his shirt pocket to double-check the copilot's identity. "His name's Curtis." No one had.

"Anyone know him or where he lives?" Rob asked, more anxiously this time.

"That name rings a bell," Sparky offered. "Yeah, he's from Texas—Houston, I think." Sparky was famous throughout the airline for never forgetting a name. He had friends in every corner of the globe. "That's one helluva commute! Bet he's riding jump seat on two thirty-six—it makes a stopover in K.C." He glanced at the clock. "It's running late—let me check their latest ETA." Kansas City was Trans Globe's domestic hub. Anyone flying from Texas, or anyplace else in the West, to Boston would have to stop and sometimes make a plane change there. Sparky pecked at his computer keyboard. "Two thirty-six is estimating at eight twenty-seven, Rob—three minutes before your departure time. We weren't advised of any connecting passengers, but if he's riding jump seat, reservations wouldn't know about him. I'll call Houston ops and see if he signed up for the jump seat."

"Yes, do that," Rob said, annoyed, thinking Curtis should have let him or Crew Scheduling know he'd be late. He could've called from Kansas City, or from the plane. He should be involved with the paperwork and preflight—that's part of the international checkout.

Sparky said, "Ever since Yeganeh centralized Scheduling and furloughed half the staff, they've been hard pressed to notify crews of flight assignments. We've had some mix-ups lately."

"Well, if he isn't on two thirty-six, call Scheduling and tell them to call out a reserve, pronto! Heck, it could take hours to get a replacement here." Rob banged the heel of his fist on the counter, mentally berating himself for not checking on Curtis's whereabouts earlier. Trans Globe had no rule against commuting to work by air, even from as far away as Houston. Rob himself had commuted to JFK occasionally, earlier in his career, but he knew there were constant pitfalls such as weather, Air Traffic Control and mechanical delays, and full airplanes. He had always allowed plenty of time, not just for Trans Globe, but for his own peace of mind as well.

A minute later Sparky called out, "You're in luck. He's aboard two thirty-six."

"Good. When they contact you for their gate assignment, ask the crew to get a message to Curtis to get his butt straight over to Gate Nineteen as soon as they block in."

"Will do, Rob."

"Thanks, Sparky."

Now Rob had to hustle to accomplish the first officer's duties as well as his own. He signed the flight release, an action by which he officially assumed total responsibility—from brake release in Boston to engine shutdown in Paris—for the hundred-million-dollar airplane and for the safety of the two-hundred-plus souls he would transport. He could not imagine any other profession, except that of a ship captain, in which a salaried employee is given such unsupervised responsibility. He handed the release to Sparky to file, quickly plotted the anticipated track on the navigation chart, then double-checked his work. "Been a long time since I've had to carry the flimsy," Rob joked as he neatly folded this chart and tucked it and the other documents into a big manila folder, which he slipped into his flight kit. "That's always been the copilot's job." Quickly heading for the door, he called out, "See you Sunday, Sparky."

"Have a good trip, Rob, and there'll be champagne waiting."

Rob mentally ticked off the tasks he needed to accomplish to prepare the airplane for flight: *preflight the cockpit, conduct an exterior walk-around, obtain the ATC clearance, load the flight computers. Curtis, this new-age copilot, will only have to jump into his seat and strap in. We should push back darned close to on schedule.* He checked his watch, and decided he had just enough time to brief the flight attendants.

Rob returned to the corridor and walked quickly to a door marked FLIGHT ATTENDANTS' BRIEFING ROOM. He considered it important to show his face and say hello to the cabin crew, describe the route and weather, and check the timing of their meal and beverage service. The door stood ajar, and from the room a male voice intoned " . . . pass out the French customs forms after we serve breakfast."

Rob paused outside the door and removed the cabin crew list from his shirt pocket. This list identified the flight service manager and eight flight attendants, and specified the emergency door or overwing exit to which each was assigned. A good reminder, he thought, that a flight attendant's primary role is safety, not to serve or entertain passengers and cockpit crew. It read:

POS	EMP#	NAME
FSM	3417	Prazar G G
L-1	5129	Johnson M L
R-1	6578	Morris L A
L-2	6007	Delorey C B
R-2	7684	Smith-Stansfield R G
L-3	7226	Bohanan J C
R-3	6843	Gizzarelli M E
O-1	6538	Reid-Seaton K S
O-2	7304	Pagano M T

Rob quickly glanced through the list of names. Gregory Prazar, darned good service manager; Margot Johnson, pretty lady, married to Steve, a Trans Globe pilot. Didn't know Morris. Delor . . . He blinked. Could it be? Charis? After all these years? He pictured a tanned, lissome young woman, remembered jogging side by side on the groomed paths in Kensington Park, her flowing hair the color of sun-dried hay. He remembered . . . But that was fifteen years—a lifetime—ago. He hesitated a moment, tapped on the door, then swung it open.

CHAPTER FOUR

CHARIS

Their eyes met immediately, then, as if she had been awaiting Rob's entrance into the briefing room, Charis sprang from her chair and moved to him with those quick, light steps he suddenly remembered so well. His arms hesitantly encircled her waist as her hands reached up to his shoulders. He gently kissed her cheek, aware at that instant that he had never before embraced her. He had wondered, sometimes, should they meet again, like this, face-to-face, what that greeting might be like, what wounds time may have healed. He'd intended, should they meet, to be restrained—aloof, perhaps. After all, she had married, and probably had children, a minivan, and a house with a huge mortgage. But now he felt that reserve crumbling. He pulled back slightly, conscious of the throb of his own heartbeat, revisiting her warm green eyes, even the little flecks of brown. Controlling his emotions, he said, "Charis. This is a surprise! What brings you to Boston?"

"Just to see you once more, to wish you a happy retirement," she replied softly. "To say good-bye. I hope you don't mind."

"Of course not." His knees felt strangely unsteady, not unlike that moment thirty-three years ago, taking off from Phuoc Vinh, when Viet Cong bullets had ripped through his C-130, setting an engine on fire.

Her soft fragrance, the warmth of her body against his, triggered the realization that he'd held no woman this close in a very long time. "This is . . . hard to believe. It's been . . ." he stammered, trying to regain his composure. "But aren't you based in L.A.?"

She gently slipped out of his arms, took a deep breath, and replied, "Yes, I've been flying Honolulu turnarounds, but I worked out a trade, just for this trip. I remembered your birthday and checked FLACCS to see when your last trip would be, and . . ."

"And here you are," Rob said. And still lovely, he thought. Slender, but strong-looking, too. Shiny white teeth. He noticed, also, a tiny wisp of gray in her hair, shorter now, and tiny wrinkles at the corners of her eyes. She looked crisply professional in Trans Globe's sedate navy blue uniform and white blouse, and he noticed approvingly that she'd worn a skirt rather than the optional slacks. "I don't deserve so much attention, but I am glad to see you."

In a hushed voice she said, "And I wanted to apologize for . . ."

"No, Charis, there's no need," he whispered.

In the taut silence Rob became aware of eight pairs of eyes transfixed on them. Unable to halt the blush spreading over his cheeks, he turned to the entranced group and said, "Sorry, everyone. You can see Charis and I are, uh . . ." He cast a reassuring glance at Charis, "old friends. Gregory, I interrupted you in mid-sentence. Please continue your briefing."

The short plump service manager laughed and said, "Captain, we wouldn't have missed that for the world. Actually, I'd just about finished." Gregory looked around at the flight attendants seated in a semicircle. "I think most of you know Captain Robertson. If you'd like to say a few words, sir, please go ahead."

As Charis returned to her chair, Rob said, "Please call me Rob," then briefed them on the flight time, route—which, he emphasized, stayed far away from Pauline—and destination weather. He mentioned that the pushback might be delayed a few minutes because of the tardy first officer, then, trying to sound unperturbed, added, "You've heard about the destruction of that Libyan airliner and seen the tightened security. I'm not anticipating any trouble, but before our passengers board, take a look around, check the overhead bins and the compartments in the lavs and anyplace else you can think of. If you find anything unusual, don't touch it. We'll call in the experts." He looked around. "And let me know if any passengers are acting strangely. Remember, you're our first line of defense."

Gregory joked, "It would be unusual if we didn't have one or two bizarre individuals on these all-nighters. Just kidding, Captain. We know what you mean."

One of the flight attendants bantered, "At least there isn't a full moon."

"That really brings out the weirdos," another agreed.

"Actually, there was a new moon last night," Rob noted, "but it doesn't mean we shouldn't be cautious. For one thing, it marked the beginning of Ramadan, Islam's holy month. Muslim nations have been calling for the president to show some restraint in Afghanistan, but he said he's not halting the bombing. A lot of people may be angry."

"I hear some airlines want to arm their pilots—stun guns, at least, if not real ones," Gregory remarked. "Are our pilots going to get them?"

"Not soon, certainly," Rob answered. "That'll probably need congressional approval."

"Do you know what caused that crash last week in New York?" someone asked.

"No, but I don't think it had anything to do with terrorism," Rob replied. "They encountered severe wake turbulence, and the plane's vertical stabilizer may have had previous structural damage. Look, I've got to get going. Don't hesitate to let us know if the temperature in the cabin isn't just right. Oh, and whenever anyone needs a break," he added, glancing at Charis, "come up front and visit. It's going to be a long night, and we like company. Two knocks on the door to come in, three for trouble, or three dings on the call button. Gregory, remember to block the aisle with a service cart whenever Curtis or I use the lav; Margot, since you're L-1, don't let the agent pull the jetway until he arrives." Rob paused at the door. "See you on board," he said to the group, and smiled quizzically at Charis as if to say, "I may not understand what's happening, but I'm mighty glad to see you."

He returned to the corridor, retrieved his flight kit, climbed the stairs on oddly springy legs, strapped the flight kit onto his suitcase, and headed down the concourse to Gate 19.

Passengers, or their carry-on luggage, occupied every seat in the waiting area adjacent to the gate. Rob greeted the two boarding agents, explained about the late-arriving first officer, then hurried down the long jetway and into the Starliner. He paused a moment to gaze at the rows of empty seats that soon would be filled with fragile human beings, the men, women, and children for whose well-being he would bear ultimate responsibility. Then he turned left and stepped into the cockpit. He stowed his suitcase in the storage bin, opened his flight kit, and wedged it into its bracket on the floor beside the left seat. Next he performed the safety check, ensuring that the landing gear handle was down and that the three green lights indicated "down and locked," that the flap handle was up, the speed brake lever was in the forward detent, and that the electrically powered hydraulic pumps were off. He checked that the auxiliary power unit (APU) properly supplied electrical power and pressurized air to the appropriate systems. Then he scrutinized the logbook to ascertain that all mandated inspections had been completed, and scanned back through a dozen pages to determine if the aircraft had exhibited any nagging ailments or other problems during its recent flight history.

His presence preceded by the pungent odor of jet fuel that permeated his clothing, the fueler stepped into the cockpit doorway. "Don't mean to interrupt you, Captain."

"Quite all right," Rob replied.

Handing Rob the fuel slip, the man joked, "See you put on a little extra gas for the wife and kiddies."

"Better safe than sorry, they say," Rob replied, not bothering to inform the man that he had neither. He double-checked that the fueler's computations were accurate, and that the cockpit fuel gauges agreed with the paperwork, verifying that the correct amount of Jet A-1 had been loaded and properly distributed. Neither engine had required oil. "Looks good to me," Rob said as he signed the triplicate fuel slip, tore off the top copy to add to the flight documents, and handed the others to the fueler, who thanked him and left.

Rob removed his flashlight from his kit and tested it. Then, after deciding that the autumn air did not require an overcoat, he returned to the jetway, opened the heavy steel door, and descended the steep metal stairs to the tarmac to begin the exterior walk-around.

As he began the inspection at the Starliner's nose wheel, his thoughts drifted back fifteen years . . .

He'd been assigned to fly 707s back then, and had been elated when his seniority finally enabled him to hold a highly desirable international trip: the all-nighter to London, on to Athens the next day, back to London the following morning, and returning to Boston the last day, with lengthy layovers in the European cities.

On a sunny June morning, following the long overnight flight from Boston, as the crew bus trundled from Heathrow to the London hotel, he had leaned back in his seat, enjoying the scenery. Charis—Charis Burns, then—sat across the aisle, thumbing through a guidebook. She'd turned to him and said, "There's so much to see. It's my first trip to Europe. Do you have any suggestions, Captain?"

"Everybody calls me Rob," he replied, "and you're Charis, right?" He'd remembered her unusual name from the crew briefing.

"Yes."

He teased, "You didn't come up to the cockpit and pay us a visit on the way over."

"I started up three times, but twice passengers stopped me, wanting drinks, and on the third try a lady needed a baby bottle warmed."

"Well, I appreciate it that you took good care of our passengers." He told her that he didn't know London very well, but suggested she visit some of the usual sights such as the Victoria and Albert Museum and, of course, the changing of the guard at Buckingham Palace. He mentioned in passing that on a previous London layover he'd picked up two tickets for Wimbledon, for today's matches. "My wife plays tennis," he explained, "and she'd planned to come along this trip, but at the last minute she had a headache and didn't feel like traveling." Over the past few months Jane had been preoccupied and distant, almost indifferent to him, and he'd bought the tickets to surprise her, certain that a junket to

Wimbledon would please her, help make things right. It seemed puzzling that she'd declined. Using his employee travel privileges, she'd occasionally accompanied him on flights—if the passenger load permitted—but, he now realized, not recently. There always seemed to be a tournament or some special event going on at the club. "I tried to talk the F/O and engineer into going, but neither one's interested in tennis. Don't suppose you'd care to pinch-hit?"

Charis, swinging the guidebook in a mock forehand, replied, "I'm from San Diego, where everybody plays tennis. I'd love to, but are you sure she won't mind?"

Rob had noticed Charis's tanned face and trim figure. "Yes, I'm sure. She told me to find someone"—but more likely one of the cockpit crew, he thought with a smile—"to take her place. Let's see." He checked his watch. "It's seven-thirty London time now. We'll reach the hotel in about fifteen minutes. There'll be time for a good nap. I'm not sure how long it'll take to get out to Wimbledon but the matches begin at two. Shall we meet at one in the lobby?"

"Fine."

"You might want to bring a light jacket—the forecast calls for a chance of showers later on."

At the hotel Rob had taken his usual postflight snooze, awakened shortly after noon, quickly shaved, showered, and dressed, then went downstairs to meet Charis. She walked into the lobby at exactly one o'clock, radiating a youthful, healthy glow. She wore a pale green dress and an ivory-colored sweater with the sleeves pushed up halfway. A short necklace with blue and brown porcelain beads dangled in front. She carried a small leather purse and had looped a jacket over an arm. Her hair, surprisingly long, and the pale yellow color of sun-drenched fields of flax, was snugged into a ponytail and tied with a ribbon, beneath which it tumbled freely over her neck and back. He wondered why, on the crew bus, he hadn't noticed her hair, then remembered that it had been wound tightly into a bun. Trans Globe had strict rules about hair length, presumably to ensure that flight attendants didn't accidentally drape their tresses across a passenger's dinner as they bent to serve. Her eyes—green, with flecks of brown—sat far apart beneath a broad forehead; high cheekbones and a small, straight nose completed the enchanting picture. Rob could not suppress a sudden flush of delight that the copilot and engineer had declined his invitation, nor a twinge of guilt, roused by the notion, however guileless the circumstances, that he'd be watching the world's top tennis players in the company of this charming young woman while Jane remained ill at home.

"Did you have a good sleep?" Charis had asked.

"Yes," he replied, "but four hours wasn't enough—I'm still a little groggy. International flying's rough on the body. How about you?"

"Slept like a log."

They had snacked on coffee and scones at the Notting Hill Gate Station cafeteria, then ridden the Underground to Wimbledon and walked from the station to the All-England Lawn Tennis and Croquet Club.

The tickets afforded them good seats in the grandstand, overlooking the manicured grass court where, in succession, they'd watched first Becker and then Navratilova breeze by less acclaimed opponents. They couldn't resist the customary strawberries and cream, then meandered past the two dozen side courts where other early-round matches were being played. Seated, or standing sometimes, only yards from the action, they marveled at the whack of powerful serves, heard the players' muted profanities and, less often, laconic compliments ("Good shot!" or simply "Yeah!"), felt the heightening tension as each hard-fought match progressed. During exciting rallies Charis occasionally touched or patted his hand, sending oddly delicious shivers up his arm.

Throughout the afternoon, Rob's conscience grappled with this surfeit of contentment. He sensed how his wife would be miffed that she'd missed out—recently, tennis had replaced golf as her favorite pastime. Jane loved the competition, "but," she'd charged, "you just don't take it seriously. And besides," she'd added, "you're always off flying." To fuel her competitive spirit, Jane invariably teamed with Roger Henderson, the cocky, mop-haired club pro, as her partner for the weekend mixed doubles tournaments, which they frequently won. The mantel above the living room fireplace sagged from the weight of her shiny trophies.

June's lingering daylight permitted the matches of what the program proclaimed as the All-England Lawn Tennis Championships to continue until nearly nine P.M., when cool, deepening shadows finally forced a halt to the action. Before leaving the immaculate grounds, Rob bought general admission tickets for the matches two days hence, when the crew would return to England following the round-trip to Athens.

Rob and Charis returned to London on the Tube, then stopped at a smoky, dark-paneled pub called The Fife and Fiddle for a quick dinner of fish-and-chips and one glass each of Guinness stout. "Dutch treat," she'd insisted. He learned that she had graduated from San Diego State, run on the cross-country team—"I was too skinny to be a cheerleader," she'd joked—then taught eighth-grade social science and phys ed for two years. But she had "an itch to travel," as she described it, and discovered that flight attendants earned more money than schoolteachers. She had been hired by Trans Globe three years ago and based in L.A., but last month, "after my male friend split," she explained, she'd applied for a transfer and been assigned to Boston, and had just moved into an apartment in the Back Bay with two other flight attendants. She played tennis only for fun, still ran for exercise and occasionally entered footraces, she said, but rarely went to movies, preferring books like Michener's Hawaii.

Charis smiled easily, and displayed lovely, perfect teeth. When Rob complimented her, she laughed. "My parents get the credit—they call it my thousand-dollar grin."

A light drizzle was falling, and streetlights cast a misty glow as they meandered back to the hotel. When the elevator stopped at her floor, she'd held out her hand and said warmly, "Thank you for a fine day, Rob."

The next morning, Rob and his crew had flown to Athens, arriving in mid-afternoon. Several crew members went shopping, the old city being a bargain-hunter's paradise, while others chose to lounge around the hotel's sun-baked outdoor swimming pool. Only Charis expressed an interest in sight-seeing.

Outside the hotel, the streets were crammed with vehicles of every description—trucks and buses belching diesel fumes, cars, and hordes of motorbikes whose drivers seemed intent on generating the maximum level of noise. Rob hailed a cab, which delivered them to the base of the Acropolis, then they tramped up the steep, graveled path, gradually leaving behind the blaring reverberations of modern civilization as they approached the summit of the ancient site.

The early Greeks chose well this setting, Rob mused while climbing the marble steps, rounded and smoothed from twenty-four centuries of footsteps. The rocky monadnock towered above the city sprawled around its base and presented a commanding view of the surrounding plain that stretched from the Aegean Sea to haze-shrouded mountain peaks in the north. The pearly marble of the Parthenon glowed in the brilliant sunlight. Not a single cloud passed to moderate the blinding rays. "Ever since a college art class," Charis remarked, "I've dreamed of coming here." She seemed to particularly admire the Erechtheum, while Rob silently observed that her slenderness might not have suited the sculptor of the full-figured caryatids.

They both perspired from the heat and exertion; somehow the beads of sweat on her brow added to her appeal. But her true beauty, he realized, was that she seemed so unaware of herself, without airs, open. He commented on how nimbly she scampered about the tumbled ruins. Laughing, she called out, "I should have warned you— my daddy said I was part mountain goat!" They ran fingertips over the weathered stone, examined treasured artifacts in the little museum, wondered how many other voyagers, beginning with the golden Age of Pericles, had basked here in the bright sunshine.

A vendor appeared, pushing a creaky wooden cart laden with soft drinks, packaged snacks, and heaps of plump green grapes. "From hills of Dimitsana," he explained, pointing toward knobby ocher slopes on the distant horizon.

"May we taste one?" Charis asked. With the vendor's nodding approval, she plucked a single grape with her long fingers, smilingly ordered Rob to open wide, and placed it in his mouth.

"Delicious," he said, and purchased a large bunch of the grapes and two sodas.

Charis had worn tennis shoes without socks and the same sleeveless cotton dress, and when they sat on the steps of the

Propylaea to snack, she slipped her feet out of her shoes and hitched her dress up to mid-thigh to bathe her legs in the sunshine. Rob chivalrously averted his eyes, but not before noticing a small tattoo—an orange poppy—on her lovely thigh.

The grapes, they agreed, tasted like sweet wine, juicy and mellow, and as the sun dipped slowly toward those faraway slopes, they chattered lightheartedly of life, sports, the world, their airline. Too soon, wispy columns of smoke curled from the chimneys of thousands of dwellings in the sprawling city, heralding the dinner hour.

They took a different footpath down from the summit, winding past houses with whitewashed and sand-colored stucco walls. The smell of olive oil warming over charcoal flames escaped from open windows, tantalizing their taste buds. The path emerged into the Plaka district, where they window-shopped along the tangled network of narrow streets lined with tourist shops before stumbling onto a bustling, open-air taverna. There they dined on green salad heaped with black olives and strong feta cheese and sizzling-hot shish kebab pierced by flame-blackened skewers, and shared a small carafe of red wine.

They strolled back to the hotel, enjoying the mellow night air. He walked her to her door, where again she thanked him and, much to his surprise, lightly kissed his cheek. His ears reddened, but he could not deny the pleasant sensation.

Early the next morning the crew flew the turnaround to London, arriving in time for Rob and Charis to retrace their journey to Wimbledon for another afternoon of tennis watching, cut short by an untimely shower. Back in the city, they stopped again at The Fife and Fiddle. The walk back to the hotel took them past Kensington Park, where dozens of people were jogging, and she'd asked if he was a runner. "Just a beginner," he'd replied.

"Will you be flying this trip next Tuesday?"

"Tuesday? Yes, I will." International crews usually flew together for the entire month.

"Why don't you bring your running gear," she'd suggested. "We could run together. I know London is safe, but I'm never comfortable running alone in big cities."

The following week, when they ran in the park, Rob was not surprised to find that her natural pace was faster than his, that he had to push himself to keep up. From that day on, he increased his mileage on the back roads of Deerwood.

Completing the month, Rob and Charis were to fly the BOS-LHR-ATH-LHR-BOS pairing twice more. He enjoyed their runs in the park. They became friends—good friends—but not, although it may have seemed inevitable, lovers. Rob, forty-four at that time, didn't ask her age, but judged that he was seventeen or eighteen years her senior, and employed that spacious age differential as an invisible barricade to overfamiliarity, as a dictate to behave in a circumspect, paternal manner.

Once, as they ran side by side on the broad pathway in Kensington Park on a warm, sunny afternoon, he'd said, "Tell me about your name—it's one I've never heard before."

"My dad's an amateur photographer. He has an old book of pictures of the West, and there's a photo of the author's wife, who was called Charis. He just liked the name."

"I do, too. It fits you."

"What's your real first name, Rob?"

He'd chuckled and replied, "Promise not to tell anyone? It's Francis. That's why I use Rob."

They'd run silently for a few minutes, then she'd asked, "Does anyone call you Robby?"

"No one's called me that since I was a kid."

"May I?"

"Sure, if you'd like. . . . Yes"

In addition to runs in the park, those long London layovers found them exploring museums and castles, or attending a concert or play. Of course, Rob made it a point to invite his entire crew along on such forays; not everyone accepted, but except for the running, he and Charis were seldom alone. In this way he sought to suppress the ingenuous contentment he found in her company, to disavow any intention of amorous involvement. He did not forget or forsake his marriage vows. Charis was the daughter he and Jane had once wished for, he reasoned. And although he sensed that Charis's attention signaled something beyond simple companionship, and although he basked in the sensual aura of her presence, he had maintained a prudent distance, fearing to cross that unmarked threshold beyond which there might be no return.

. . . Rob grabbed his hat as a brisk gust of wind whipped across the ramp, rudely chasing thoughts of Charis from his daydreaming mind. He refocused his attention to the job at hand—the exterior inspection of his aircraft.

On airliners that utilized a flight engineer (second officer, in the parlance of some airlines), that person conducted the exterior inspection. But on two-man airplanes like the Starliner, the pilot who would not be flying the forthcoming leg ordinarily performed the walk-around; the "pilot flying," to use the flight manual terminology, preflighted the cockpit. Tonight, because of the time crunch caused by Curtis's late arrival, Rob would handle both jobs.

Trans Globe captains routinely split the flying duties with their first officers. Rob customarily flew the first leg of a trip himself whenever he had an F/O with whom he had not previously flown. This gave the other pilot an opportunity to see how Rob did things, what sort of cockpit atmosphere and level of discipline Rob maintained, and also allowed Rob to observe how well the F/O handled his duties. Trans Globe's flight procedures were highly standardized, but every captain ran his ship a bit differently. Tonight, however, because it was his final trip, Rob would violate his own routine and ask Curtis to fly the leg to Paris, saving the homeward flight—the last Atlantic crossing and final landing—as a parting gift for himself.

Rob methodically moved clockwise around the airplane, shining his flashlight to seek out possible fuel seeps, hydraulic leaks, dents in the Starliner's aluminum skin, service panels left unsecured. He examined the landing gear, tires, and brakes and peered into the inlets and tailpipes of the huge engines, suspended on pylons beneath the great wings that stretched too high above him to touch at full stretch. Whenever he conducted the walk-around, the immense size of this airplane always astonished him.

Aft of the wing, two baggage handlers hoisted large cardboard boxes onto the conveyor belt, which extended into the Starliner's rear cargo compartment. One of the workers, overcoming the shrill whine of the APU, bellowed, "Hey, Captain, did you hear about Air Northeast at La Guardia?"

"No," Rob boomed in reply. "What happened?"

The baggage handler gestured toward his coworker. "Chuck says they found a hand grenade in some jerk's luggage!"

"Sounds like security was on the ball," Rob commented, glad that another possible tragedy had been averted. Still, he had little doubt that a clever, determined individual could find a way to slip a weapon or explosive device past less vigilant checkpoints.

"Have a good one, Captain."

"Thanks." Thoughts of possible violence troubled Rob. Attacking a commercial airplane, wreaking senseless savagery against innocent passengers and crew in the name of politics or retribution, without regard for the victims, seemed to him the most abhorrent crime of all. A modern airliner is very sturdy, he knew, but it is extremely vulnerable to the effect of an internal explosion. When the Starliner is at cruising altitude, typically thirty-three thousand to thirty-nine thousand feet, the aircraft interior is pressurized to about seventy-five hundred feet, creating a differential pressure of more than eight pounds per every square inch of the entire pressurized surface—fuselage, bulkheads, cabin and cargo doors, passenger and cockpit windows. Even a small explosion within the aircraft would likely rupture the adjacent structure, instantaneously causing a loss of pressurization. The passenger emergency oxygen system is designed to sustain those in the cabin for only the several minutes required by the pilots to rapidly descend the aircraft to a lower altitude where the air is sufficiently thick for normal breathing. Like all Trans Globe pilots, Rob had been trained well to handle this contingency, but an explosion might bring other consequences with which no pilot could cope: severed flight controls, rendering the aircraft uncontrollable, or, worse, the disintegration of the fuselage. A sudden cold chill prickled Rob's back; he wished he'd worn his overcoat.

Glancing up at the terminal windows, he thought about the passengers beginning to stream into the jetway. And their courage—not unlike that of our ancestors who crossed the ocean in fragile wooden boats—for aspiring to span the sea inside a thin aluminum tube called a fuselage. He questioned the veracity of Madison Avenue's antiseptic, sugarcoated presentation of commercial aviation. He remembered earlier times, when passengers trudged across the cold, windy ramp holding tight onto their hats, heard the roars of other airplanes, whiffed the exotic fumes of high-octane fuel, and actually looked at the airliner they were to board before they climbed steep stairs into the marvelous flying machine that would magically carry them aloft, far above the mundane perimeters of earthbound existence.

Nowadays, despite the horrors of 9/11, they are seduced by televised promises of gourmet meals, dreamy glides through storm-free skies, unflaggingly solicitous and cheerful cabin attendants, and unerringly competent pilots. Their journey begins in a glitzy terminal lined with specialty shops and looking more like a shopping mall than an airport. Any anxieties passengers might harbor are mollified, perhaps, at the handy saloons, smothered under blaring TV screens in the waiting areas, or soothed with Muzak. They board through a windowless jetway seemingly designed to belie any sensation of actually entering an airplane. How are passengers to comprehend the magnitude of this utterly profound, almost inconceivable venture: entrusting their fragile bodies to fallible human beings, to inscrutable laws of physics and aerodynamics, to invisible vectors of lift and drag, to turbofan power plants whose intricacies few could explain?

To Rob, the Starliner seemed like a giant, living thing: the fuselage its body, the two powerful engines its stalwart twin hearts. Jet fuel supplied liquid nourishment; air-conditioning packs provided life-sustaining air. Hydraulic fluid, like precious blood, coursed through its veins, while thousands of electric wires relayed nerve messages. He marveled at the audacity, the brilliance of the mind of man for conceiving such a machine. It seemed almost beyond belief that he—and Curtis, when he finally got himself here—would soon stir this immobile, Brobdingnagian contrivance to life, command it to hurtle off the ground, to climb into the thin air seven miles above the earth's surface, to cruise there at more than five hundred miles per hour, and to not again touch terra firma until it had spanned a vast ocean and reached a foreign land.

A land where he might spend one last day with Charis.

CHAPTER FIVE

CASH

The cockpit hummed with the steady drone of instrument-cool-ing fans and the soft rush of toasty air from the distribution vents. Warning lights on the overhead panels glowed green to indicate sys-tems operating normally, yellow or red in those not yet activated. Hidden behind side panels, the hundreds of wires that energized the instruments, lights, and switches blended to emit a faint, warm, elec-trical odor. The varied ingredients combined to give the cockpit of each type of aircraft its unique aroma—something pilots take for granted but for Rob a fragrance he knew he would always miss. He hung his jacket and hat in the narrow closet, then settled into the left seat, loosened his necktie, and unfastened the top button of his shirt. His reading half-glasses, attached to a cord looped around his neck, hung on his chest. He appeared utterly comfortable in this familiar environment, but his fingers thrummed against the tops of the fold-ing armrests. With a six-hour-and-thirty-minute flight plan to Paris, being a few minutes late would make little difference in the great scheme of things, he knew, except to reflect unfavorably on his air-line in the government's on-time statistics. Still, he was not pleased with this man Curtis for being late, forcing two hundred and thir-teen passengers and his crew mates to wait.

Ten minutes before scheduled departure time, Rob radioed for the flight's Air Traffic Control (ATC) clearance, jotted it down in shorthand (cl CDG v/Log7 ENE J55 PQI J564 Goo FPR M240 ex370/10af sqk2110) on the flight plan as it was issued, then responded, "Roger, Trans Globe eight-ten cleared to Charles de Gaulle via Logan Seven departure Kennebunk, Jet fifty-five Presque Isle, Jet five sixty-four Goose, flight plan route. Maintain flight level two-four-zero, expect three-seven-zero ten minutes after departure, squawking two one one zero."

"Trans Globe eight-ten, readback correct, contact Ground Control on one twenty-one point seven, and everybody working the night shift wishes you a great last trip, Captain."

"Thank you, and thanks for many years of help," Rob replied, wondering how the Boston tower personnel knew this, then realizing that, undoubtedly, Sparky had spread the word.

Rob double-checked that the ATC clearance exactly matched the routing and altitudes he had loaded into the Flight Management System (FMS) computers. He understood that there were good reasons for having two pilots in airplanes—catching the other pilot's occasional error, confirming routing and altitude changes, agreeing on courses of action when problems arose, plus the obvious safety factor should either pilot become incapacitated. Aviators were not superhuman; several months ago a senior Trans Globe captain had suffered a heart attack in flight, and other maladies such as food poisoning occurred from time to time. Besides, company procedures specified that one pilot load the data into the FMS, the other confirm its accuracy. But because his first officer had not yet arrived, and with departure time approaching, tonight Rob had to bend the rules and perform both tasks himself.

The tempting aroma of coffee drifted through the open cockpit door, then Margot appeared, carrying a tray with a steaming pot, paper cups, a cream server, and individual sugar packets. Yeganeh's reign may have wrought unpleasant changes, Rob mused, but at least Trans Globe still served fine coffee.

"Coffee, Rob? Just brewed a pot."

Rob swung around. "Hi, Margot. Yes, please. Maybe after thirty-two years I'm hooked on that stuff."

She had a compact Afro and each of her wrists bore several gold bracelets that gleamed against her dark skin and jangled lightly as she eased sidesaddle into the first officer's seat. She set the tray on her lap and filled a cup, asking, "Black, right?"

"Yes, thanks, just half a cup. All set in the cabin?"

"Finally. Some passengers carry on so much stuff." She handed the cup to Rob. "How much longer before our first officer arrives?"

Rob checked his watch again. "Two thirty-six should land in a few minutes—it's an hour late tonight. The perils of commuting." He sipped the coffee. "What's Steve up to these days?" Margot's husband was one of the first black pilots hired by the airline.

"Still flying F/O on the 'nine, but he's in line to train on the Starliner in the spring."

"Then you two could fly together sometimes."

"That would be *so* nice. He's due in at ten from a three-day domestic trip, and I'm about to leave for Paris." She sighed. "So much for the romance of flying."

"I see what you mean."

She arched her eyebrows. "Now, who is this Charis? You looked flabbergasted to see her at briefing."

"Did I?" Rob's face colored again. "I was surprised. We're just, uh, old friends. Flew together a few times, oh, about fifteen years ago. Haven't seen her since—well, only at a distance, not to talk to."

"Uh-huh," Margot said skeptically.

"She said she'd traded into this flight, uh, just to . . ."

"Trans Globe eight-ten, Trans Globe ops. Over." Sparky's staccato voice crackled from the overhead speakers.

"Go ahead ops," Rob radioed back.

"Two thirty-six just touched down, be pulling into Gate Sixteen in a couple of minutes. We'll get your man there *tout de suite*. See you Sunday."

Margot said, "I'd better get back to the cabin."

"Thanks again, Margot."

The coffee may not have changed, Rob thought, but airplanes had, and the Starliner's futuristic technology had caused him some anxiety when he first transitioned to it after many years on 707s. He was not of the computer age, and had fretted that he'd be the dog too old to learn new tricks. But he'd caught on fast, and now enjoyed flying the Starliner with its "glass cockpit" and state-of-the-art, digitized, computer-controlled avionics. Now, in place of banks of individual instruments and gauges, flight information was shown on six flat-panel, multicolor, eight- by ten-inch liquid-crystal screens. The two on the center panel presented engine data and parameters and the status of various aircraft systems. One of the two screens on the captain's instrument panel displayed primary flight data including airspeed, vertical speed, altitude, and aircraft attitude; the other provided positional awareness information such as routing and navigational facilities. A repeat of the weather radar could be superimposed on this screen, showing the location of storms in relation to the planned route. The first officer's panel held identical displays.

This modern electronic equipment made flying much easier, but sometimes Rob yearned for the venerable Boeing, about which, he sometimes joked, "the throttles were hooked up to the engines and the rudder pedals and yoke moved the flight controls, instead of everything having to get permission from the darned computer." In the Starliner cockpit, assisted by devices such as the FMS, Inertial Navigation System (INS), Ground Proximity Warning System (GPWS), Traffic Alert and Collision Avoidance System (TCAS), Electronic Flight Information System (EFIS), Aircraft Alerting and Reporting System (ACARS), Full Authority Digital Engine Control (FADEC), and the Global Positioning System (GPS), Rob sometimes felt he'd become merely a systems manager, rather than a pilot and captain prized for his airmanship.

Some industry journalists had deemed the Starliner "the most efficient and sophisticated airliner in the world." Unlike the previous generation of jet transports, such as the 707, which required a three-man operating crew, the Starliner utilized only two pilots (with a relief pilot on certain long-haul operations in which fatigue could be a factor). Automation of the fuel, electrical, air-conditioning, and other systems had rendered the flight engineer position superfluous, just as earlier advances in radio and navigational equipment signaled the dismissal of radio operators and navigators. In addition to reduced crew costs, the Starliner carried forty percent more passengers and provided more below-deck cargo volume than a 707, yet burned a third less fuel.

Aircraft performance data were also incorporated into the Flight Management System, simplifying routine tasks such as selecting optimum climb and cruise speeds and cruising altitude based on air-craft weight, ambient temperature, and wind. Should an engine fail, best single-engine performance parameters would be presented on the screens. As for electronic sophistication, the precise location of every navigational aid and major airport in North and South America, Europe, and the Middle East was stored in the Starliner's computers. It was theoretically possible to program the FMS such that immediately after liftoff, one could engage the autopilot and auto-throttles, command the airplane to climb to the selected alti-tude, cruise at the selected speed on the chosen route, descend at a predetermined point, follow a standard arrival routing, then inter-cept and precisely track the instrument landing system all the way down to an automatic landing. The airplane even had auto-brakes! Of course, it was unlikely that aerial traffic conditions would allow such unfettered freedom of action, and a pilot or a well-trained monkey would still be needed to raise and lower the gear and flaps. Oh, and somebody had to taxi the magnificent contraption to the terminal.

No, flying wasn't that simple to Rob. It had never been simple. People may say that modern aviators merely push buttons, but to him an airplane without flesh-and-blood pilots to give it life was just a huge immobile object. Aircraft such as the Starliner, the giant 747, supersonic single-seat fighters like the F-16, all were technical won-ders and beautiful to behold, but only human pilots possessed the heart and brains to make them sing, to transform those tons of static inertia into soaring, sensuous motion, to accomplish worthwhile feats. And to make the crucial, in-flight decisions that safe flight demanded. He remembered Ernest Gann's admonition in *The High and the Mighty:* An airline pilot is paid for more than sitting grandly aloft and watching the lovely clouds float by.

Rob cinched his seat belt and shoulder harness and was down-ing the last swallow of coffee when Curtis burst into the cockpit. "This friggin' airline!" he growled. "You never can count on it when you have to get someplace on time. Kee-riste, they get a few clouds in K.C. and the whole goddamned system falls on its ass." He slammed his suitcase into the storage bin, not taking care to avoid mashing Rob's luggage, and tossed his shoulder bag on top.

Rob, annoyed, almost bellowed, "Look, Buster, even if two thirty-six had arrived on schedule, you'd have barely made check-in time, and with *that* commute any damned fool would have caught an earlier flight, especially with lousy weather in Kansas City." Instead he extended his hand and introduced himself. "I'm Rob Robertson," he said calmly, knowing that for fifteen or more of the next forty-plus hours—his final working trip in the employ of Trans Globe Airlines—he and Curtis must function as a team, professionally, side by side, in the constricted proximity of the Starliner cockpit. Why start the journey on a sour note?

"Call me Cash," Curtis replied, nearly cracking the bones in Rob's hand as he gripped it, flashing a broad grin of square teeth with narrow gaps between. He was short and stocky, thirtyish but already showing signs of a beer belly, with a ruddy complexion and curly brown hair. His nose was sunburnt and beginning to peel. A gold earring—not specifically forbidden by Trans Globe's SOPs but the first such adornment that Rob had seen on a male Trans Globe pilot—pierced his left earlobe. Cash wore no hat— probably to avoid mussing his hair, Rob surmised dourly. Hats were a nuisance, but they were part of the uniform. Cash's left wrist sported an oversize watch with a multitude of buttons, a type usually favored by novice pilots. Rob expected an apology from Cash for his tardiness, for delaying the passengers and the other crew members, but none came.

As Cash tossed his jacket in the direction of his suitcase, Rob said, "According to a note from the chief pilot, this trip's your international checkout, correct?"

"Yeah, sure is. Never been out of the States before, except for the border towns in May-hee-co," Cash replied. His accent carried a hint of a Southern drawl.

"Okay, we'll discuss the flight-planning procedures later. Sorry to rush you," Rob said, aiming a finger toward the clock on the right instrument panel, "but it's already past block-out time.

Everything's set for engine start. You can fly this leg if you'd like. Get yourself comfortable, and as soon as you're ready we'll run the checklist and crank 'em up."

The first officer raced through his preflight checks, then stated, "Ready, Skipper."

"Don't forget your oxygen mask," Rob suggested, knowing that when cruising at thirty-seven thousand feet they'd have about thirty seconds of useful consciousness following a rapid decompression. And smoke or fumes could quickly fill a cockpit at any altitude. Either situation would be no time to be fumbling with one's oxygen mask.

"You look anxious and I didn't want to take the time," Cash muttered, quickly adjusting the fit of his mask and testing the oxygen flow and built-in microphone before hanging it back on the quick-release strap alongside his right shoulder. "Checklist," he called.

"Before Starting Engines checklist," Rob answered, emphasizing the proper terminology, and hoping to demonstrate subtly the kind of cockpit discipline and precision he expected. Knowing, however, that other pilots, even veteran ones, occasionally gave inexact responses, he held back his increasing annoyance with Curtis.

After completing the checklist, Rob turned to face his first officer. "One other thing. I've always aimed to fly by the book. If I do anything you don't agree with, or if you think the book is wrong, tell me. I'll do the same for you. CRM, they call it nowadays— Cockpit Resource Management—but that's why they put two seats in this cockpit. Okay, Cash, what say we take all these good people to Paris. Call for push-back clearance, please."

After push-back and engine start, Rob taxied the Starliner to the departure runway. He prided himself on taxiing smoothly, not too fast but not too slowly either, making easy turns, stopping the three-hundred-thirty-thousand-pound giant almost imperceptibly. Company policy forbade superfluous cockpit conversation during ground movement and in flight below ten thousand feet; Rob noted approvingly that Cash respected that rule, their only communication being in regard to checklists and responding to instructions from ground control and the tower. When Boston Tower radioed, "Trans

Globe eight-ten, position and hold," Rob taxied the aircraft onto the runway. To compensate for the distance to the main gear tires, eighty-five feet behind the cockpit, he continued past the center stripe before gently prodding the airplane into a ninety-degree turn, which ended with the Starliner aligned precisely on the center of the long runway. The white centerline and edge lights converged far in the distance.

"Trans Globe eight-ten, cleared for takeoff."

"You have the flight controls," Rob advised Cash, simultaneously releasing the brakes and easing the two throttles forward until the needles on the Exhaust Pressure Ratio (EPR) indicators overlapped the triangular indices marking the FMS's calculated thrust level.

It still gave Rob a heady feeling to command, using just a hand, the two powerful Vickery engines with their combined one hundred and ten thousand pounds of thrust. Although he was "giving the leg" to the first officer, following Trans Globe's policy the captain retained control of the throttles and brakes during the ground roll, since only he was authorized to "reject" the takeoff. During that half-minute, Rob had always most keenly felt the responsibility of being captain of an airliner. If an engine failed or another serious mechanical problem occurred below V_1, which the manual defined as "the critical engine-failure speed," he must abort the takeoff and attempt to stop the speeding, fuel-laden aircraft on the swiftly shrinking runway. Rob mentally rehearsed the reject procedure: Close the throttles, apply maximum pressure on the foot brakes, deploy the wing-mounted speed brakes, use reverse thrust on the operating engine—all while maintaining directional control of the airplane. According to the performance charts, if an engine failed at exactly V_1, and if the reject procedure was executed flawlessly, sufficient runway would remain for stopping the aircraft, although in the real world, Rob recalled, few high-speed aborts had been entirely successful. Should circumstances demand that procedure tonight, past the distant end of runway 14L the dark, frigid waters of Boston Harbor awaited his slightest mistake.

However, should an engine fail after V_1, the takeoff must be continued, despite the asymmetric loss of half the power—the engine beneath one wing straining at maximum thrust while the other generated only drag. Full pressure on the rudder pedal on the side with the "good" engine would be required to keep the airplane from yawing grotesquely toward the failed one. Climb performance would deteriorate. The climb profile and airspeeds must be flown precisely to ensure clearance over terrain and tall structures bordering many airports.

Rob understood that tonight two hundred and thirteen passengers and ten crew members had placed their trust in his decision making, reflexes, and airmanship. And for him to act was not simply a matter of waiting for an instrument to falter. His senses were tuned to the sound, feel, motion, and rate of acceleration of the airplane. No computer could replace the human pilot in making this split-second decision. Perhaps the job demanded a younger man, maybe the FAA's "age-sixty rule" made sense, but tonight he was primed to react instantly to any contingency.

Gaining speed remarkably quickly for a machine weighing one hundred and sixty-five tons, the Starliner hurtled down the runway. Twenty seconds into the takeoff roll, Rob lifted his left hand from the nose-wheel steering tiller and simultaneously called "Eighty knots," the speed at which the rudder became effective, meaning that Cash should assume directional control with the rudder pedals. When the airspeed needle indicated 143 knots, Rob called "Vee-one," and a few seconds later, at 153 knots, the rotation speed, "Vee-rotate." Cash pulled back on the control column, the nose of the aircraft rose, and the Starliner lifted thunderously, magically away from the runway lights. Safely airborne, Rob said, "Your throttles."

Cash moved his left hand to the throttles, called "Gear up," continued back pressure on the control column with his right until the aircraft's nose seemed glued at fifteen degrees above the horizon. Trans Globe Flight 810 soared into the night sky, bound for Paris.

Rob monitored Cash closely, as he would any copilot with whom he not previously flown, and was relieved to observe that, despite his cavalier attitude, Cash handled the aircraft well. However, passing through ten thousand feet, with the aircraft "cleaned up" and with the proper climb and navigational modes selected, Cash engaged the autopilot and auto-throttles. This was acceptable procedure, but not what Rob would do. Most Trans Globe pilots hand-flew the aircraft during the initial climb, usually a period of less workload, making it an opportune time to hone basic flying skills. But Rob silently excused Cash, knowing he'd already had a long day.

A few minutes later, Cash asked, "Where do we stay in Pa-ree, Skipper? Downtown, or are we stuck in a motel out near the airport?"

"At the Gallia, not far from the heart of the city," Rob replied. "It's a fine hotel, but the rooms they assign to crew members are rather compact, to put it mildly."

"Do our stews stay there, too?"

"The flight attendants? Yes, why?"

"Hey, man! The crew that stays together plays together." Cash unleashed a cackly laugh that sounded like an agitated turkey. He reached across the center console to slap Rob on the shoulder.

Rob, ignoring the disrespectful familiarity, inquired, "How long have you been on the Starliner?"

"About a year, domestic only. Say, Skipper, I gotta take one hel-luva piss. Will you watch the store?"

"Sure, I've got it," Rob answered without enthusiasm.

"I wanna check out the stews, too. Kee-riste, man, with this many chicks there's gotta be at least one nympho!"

Rob waited silently while Cash guffawed at his own stale joke. As captain, Rob felt protective of his cabin crew, and the notion of this vexatious Texan propositioning anyone—especially Charis—rankled. Controlling his irritation, he said, "Sorry to reduce your odds, but the service manager and one of the flight attendants are male."

"It figures," Cash responded. "Hell, the way things're going, by the time I make captain all the stews will be guys and all the pilots gals. Hey! Maybe that won't be so bad." Cash slapped his thigh and again cackled loudly.

"Look, Cash. They're busy starting the meal service. They don't want you or anybody else in their way. Our passengers come first, and they're anxious for dinner and drinks."

"Me, too. Nothing but a couple of little old bags of pretzels all day." He burped noisily. "Okay, Skipper, won't be long. What's the signal to get back in?"

"Two knocks."

"Two knockers on the door? I'll get one of the stews to lead the way." He exited the cockpit whistling cheerfully.

Alone with his thoughts, Rob decided he would not let Cash get under his skin. Nothing, nobody, would spoil this trip, his farewell to airline flying. A moment later, Boston Center cleared Trans Globe 810: " . . . direct to Presque Isle, flight plan route, climb to and maintain flight level three-seven-zero." Rob repeated the clearance, selected >PQI on the FMS, and reset his altimeter to 29.92 inches as the aircraft ascended through an altitude of seventeen thousand five hundred feet.

Cash returned to the cockpit carrying a plate of hors d'oeuvres. "Margot handed this to me and said to get out of her way," he wisecracked. "How about a shrimp?"

"No thanks," Rob replied.

Buckling into his seat, Cash fumed, "Man, ol' Smokey's out of luck this trip—every one of the stews is either p.g. or old enough to be my mother." He grinned mischievously, observing Rob's reaction. "One gal's pretty well preserved. Said she knew you, Skipper, you sly devil."

Rob motioned toward the control wheel, said, "You've got it," and updated Cash on the revised clearance. Then, looking away, he said, "Charis and I are old friends, just friends."

"Sure, Skipper, I understand," Cash said, stifling a giggle.

Both men were silent while Cash devoured the hors d'oeuvres, then Cash grumbled, "Anyhow, all the other babes are hitched." Switching to a falsetto, he added, "I guess that leaves only Gre-go-ry," and again burst into that cackling laugh.

Rob waited for the laughter to stop, then said evenly, "He's a fine service manager." Turning to look directly at his copilot, he continued, "Look, Cash, let's get one thing straight. I don't want you treating any member of my crew rudely. Understand?"

"Oh sh . . ." Cash stopped, seeming to recall the rules of flight deck decorum. "Sorry 'bout that."

"Okay. Forget it. Let's change the subject," Rob suggested curtly, wanting to avoid any friction. He knew of pilots who'd had such vociferous disagreements, usually over politics, that the flight attendants had intervened. Whatever the subject, such behavior could result in a breakdown in cockpit discipline and a loss of vigilance. "Heard about the latest incident?"

"Just rumors. What happened?"

"A Navy fighter plane shot down a Libyan Airways Skybus over the Mediterranean. No survivors, evidently."

"Libya—that's in Africa, right?"

"Yes, North Africa, west of Egypt."

"I'll bet they were trying a kamikaze attack on our ships," Cash said. "Just like nine-eleven."

"I don't think so," Rob replied. "The airplane was full of people returning from a pilgrimage to Mecca. It'd stopped to refuel and had just taken off."

"Well, they've got that crazy guy, Kadami, something like that," Cash said, scratching his nose. "I'm amazed anybody could teach A-rabs learn how to fly airplanes. Kee-riste, they live in tents and all they do is pray and ride around on camels."

"Gadhafi," Rob said. "And they're not backward. They've made major contributions to astronomy and mathematics, and for about six centuries they ruled a big chunk of the world. Ever heard of the Ottoman Empire?"

"Nah. We didn't learn stuff like that in Texas."

Feeling that this conversation was going nowhere, and with the aircraft settled into cruise flight, Rob spent the next fifteen minutes reviewing international procedures with his first officer, use of the High Frequency (HF) radios for position reports, and programming the FMS for overwater navigation. Satisfied that Cash had a good grasp of the operation, Rob suggested, "Tell me about yourself."

Cash said he'd grown up in Dallas, "Big D," as he called it. He'd attended A&M for a couple of years but didn't graduate, learned to fly at Pitts Aviation, then had worked for Trans Tex commuter airline before being hired by Trans Globe "nine or ten years ago." Twice divorced, two kids were with "number one ex." His second wife had been Nancy Follansbee. "Name sound familiar?"

"Isn't she pretty high up?" Rob asked. "The assistant director of In-flight Service?"

"Yeah, something like that. She went over to the other side, but at least I got to screw management for a while, instead of them always screwing me." Again the cackling laugh, but this time Rob could not suppress a smile.

After several minutes of silence Cash inquired, "You married, Skip?"

"Widower. I live alone," Rob replied.

"Man, you oughta move down my way if you're not getting any." Cash described "good ol' Texas gals" as being the best looking and having "great boobs," and assured Rob there were "plenty of gals to go around—even some your age. My condo's full of 'em."

"I'll keep that in mind."

As Trans Globe 810 sped by the distant lights of Saint John, New Brunswick, Margot came to the cockpit to take the pilots' dinner requests. She checked her chart to determine which entrées had not already been selected from the first-class menu. "The veal's gone," she said, "but there's one filet mignon left, one veggie plate, and the seafood dish."

"You mean we don't have to eat those rotten crew meals?" Cash asked.

"Oh no, not on international," Margot replied, "and the food's pretty good. Well, not what it used to be, before Mr. Yeganeh took over."

"Hey, don't knock ol' Frank," Cash said. "He saved the airline, didn't he? We've got jobs, right? And food, and I'm hungry as a newborn colt."

Rob said, "Cash, since you're flying this leg, you have first choice."

Margot raised her eyebrows. "Your last trip, Rob, and you're giving him first choice?"

"Last trip?" Cash queried. "You're quitting?"

"Yep, retiring. When we return on Sunday, that's it."

"Congrats, Skipper, and ma'am, bring me the closest thing to a steak. Please!"

Ten minutes later, when Margot served the filet, sizzling hot from the convection oven, Cash eyed it dubiously. "Damn! Did Yeganeh downsize the goddamned steaks, too? Back home in Texas they'd stick a toothpick in this little-bitty thing and call it an appetizer."

For safety reasons, company policy dictated that pilots not eat simultaneously, when time allowed, and that they choose different meals. With just two pilots, the airline could not risk both coming down with food poisoning, especially in mid-Atlantic. Rob requested the seafood dish.

Before Yeganeh's tightfisted approach, Trans Globe's international in-flight meals had been the epitome of airline cuisine, always ranking high in industry surveys. Now there were fewer choices and courses, and even first-class passengers were served unexceptional wines, rather than the *grands crus* of yesteryear. Such frugality may have saved a few dollars, Rob acknowledged, but surely it cost the airline dearly in passenger loyalty.

CHAPTER SIX

REVELATIONS

Two hours and twenty minutes into the flight, Trans Globe 810 approached Goose Bay, Labrador, a small, remote community but one with a vital airfield. Gazing down at the dim lights, twinkling in the frigid air like a cluster of stars, Cash sneered, "Do people actually live down there?"

"Yep, but not many," Rob replied. "The combined population of Goose Bay and the town next to it—Happy Valley, it's called—is only about seven thousand. The nearest settlement of similar size is more than two hundred miles away."

"Happy Valley? Wonder what they're happy about. Man, it sure looks cold and desolate." Cash shuddered. "I'd die of boredom—if I didn't freeze to death first."

"It does look wintry tonight," Rob acknowledged, "and I know nothing about the 'Happy' part, but I do know that on September eleventh, when our government closed U.S. airspace, the airport workers and the folks who live nearby did a tremendous job of dealing with the dozens of airliners that landed here. I don't know how many diverted to Goose, but I read that thirty-eight planes with over sixty-six hundred passengers inbound to the United States landed at Gander. After the local radio station announced what was happening, the townspeople brought food and blankets and sleeping bags to the airport. The passengers and crews were stranded for three days, and they were put up in schools and other public buildings, and some folks even took them into their homes. The school bus drivers had been on strike, but they came back and worked twenty-four hours straight without pay. I suspect the passengers and crews stranded at Goose got the same hospitable treatment."

Cash said, "I won't knock it again. Sounds like a great place to land in a pinch."

"It was the same story at Halifax, Nova Scotia," Rob added. "I saw a photograph in *Aviation Monthly* showing about forty planes parked nose-to-tail, occupying every square inch of taxiway and ramp space on the airport."

"Halifax. Ain't that where that Swissair with the electrical problems was trying to land—the one that went into the drink?"

Rob nodded, thinking about the valiant fishermen of tiny Peggy's Cove who went out in their boats in the dark of night in a desperate search for survivors.

Leaving behind Goose Bay's dim cluster of lights, Trans Globe 810 soared east into the deepening darkness. Rob scanned the ebony umbrella of sky and asked, "Do you know the stars?"

"Nah. The only heavenly bodies that turn me on are the ones in bikinis." He squinted at the sky. "Besides, we don't have stars this bright in Houston."

"They're there," Rob said, "it's just that your night sky is aglow from the millions of lights and neon signs." He pointed out the great constellation Ursa Major, so familiar to pilots and shepherds, sparkling clean against a black velvet background. "See those four bright stars at eleven o'clock? Imagine they form a bucket and the three stars to the side are the handle. That's the Big Dipper, and if you trace an imaginary line from the nearest two stars, it leads you right to Polaris, the North Star."

"I'll be damned," Cash remarked. "Always wondered about that."

"And see, Polaris is the end of a handle of a smaller bucket, called the Little Dipper, Ursa Minor," Rob explained. He leaned forward for a better view through the broad windshield. "Those stars that make a W? The constellation Cassiopeia. That prominent star overhead—Capella," Rob continued, aiming a finger as he identified each entity. "There's the planet Saturn to the right, and that fuzzy-looking spot—it's a cluster of stars called the Pleiades."

"How'd you learn all this stuff?"

"I've spent a good part of my life crossing the Atlantic in the middle of the night, and eventually I absorbed a few things, I guess," Rob joked. "Oh, that's Jupiter ahead and those two bright stars are the twins, Castor and Pollux, in the constellation Gemini. Admittedly, it takes a fertile imagination to turn an array of stars into something like Taurus, the Bull."

"Especially when sober," Cash teased.

"There's one that's easy to recognize, coming up on the horizon. See those stars in a row? That's called Orion's Belt, part of Orion the Hunter, pursuing Taurus." Close behind tagged faithful Sirius, the Dog Star, brightest star in the heavens.

"Hope I don't have to pass a quiz to get my international check-out," Cash protested.

"No, of course not," Rob replied, thinking it was going to be a long night. Ahead of and beneath Flight 810 lay more than two thousand nautical miles of inky black ocean, and for the two pilots, hours of constant attention to navigation and aircraft systems, with routine position reports each ten degrees of longitude, until reaching landfall over Ireland.

Although the cockpit stayed comfortably warm, the air surging past the inch-thick Plexiglas windshield registered a temperature of sixty-seven degrees Fahrenheit below zero. Yet here the Starliner purred, operating most efficiently in this frigid, rarefied atmosphere. Low ambient temperatures increased the turbojet engines' thermal efficiency, and the thinner air at high altitude spawned less aerodynamic drag on the airframe.

Gregory called on the interphone. "Captain, we're ready to start the movie if you want to talk to the passengers first. Maybe that'll make those Singing Squares cool it."

"Will do," Rob replied, then reached for the public address microphone and handed it to Cash. "It's your leg. Why don't you tell everyone where we are and that we should arrive close to schedule. And then we won't bother them again until morning."

In the cabin, the flight attendants completed the dessert service, picked up meal trays, and dimmed the lighting. Now came the quiet time. Some passengers would watch the movie, others might sleep or read. In this serenity, thoughts of Charis rekindled in Rob's mind . . .

He recalled that moment one year, precisely, after Jane's funeral, when on a whim, using the pretense of being just curious about her present domicile and the trips she'd been flying, he had keyed Charis's employee number (which still somehow stuck in his memory, like his Air Force serial number) into the FLACCS computer. And standing awestruck as DELOREY, C.B. flashed on the screen, not the BURNS, C.R. he'd expected. And how he'd briefly hoped he had typed the wrong numbers. The changed last name meant, he'd realized, feeling oddly disheartened, that she had married. He'd long conceded, of course, the inevitability of marriage for such a lovely and spirited young woman; still, the sight of this startling information stunned him, as if the gate to some undefined, noble passage had slammed closed. He had, at that moment, petulantly vowed to exclude her forever from his solitary longing, but lofty intentions could never suppress bittersweet memories from popping uninvited into his head, as they had earlier in the shower. Why now, he wondered, on this, my final trip, has she come? To bid me farewell? To apologize? Whatever her motive, he hoped she would visit the cockpit soon.

While stars overhead glittered like tiny diamonds, a radiant glow swirling high above the bleak northern horizon claimed Rob's attention. Luminescent pastels of light kindled in the sky and unfolded into slowly waving banners that floated across space, curving and coiling in great emerald and magenta arcs. The aurora borealis.

"Golly, Cash, take a look at this."

The first officer leaned across the center console for a better view. "Man, that sure beats *Star Wars*. I get visions like that when I'm making love to a beautiful gal."

Cash may have ticked me off earlier, but he is a character, Rob decided, smiling to himself as he wondered what sort of predicament Cash's seemingly irrepressible urges would get him into in Paris, a city of countless temptations.

"Want me to tell the passengers?" Cash asked.

Rob looked at his watch. "It's late. Everyone's either asleep or watching the movie."

As the aurora grew more brilliant, Rob silently acknowledged the pilots' unheralded side benefit of occupying the best seats in the house when presented with a spectacular view of the earth or sky. Yes, sights like this he would miss. He recalled the Robert Service poem:

> *Were you ever out in the great alone*
> *When the moon was awful clear,*
> *And the icy stillness hemmed you in*
> *With a silence you most could hear . . .*
> *While high overhead green yellow and red*
> *The north lights swept in bars . . .*

Two soft raps on the cockpit door interrupted Rob's reverie. He pushed the door lock release button, and turned to see Charis's slim figure silhouetted in the doorway. She stepped into the darkened cockpit, carrying a tray with three paper cups of steaming liquid.

"Coffee, gentlemen? Margot told me how you like it."

Rob said, "Yes, please. Charis, you've met Cash, I believe."

She laughed lightheartedly. "Yes, we met. He told me all about himself." For once, to Rob's surprise, Cash had no clever retort.

Rob noted approvingly that Charis did not reach across the center console, where a spill might frizzle the delicate electronic gear, causing all sorts of problems, but instead served each from the side. Then, keeping the third cup for herself, she slid onto the observer's or "jump" seat—an extra seat utilized by FAA and company check airmen when evaluating the operating crew, and by commuting pilots when the cabin was full—behind and to the left of Rob's seat.

Rob twisted around. "Thanks," he said. "Good timing, too. We've been watching the northern lights." He pointed at the luminous swashes of colors spooling through the heavens.

She leaned forward for a better view. "It's beautiful," she said, and watched in silence for several minutes. "What causes the sky to glow like that?"

"Been waiting years for someone to ask," Rob joked as he reached into his flight kit. He pulled out a small notebook, then switched on the narrow-beam reading light. "According to the *National Geographic,* auroras appear when electrons high above the Earth's magnetic poles are energized by the solar wind and crash into gaseous atoms and molecules."

"Yeah, so what causes them?" Cash asked in mock seriousness, then slapped his thigh and laughed.

"Touché," Rob said softly, extinguishing the reading light.

They sat quietly for several minutes, admiring the evolving, iridescent display, until Rob broke the silence by asking, "Did that singing group ever quiet down? Gregory said they took it upon themselves to provide in-flight entertainment."

"Yes, they're quiet now, thank goodness." Then Charis leaned closer. Resting her hand on his shoulder, she said in a low voice, "How long has it been, Robby, fifteen years?"

"Yes, I believe so. Fifteen years."

"I had to see you once more . . . I had to tell you . . ."

"No, it was my fault. Besides, nothing really happened between us."

Diaphanous ribbons of crimson and orange slowly curled across the firmament as again they silently admired the celestial spectacle.

"How have you been?" she asked.

"I'm doing okay. And you? You look fine." He thought: *As lovely as you looked before.*

"Thank you. Do you still follow tennis?"

"No, not anymore, Charis. I developed an aversion to tennis."

"I don't have time for it either." After a moment she asked, "Do you still run?"

"Yep, that I do, nearly every day. You were the one who got me hooked . . ."

And he remembered a gray afternoon in London when the light mist had erupted into a deluge. Caught in Kensington Park, they had cut across the manicured grass to the nearest gate and, spotting a pub farther down the street, raced for it.

*The bartender, a huge man with a huge handlebar mustache, had
eyed them coolly when they'd clambered, laughing, in just their
dripping wet running clothes, onto stools at the bar. But then he'd
reached under the counter, pulled out two clean dish towels for them
to dry themselves with, and suggested, "'Ow about an 'ot toddy?"*

". . . in fact, I brought along my gear."

"I did, too." Her manner brightened. "Would you mind if I
joined you? Running alone in some cities can be unnerving. There
always seem to be people who think that seeing a female runner is
an invitation to make comments."

He savored the notion of running with her, and, afterward perhaps, dining together—along with some of the other crew, of course.
"It'll be like the old days," he replied, mindful that, over time, their
situations had reversed—that now she was the married one and he
was single. "There's a good place to run along the Seine, away from
traffic."

"Fine," she said. They were silent for a moment, both watching
the spiraling, multicolored bands weave across the sky. Then she
asked, "Are you looking forward to retirement?"

"You know, it really sneaked up on me. I hadn't thought of myself
as over the hill, at the end of my career. It seems like just yesterday that
I started flying. But everyone has to quit at some point, and I'm okay
financially."

"What will you do with all your spare time?"

"Oh, I'll have plenty to do, especially for the next couple of
months. I grow Christmas trees . . ."

"Real Christmas trees?" Cash interjected. "Man, all they grow
down in Texas are them wobbly plastic things. My condo won't
allow live trees. Fire hazard. Too dangerous."

"Yep, the real thing," Rob said. "Plastic trees are an abomina-
tion. Anyhow, next week we'll begin harvesting this year's crop, bal-
ing the trees, and getting them to market."

"Harvesting!" Cash exclaimed in mock horror. "You mean
you're gonna kill those poor little trees?"

"Do you eat carrots? Same principle."

"Now I remember," Charis said. "You were just getting

started—you told me about that the day we met, when you took me to Wimbledon, remember? You had two tickets because your wife had planned to come but had been ill."

"You have a good memory," Rob said, again visualizing that day. "Christmas trees don't require much day-to-day care, and I didn't want that good farmland to sit idle and besides, I like to grow things. I don't need the extra money now, but back then I figured an airline pilot should have a backup source of income, just in case he or she busted a physical one day, or botched a check ride, or put a dent in the company's expensive sheet metal, and bam," he snapped his fingers for emphasis, "his career is finished."

"I see what you mean."

Rob glanced at Cash. "I hope you're listening."

"Yeah, but me, I spend my spare time chasing girls," Cash replied with a toothy grin.

"Then maybe some traveling," Rob continued. "There are places I've longed to visit, the Serengeti, Machu Picchu, maybe Tahiti some day. But I'll keep growing trees. In the spring we'll plant five hundred seedlings. It takes seven or eight years to grow a good-sized Christmas tree from a ten-inch seedling. But otherwise, I haven't made any definite plans."

"I'm sure your wife—Jane, isn't it?—will be pleased to have you home," Charis said. "Not flying across the ocean, watching Grecian sunsets with impressionable young flight attendants." She patted his shoulder lightly.

Rob looked down, then in a hushed voice said, "Jane's dead. She was in an automobile accident."

Charis leaned forward and clasped his shoulder. "Oh, Robby. I didn't know. I'm sorry." In the dim light Rob saw a tear, glistening like crystal in the starlight, inch slowly down her cheek.

Far to the north, an incandescent violet band slowly uncoiled across the blackness and hung like a gossamer curtain draped over a heavenly window while stars twinkled in the background like tiny decorations.

Cash brought Rob back to the moment. "Sorry about your wife, Skipper." He pointed to the inertial navigation system readouts. "We're passing fifty west."

Charis gently touched Rob's shoulder. "I'll be back later."

Rob rechecked the aircraft's position on the INS indicators, noted the time and jotted it on the flight plan, and calculated an estimated time of arrival (ETA) for 40° west, the next reporting point, by correlating the flight plan's and FMS's estimated leg times. He confirmed the numbers with Cash, compared the fuel remaining, as indicated on the gauges, with the precomputed burn, and advised him, "We're two minutes under flight plan, and the fuel's nineteen hundred pounds to the good." Then he picked up the microphone and called, "Gander Radio, Trans Globe eight-ten, position. Over."

When he had completed the position report, Rob turned to Cash. "Sorry. It was impolite of me to hold a private conversation here in the cockpit. As I mentioned earlier, Charis and I are old friends. It'd been a long time."

Cash said, "Hey, she looks pretty good for her age, Skipper. A little skinny for my taste, but what she's got is in the right places." He let out a whistle, looked at Rob, grinned. "I think she likes you."

"Well, it doesn't matter. She's married to some guy named Delorey. Flies for Trans-Continental, as I recall. You may have heard of him. I guess he's a fanatic about old warbirds, even owned a couple of World War Two fighters, a Mustang and a British Sea Fury that he raced in that Unlimited Class. Meant to ask her about him."

Cash stared at Rob in disbelief. "Did you say Delorey? *Sam* Delorey? She married him?"

"Yep. I read an article about him, oh, years ago. It said he planned to replace the engine in that Sea Fury with a forty-three sixty and try setting a new speed record for prop-driven airplanes."

"Holy shit! He almost did. Yeah, almost. You didn't know about that?"

"Know what?"

"Oh man. He was making a practice run over the desert out west of Tucson, right down on the deck and going like a bat out of hell when that fucking engine blew, and he splattered that god-damned Fury with himself still in it all over the desert. Yeah, about seven or eight years ago. Nothing left of man or flying machine but little-bitty pieces."

Rob gasped. "Oh God," he said.

CHAPTER SEVEN

MEMORIES

Every evening, Oceanic Control establishes a family of east-bound trans-Atlantic routes, called tracks, each identified by a separate letter code, starting with Z for the most southerly route, then working backward. Westbound tracks, used primarily in the day-time, are assigned the beginning letters of the alphabet. Typically there are five or six tracks in each direction, and they are revised daily to take advantage of the most favorable winds and to avoid severe weather. Each track is separated horizontally from the adjacent one by one degree of latitude, which equals sixty nautical miles. Aircraft are normally separated by two-thousand-foot altitude increments from other aircraft following the same track and ten-minute time intervals from those assigned the same flight level. Reporting points are designated at each ten degrees of longitude, enabling Oceanic Control to continuously monitor aircraft separation.

Technological advances of the past two decades had greatly simplified overwater navigation, the most significant being the Global Positioning System (GPS), which utilizes signals from an array of twenty-four solar-powered satellites orbiting twelve thousand miles above the earth. The GPS receiver compares the time a signal is sent from the satellite until it is received. With this relatively low-cost

device (inexpensive handheld receivers are in widespread use by sur-
veyors, long-haul truck drivers, and many others, including private
pilots), a speeding aircraft's latitude and longitude can be determined within a few meters, almost anywhere on earth, if signals
from four satellites are received. Three signals produce a less refined
position.

Occasionally, however, an aircraft's GPS receiver will fail, or a
critical satellite might cease transmitting. With dozens of aircraft
overflying the North Atlantic at any given moment, the failure of a
critical satellite might cause navigational chaos, ruling out the use of
GPS as an airliner's sole derivation of navigational data. Thus, on
the Starliner, the GPS functions to continuously refine the calculated
positions of two highly sensitive Inertial Navigation Systems.

Each INS is a self-contained unit employing a laser gyro. During
preflight preparations, pilots load the aircraft's gate position into the
INSs, using geographical coordinates accurate to the nearest tenth of
a minute of latitude and longitude. Typically, after an eight-hour
flight, even with no further updating, the aircraft's calculated INS
position will be accurate to less than two hundred feet—well within
the limits for overwater navigation.

In addition, the Starliner's two Flight Management System
(FMS) computers incorporate a vast database of ground-based navigational facilities such as Automatic Direction Finding (ADF) and
Very High Frequency Omnirange (VOR) stations, Distance
Measuring Equipment (DME), and Instrument Landing Systems
(ILS) as well as standard departure and arrival routes, instrument
approach procedures, and suitable civil and military airports. The
information from all sources is absorbed and blended into a "present position," with greater weight given to the more accurate sen-
sors. The FMS displays the desired navigational data on eight- by
ten-inch liquid-crystal displays on each pilot's instrument panel. In
addition, the FMS will detect a sensor that differs significantly from
the others—either in distance or in rate of divergence—and warn the
pilots.

Tonight, from overhead Goose Bay, Trans Globe 810 had flown
to an imaginary fix code-named LOACH, the track entry point, then
had followed track V to 58 degrees north latitude/50 degrees west

longitude, continued to 59N/40W, 59N/30W, and was now approaching 58N/20W. Next would come 56N/10W, and from that point, airways led to landfall over Aran Island, near the rugged coast of Ireland.

During the long night, each of the flight attendants had visited the cockpit, taking a brief respite from the crowded cabin, but now silence reigned on the flight deck. Except for an occasional position report on the High Frequency (HF) radios, even the airwaves were hushed. The pilots also routinely monitored the two Very High Frequency (VHF) radios. One was tuned to 131.8 megahertz (MHz), the air-to-air "common" employed by pilots to relay useful flight information, such as areas of turbulence, and sometimes by less disciplined airmen engaged in shop talk. The other VHF was set to 121.5 MHz, the international frequency reserved for emergency transmissions. In his thirty-two years of airline flying, Rob had never had need to make a distress call, although on several occasions he had heard such transmissions from other aircraft.

As Trans Globe 810 continued its eastward journey, the magnificent display of the aurora borealis gradually diminished, then finally disappeared, and the sky returned to blackness salted by the scattered millions of stars. Rob scanned the heavens for meteors, aware that the Leonid showers would be at their maximum on the eighteenth—just two nights away; but tonight, only a few, fleeting shooting stars had streaked across the firmament before the first hint of dawn, a deep blue mellowing of the darkness, washed the horizon.

The autopilot, directed by the two electronically linked FMSs, precisely followed its designated invisible path high above the North Atlantic. As the miles to the next reporting point hypnotically counted down on the digital readouts, Rob recalled that fateful trip, fifteen years ago, the last time he had been with Charis . . .

Again they had flown the overnight to London, and had run in the park in the afternoon. He remembered that, returning to the hotel, Charis had nearly been hit by a speeding car when she looked left instead of right before stepping off the curb to cross a busy street. That evening, accompanied by three other crew members, they had attended the long-running play The Mousetrap. *The next day, in Athens, other flight attendants had joined them for sight-seeing and dinner. Back in London the following afternoon, en route to the hotel in the crew bus under a gray, overcast sky, they made plans to meet after short naps to go for a run.*

Rob had not slept well. When he'd roused himself and looked outside, a steady drizzle was falling. Charis answered her phone after the third ring.

"Robby, is that you?" A slow, soft yawn. "Did I oversleep?"

"Yes, it is, and, no, you didn't." Her drowsy voice triggered a vision of her awakening beside him, her long sunny hair tumbling over the white pillow, her skin warm and smooth beneath his touch. He abruptly caught himself, silently chastised himself for imagining such forbidden fantasies, and reminded himself that he was married, that Charis was just a friend. Moreover, she had made no overtures that suggested any motive beyond simple companionship, nor had he. He frowned at his vanity, for indulging in such mental gymnastics over a woman young enough to . . . "Remember? I said I'd call. Just peeked outside—it's raining cats and dogs, too darned wet to run."

Perhaps he should have left it at that. Although Rob had tried to convince himself that he harbored no illicit yearnings, and knew, somehow, that he should not pursue this relationship, he stumbled on. "Look, it's two-thirty local time. Would you care to meet, say, in half an hour, see if we can find something resembling lunch?" It was the first time they had canceled a run, not counting the day they'd been caught in a sudden downpour.

Charis, looking sparklingly fresh, her hair pulled back neatly and flowing over her neck, had walked briskly into the crowded lobby. She wore a dark knee-length skirt and a fuzzy, honey-colored sweater, with a silk scarf of lavender and green encircling her neck. Her trusty L.L. Bean rain jacket hung over her arm, and a small leather purse swung from the ends of a shoulder strap. The sight of her gave Rob a strange delight.

She paused, standing very erect, looked around, spotted him, flashed a smile, and moved toward him in her quick, direct way. A silence settled over the room as businessmen in somber, pinstriped suits, huddled in small groups, stopped in mid-sentence and turned to watch her. Charis seemed like a flower bursting into bloom in a sea of gray, and with her tanned face and dazzling smile looked

*utterly healthy compared to the pale-faced English, radiating a natu-
ral look that many women strove for, or so it seemed to Rob, but few
attained. Small gold earrings adorned her ears but she wore no other
jewelry, and a thin veneer of lipstick appeared to be her only makeup.
However guileless his intentions, Rob felt a licentious pride that this
charming lady would be his companion for the afternoon.*

*No, it went beyond pride. He felt that some rare perfection had
touched him. He was falling in love, and he suddenly understood it
had to stop. It wasn't fair to Jane . . . Or to Charis. Rob wasn't a
religious man, but a Puritan conscience coursed within his Yankee
blood.*

*Under gray skies they had queued at the bus stop in front of the
hotel, climbed the narrow, winding rear stairway to the upper level
of the dull red double-decker bus, perched in the front row like
tourists to admire the stately buildings lining the Bayswater Road.
They exited at Marble Arch, sauntered the wide, congested side-
walks dodging umbrellas, and window-shopped past haberdasheries
and boutiques, music shops throbbing with rock beats, and other
establishments jammed with merchandise and shoppers. Turning
down a less crowded side street, they found a small restaurant and
went inside.*

*Over second cups of coffee for him and tea for her, they talked
about things to see and do. They studied a small guidebook Charis
had tucked into her jacket pocket, but could not find a historic
church or building or chilly museum that beckoned.*

*"It's an indoor sort of day," she'd said. "I'd love to visit a big
department store. We're not far from Harrington's."*

*Low, dreary clouds still hovered but the rain had ceased as they
turned onto Oxford Street. They strolled along the bustling avenue
until they faced the store's imposing facade with its colossal Ionic
columns, three stories high. Harrington's occupied an entire block,
and every floor featured expensive, quality goods from various
countries: handcrafted furniture, modernistic lamps, safari apparel,
delicate china—a veritable museum of contemporary treasures.*

*"Jane would be in heaven here," Rob joked. "She spends so
much time at the North Shore Mall she says they're going to make
her an honorary shareholder."*

"*Why don't you buy something for her?*" Charis suggested.

"*That's a good idea. In fact, her birthday's next week. Been scratching my head over what to get.*"

"*What sorts of things does she like?*"

"*Nice clothes. Jewelry. Pop music, jazz. Tennis and golf accessories,*" he'd replied. "*Hmm. Pottery—she has quite a collection. Stoneware, mostly, which I must admit I'm not crazy about. Pour a mug of piping hot coffee and a minute later it's cold as ice. Well, you'll have to help me choose.*"

They'd found the pottery department on the second floor. Shelves and countertops held carefully arranged examples of the ancient craft, a potpourri of objects representing every corner of the globe. With assistance from the solicitous salesman, who—with his dark suit, dapper mustache, and bald pate—bore an uncanny resemblance to a former British prime minister, and after much diligent searching, Charis proposed, "*What about this?*" She'd selected a small, exquisitely simple sky blue vase, and spoke with an earnestness Rob had not detected before. "*See how it catches the light and how deep the color is,*" she said, then, holding the vase higher, added, "*and the blue exactly matches your eyes.*"

"*It is beautiful,*" Rob agreed, "*despite any possible resemblance.*"

"*It's called opaline,*" Charis explained as the salesman nodded in agreement, "*but I've never actually seen anything like this before except in books.*" She turned it upside down. "*See, this is from the pontil—that's the metal rod the glassblower holds it with—and that's his signature mark. That means it's authentic, and quite old, I think.*" She beamed encouragingly as she carefully handed it to Rob. "*And expensive.*"

"*Yes, this will be a lovely gift,*" he'd said, truly pleased. He motioned to the salesman, then looked at Charis. "*Jane will like this. Thank you.*"

Afterward, they'd strolled along Bond Street, scrutinizing the window displays. Charis admired the pricey, fashionable clothes, but they purchased nothing more.

The day passed quickly, and before returning to the hotel they decided to dine at Hasani's, a spotless Lebanese restaurant they had *chanced on earlier that summer. The modest eatery specialized in vegetarian fare and the chef seemed to take special care that nothing was overcooked.*

The waiter, who appeared to be of Middle Eastern descent, first brought warm pita bread, wrapped in linen to retain the heat, and a "finger-food" salad of celery sticks, cherry tomatoes, and broccoli florets, with cucumbers and carrots sliced lengthwise. The main course consisted of a heaping platter of couscous and, in a side bowl, a steamy sauce with vegetables and exotic spices (a bit heavy on the garlic for Rob's taste), also to be shared. They scooped the couscous onto their plates and topped it with the thick sauce. Later, the waiter brought a second pot of tea to accompany the raspberry sorbet.

Rob had been rather quiet throughout the meal, again at a mental impasse, grappling with his dilemma. Charis had asked, "What's wrong, Robby? If it's none of my business, just say so, but you seem very distant."

He'd procrastinated. "No, it's nothing," he said, but later, outside her door in the hotel, he'd said, "Charis, you know I've enjoyed being with you, but . . ."

"But what?"

"I've been trying to build up my courage all day. I wish there was a better way to say this. I . . . I shouldn't see you anymore."

Her manner stiffened. She eyed him quizzically. "Why, what do you mean?"

"It's nothing you've done. It's . . . My life's been in a tizzy. Jane . . ." He wanted to tell Charis, to tell someone, that things were not good, that Jane had been distant lately, remote, indifferent to him. That she was spending more and more time at her club, but at home she'd been argumentative, moody, complaining of headaches, not sleeping well, you name it. She wouldn't see the doctor—she said it wasn't physical—but he was worried, very worried, and maybe a little jealous of that Henderson character.

Charis's tone mellowed. "I don't know her, of course, but she must be a very fine person."

He groped for the precise words. "It's never been right for me to . . . to find ways to keep seeing you, and it's especially unfair now, while she is so . . . afflicted. I feel terribly guilty." More softly, he said, "I'm sorry, Charis, I shouldn't have waited until now to . . ."

"Does she know about me, I mean, that we've . . . spent time together?"

"Well, yes, sort of," Rob stammered. "Jane's never expected me to sit in my hotel room and stare at the walls. She knows that crews go out on layovers, like we've done, for dinner, sight-seeing, things like that. She knows the routine—she's accompanied me on flights many times. But lately, she hasn't wanted to go anywhere—with me." He paused, looked down. "Yes, I've told her about . . . running together, places we've seen. Maybe not everything. She knows that other members of the crew join us, sometimes, that it's not always just . . . you and me. It's my fault. I shouldn't have let things go this far."

"What do you mean 'this far'? Nothing's happened. Nothing at all. What is there to hide?" Her hand moved to his arm, then up to his shoulder. "You've done nothing to feel guilty about."

"Well, the other thing is I've been pretending that it's platonic— isn't that the word? That you were someone to run with, go sight-seeing with. Simply that. I keep reminding myself I'm almost old enough to be your fath—"

Charis touched a finger to his lips, then slipped her hand around his neck. "I already have a father, Robby. Maybe we've both been pretending." She gently eased down his head and pressed her cheek against his. "Please don't go . . . stay with me tonight," she had whispered.

He hesitated. Her lips looked so warm and inviting. Then his arms encircled her waist, one hand still clutching the opaline vase. He cherished the moment, knowing he would not forget the fragrance of her hair, the warmth of her supple body, her breasts soft against his chest, his quickening desire, and knowing, too well, what he must do. In a hushed voice he said, "I want desperately to say yes, Charis, but I can't forsake her now. I can't."

"Are you saying that's it?" She looked at him a long moment, withdrew her hand, and pulled back, out of Rob's arms.

"It has to be."

She turned away from him, tears rolling down her cheeks as she fumbled in her purse for her room key. She opened the door, stepped inside without looking back, and closed the door behind her.

The next morning, on the crew bus riding back to Heathrow, Charis had sat alone, head turned toward the window. She did not visit the cockpit throughout the long flight to Boston, during which, unknown to Rob, the ingredients of a greater tragedy had been stirred and awaited his return.

They had not spoken since that night—until tonight. Twice, in the long years between, Rob had spotted Charis. Once they had passed in the crowded terminal in Kansas City as he hurried to make a connection, and years later at JFK he'd noticed her in the boarding area for the L.A. flight as he waited to enplane for Rome from the adjacent gate. He had not tried to catch her eye or speak to her on either occasion; since then, he had often wondered why. Had he feared that she might ignore him, or was he afraid of rekindling emotions that again could only be left to smolder?

Amber lights on each of the two INSs flashed in rapid succession, alerting the pilots that Trans Globe 810 was exactly ten nautical miles from the next way point. The nearly simultaneous illuminations also verified that the navigational systems were in close agreement.

"Coming up on twenty west, Cash," Rob announced. "We're on the backstretch now." When there was no response, he peered at the first officer. Cash's eyes were clamped shut and his chin slumped down onto his chest.

Rob debated waking his copilot. The Starliner was far too complicated for anyone to fly solo. And the captain of an airliner, like that of a naval vessel, bears the ultimate responsibility in all matters concerning the operation of his craft and the well-being of his passengers. Some call it the Golden Rule: The individual with the most gold on his visor rules. Democracy does not flourish within an airplane's cockpit or on the high seas.

Still, Rob strove to work harmoniously with his crew, as did most Trans Globe captains. However, an inevitable few considered themselves infallible, if not godlike, while others could be pleasant individuals on the ground but transmuted, like Mr. Hyde to Dr.

Jekyll, into oppressors in the air. Rob knew of several accidents that had occurred in years past when a dictatorial or vain captain had made gross, sometimes fatal errors and would not accept the copilot's input, or the copilot had been too meek or intimidated to intervene. An airliner's flight deck was not always the sterile, congenial cubicle depicted in movies and on television.

Rob decided to let Cash sleep for a few more minutes. There was no point in getting upset—at this time of night a person's diurnal cycle engendered the deepest sleep. Cash was doing what his fatigued body demanded. For years, specialists in aviation medicine had recommended that pilots alternate taking a brief nap during long flights crossing multiple time zones; unfortunately, government agencies saw no need to modify regulations that dated back to the 1930s. Given a choice, Rob preferred that Cash be alert for the approach and landing rather than now, in stabilized cruise. Still, during his own airline apprenticeship, Rob had always tried his darnedest to please *his* captain. He'd arrived punctually for his flights, leapt at the chance when a captain offered him a "leg" to fly, handled mundane chores enthusiastically. Could it be a generational thing, Rob wondered? Maybe age had made him less tolerant. Perhaps his values were obsolete, but he would never understand Cash's lackadaisical attitude.

CHAPTER EIGHT

A New Dawn

At the equator, time zones are approximately one thousand miles wide. To the north or south, as the lines of longitude compress, this distance decreases, becoming zero at the poles. Approaching Ireland at 56 degrees north latitude, with a true airspeed of 474 knots or 545 statute miles per hour, and further boosted by a 130 knot tailwind, the Starliner sped into a different time zone every fifty minutes. Rob's watch, which he kept on what he called "stomach time," regardless of his destination's time zone, displayed 1 A.M. Eastern standard time when the first splash of color appeared on the horizon, heralding the metamorphosis from end of night to break of day.

While Cash continued to doze, the sky subtly warmed from deepest black to blue-green, then to a greenish bronze, the veteran captain's favorite early-morning color. Rob tolerated his copilot's catnap; after commuting from Houston to Boston via Kansas City in order to work this overnight flight, he was bound to be weary. Nor was Cash the first aviator to "rest his eyelids" during an overnight crossing, and surely would not be the last. The more important consideration, in Rob's judgment, was that Cash be wide awake for the descent into Charles de Gaulle; still, Rob would have preferred that Cash first ask his permission.

As the stars faded from sight, the sky's somber hues gradually melded to a golden radiance and soon the whole skyline glowed in warm pastels. Distant clouds became etched in orange, then at the far horizon the sun emerged, first a sliver of magenta, then quickly growing fat and blazing red, too dazzling to gaze at directly, and because of Trans Globe 810's swift easterly passage, the sun appeared to rise rapidly, seemingly twice as fast for those in the Starliner cockpit—those awake, at least—as for a person stationary on the earth's surface. Rob slid the Plexiglas sunshade along its metal rail above the windshield, positioning it to screen out the glare. The ancient dictate "Red sky in the morning, sailors take warning" ran through his mind, but he saw no reason to doubt that this fleeting, wondrous sunrise was the harbinger of anything but a glorious day ahead.

Years ago, in an idle moment, Rob had attempted to calculate the number of sunrises he had witnessed from an airplane cockpit, sometimes as now, the climax of an all-night red-eye, occasionally for those oh-dark-early-morning departures. After thumbing through several months' entries in his logbook, he'd decided that this was one bit of aeronautical trivia best left unanswered.

Despite the hundreds of dawns he had witnessed, the onset of daylight always posed for Rob the most difficult episode of an overnight Atlantic crossing. In far-off New Hampshire, unwatched clocks ticked away these long, middle-of-the-night hours. Likewise, his body's natural cadence craved deep slumber in a warm snug bed; instead, in command of this sophisticated machine, responsible for all those on board, he hurtled eastward at flight level 370, straight toward the blinding fireball that continued to ascend above the horizon, beginning its long daily journey across the heavens.

Heavy weights tugged at Rob's eyelids. It would be so soothing, so easy to close them for a few seconds—if Cash were awake—but he had disciplined himself to resist that temptation. He had learned long ago to be vigilant, to stay attentive to the slightest abnormal sound or unusual motion from the airplane, while simultaneously feeling relaxed and comfortable. Now, nearing his sixtieth year, he admitted to tiring more easily, but remained confident of his ability to revive and be fully alert for the approach and landing, the other critical segment of every flight. He knew that his duty to ensure the safe completion of Flight 810 did not cease until the Starliner was parked at the gate with its engines shut down and his passengers had disembarked.

Two knocks on the cockpit door failed to stir Cash. After Rob pushed the lock-release button, Gregory leaned partway into the cockpit and asked, "How much longer, Captain?"

"About an hour and ten minutes," Rob replied. "Shall we give a wake-up announcement, or do you want to do it?"

"Yes, please do. We'll be ready to serve breakfast and hand out customs forms in a few minutes. Is this a good time to bring in your trays?"

The mention of food roused Cash. He blinked his eyes, looked around, casually picked up the flight plan, and examined it studiously, but could not stifle a big yawn.

Rob asked, "Hungry, Cash?"

"Yeah. Starving!"

"We're ready, Gregory. Bring Cash's tray first. I'll wait till he's finished."

After the service manager left, Cash yawned again. "Man, this all-night flying's for the owls."

"You're in for a steady dose of it on international," Rob remarked, his drowsiness vanished. "Most departures from the United States are in the evening."

"Yeah, I know, but I thought there was supposed to be a relief pilot on trans-Atlantic flights."

"Not unless the scheduled block-to-block time exceeds eight hours—Boston to London or Paris takes less than eight hours, either direction. But flights to Europe from JFK and Dulles qualify for a relief pilot."

"I'm gonna bid New York."

"Times sure have changed," Rob mused. "It took five guys to fly a Connie across the pond—two pilots, an engineer, a navigator, and a radio operator. Of course, the flight time was double what it is now, sometimes more if they made a fuel stop at Gander or Shannon, or both."

"Good thing I missed those good old days," Cash grunted. He

put on sunglasses with oversize lenses. "Seven hours are about all my butt can take."

The warm colors of sunrise gradually dissolved into bright sunshine as the sun rose higher and Flight 810 continued its solitary passage, the accuracy of its course dependent on unseen satellites and the aircraft's laser gyros. Now, as the Starliner came within range of the VOR/DME stations at Benbecula, Scotland, and Belfast, Northern Ireland, Rob plotted their position, using radials and distances from the two stations, on the navigational chart, and thus verified that the aircraft's inscrutable electronic devices had, indeed, kept them precisely on course.

"How do you like that, Cash?" Rob asked, holding the chart for him to verify and pointing to the digital readouts on the FMS. "Pretty good navigating, wouldn't you say?"

"Yeah," Cash agreed, "but why do we even bother with plotting that stuff on the chart? Isn't everything in the FMS—our position, route, the distance and course to alternates?"

"Well, for one thing it's company policy, and being able to visualize where we are in relation to the nearest airfield might come in handy if we got in a bind," Rob contended. "Anyhow, things were different in those good old days. We still had flight engineers and navigators when Trans Globe first started flying 707s across the pond. The navigator still used celestial and loran, same as in propeller days. At night he would shoot the stars with a sextant—which required several minutes—plot where we *were* when he took the fix, then calculate how far we'd flown since. But in the daytime there was only the sun, and solar activity could make the loran useless. Then the company installed Doppler sets and dismissed all the navigators—Sparky, the ops agent in Boston, was one of the casualties—and pilots took over the navigational chores." He chuckled at the memory. "Everybody figured the jets went too fast to get off course, but occasionally the Doppler went haywire, leading to some gross excursions."

"Sounds too complicated for my taste," Cash muttered.

"It wasn't easy," Rob agreed. "Then when the Starliner with all its automated systems came along, the Feds decided we didn't need engineers, either."

"Well, I'm glad I missed all that ancient history," Cash said. "It's simpler to push buttons."

"Yep, and I suppose the next generation of airliners won't even need pilots. I guess that's progress."

Cash sighed. "Wish my paycheck would make some progress. Ever since the union caved in to Yeganeh, we've been the lowest-paid pilots in the industry."

"Some of that's my fault, Cash. I was on the Transition Team that . . ."

"Oh, so you're *that* Robertson. Thought I'd seen your name somewhere."

"Probably on a lavatory wall. After my wife's death, I started doing more union chores and when Yeganeh took over I was asked to help with the negotiations." Rob shook his head as he recalled the doomed agreements. "Whatever gave me the notion I was smart enough to deal with him and his Wall Street lackeys?"

"Wouldn't the airline have gone belly-up without Yeganeh?"

"No," Rob replied. "That's what he claimed, and I—we—believed him at first and trusted him, as did most employees. But later we learned that he wanted us to strike. He'd been secretly training corporate pilots and even had some foreign pilots lined up, ready to steal our jobs—at half the pay."

"Scabs, huh? Guess I'm not surprised, but still he can't be all bad."

"What makes you think so?"

"He likes animals, at least," Cash said. "I hear ol' Frank just bought himself a racehorse. One million bucks. Friend of mine read about it in one of those horse magazines."

Rob frowned. "That money came right out of our pockets."

"Ah, what the hell, Skip, as long as they don't take away the gals, I'm happy."

"After the latest round of cutbacks, I wouldn't guarantee that. But speaking of the ladies, please don't say anything to Charis about our earlier conversation."

"Sure, Skipper," Cash responded. "Wouldn't want to bust your chances with her."

"Why don't you say good morning to our passengers? We're one hour from touchdown. You might tell them we'll have a look at the White Cliffs of Dover in about twenty minutes and pass right over Dunkirk on our arrival route." Rob checked the weather report he had jotted down while Cash napped. "The latest de Gaulle temperature was five degrees Celsius, that's forty-one Fahrenheit, with clear skies. Looks like a fine day ahead."

As soon as Cash completed the announcement, Gregory returned carrying a tray with Cash's breakfast snack—coffee, a huge Danish, and a bowl of fresh fruit cut into bite-sized pieces.

"They sure feed you good on international," Cash remarked. "No wonder this airline never shows a profit." He devoured the pastry but ignored the fruit.

Rob rang the call button when Cash had finished, and was pleasantly surprised when Charis brought in his tray, the same except for a bran muffin instead of the pastry. She slid onto the observer's seat, saying, "I'll only stay a minute," and leaned forward to view the brilliant morning sky through the wide windshield. "Aren't you going to miss this, Robby?"

She looked fresh and alert in the bright sunshine, he observed, not like someone who'd been cooped up in an airplane all night. A pleasing, feminine fragrance displaced stale cockpit odors.

"I sure as heck am," Rob acknowledged. "Where else do you get such great service, beautiful sunrises, good people to work with, and," casting a skeptical glance at Cash, "we've just been discussing the pay. Of course, there've been a few anxious moments along the way, too."

"That's the definition of flying," Cash piped in. "Hours and hours of sheer boredom spiced with moments of stark terror." He cackled at this overused description; Charis and Rob smiled.

"When did you decide to be a pilot?" Charis asked.

"During the war my uncle sent me a model of an A-20 Havoc for my birthday," Rob replied, "and that got me interested in airplanes. Of course, I didn't appreciate it at that age; I'd figured on being a fireman—firefighter, it's called now. But growing up I could identify every plane that flew over the farm, and I dreamed about flying to exotic, far-off lands. When I started college, I'd never heard of ROTC, which was compulsory in those days when every warm-blooded male had to serve Uncle Sam. But ROTC gave me the chance to go to Air Force pilot training, and that kept me out of the rice paddies."

"You? A trained killer?" Cash teased.

"I never thought of myself that way," Rob replied, "but I suppose flying cargo planes in Vietnam contributed to the campaign and to killing people."

Cash said, "Make love, not war—that's my motto."

"Anyhow," Rob continued, "I did my duty, and when my hitch was up, Trans Globe was hiring. So really, I just stumbled into this job. Yep, I'll miss it. It's the best darned job in the world."

"Sounds like you'll be missed too," Charis said. "Gregory said that your friends in Boston are planning some festivities."

"Maybe Yeganeh will give you a gold watch," Cash suggested in mock seriousness.

"Yeganeh?" Rob chuckled. "No reason for him to be there. To him I'm just another garden-variety pilot. One of his underlings might show up, I suppose. Look, let's not celebrate too soon. We still have to find de Gaulle this morning, and tomorrow there's the long flight home." Rob paused a moment, then tapped his knuckles against his head. "Knock on wood, but in thirty-two years with Trans Globe I've never so much as dented a wing tip. Maybe somebody will mention that."

"That's something to be proud of," Charis agreed.

Rob glanced at Cash. "Of course, there's plenty of guys who'll be glad to have me leave so they can move up a number."

"Not meaning to be disrespectful, Skipper, but that's how the seniority system works," Cash remarked, laughing. "Your seat cushion won't even cool off."

Charis touched Rob's shoulder. "I'd better get back to work."

The flight proceeded over Ireland. From seven miles up the fragmented, grassy fields looked like pieces of a huge, emerald green jigsaw puzzle. They crossed the Irish Sea, passing from Dublin Control to London Control, then continued along airway Upper Blue 39 over the verdant hills of southwestern England. As they passed twenty-five miles south of the vast London metropolis, Rob rummaged through his flight kit and located a battered road map of England. He traced with his finger a highway running south of the city, meandering through several towns, identified the corresponding locations on the ground below, then pointed out a village where a bridge crossed a river. "That's Hadley-on-Stone. My uncle was based there during World War Two. A few years ago, on a London layover, I rented a car and drove out there, but any vestiges of a military base had disappeared. Just houses where the runway used to be."

"It's getting the same in Texas," Cash muttered. "Houses everywhere."

Rob put away his map, dimly remembering—despite his tender age at the time—how he'd cried the day when his parents told him that Uncle James's plane had been shot down. Neither the wreckage nor his body was ever found.

The aircraft passed south of the White Cliffs, dazzling in the morning sunshine, with the jagged coastline and checkered fields of France sliding into view ahead. Midway across the English Channel, London Control radioed, "Trans Globe eight-ten, contact Paris Control on one twenty-six point two, cheerio."

Rob dialed in the new frequency. "*Bonjour,* Paris. Trans Globe eight-ten, flight level three-seven-zero." Like many international pilots, he attempted, as a courtesy, to greet each new controller in his or her native language.

A woman replied with what sounded like, "Bonjour, Trans-Globeighten-proceeDieppe-standardrouteMerue-nowmaintain-leveltwofourzero, over."

"Huh? What'd she say?" Cash asked, looking baffled.

Rob repeated the clearance to the controller, slowly for Cash's benefit, and reported, "Leaving flight level three-seven-zero for two-four-zero." He turned to his copilot. "Start her down, Cash. Things happen fast now. We'll both need to listen carefully. These controllers switch instantaneously from speaking French to Air France pilots to English for everybody else—Greeks, Turks, us. It's the same deal in each country, and the accents can be difficult. Wait till you fly into Cairo some day!"

"You'll have to interpret for me, Skipper. No Texan could understand anybody talking that fast."

"Just be glad that English was adopted as the international aviation language after the war."

"I am," Cash conceded. "Good thing our side won."

Paris Control cleared the flight along the standard arrival path to Aéroport Charles de Gaulle. Only a thin, smoggy haze over Paris, sprawling across the horizon twenty miles south of the airport, marred the otherwise ideal conditions.

Nearing the airport, Rob suggested, "Because we'll be landing on two-seven, what say we ask for an early turn in? Otherwise they'll vector us halfway to Prussia."

"How come we're always trying to save time?" Cash moaned. "Don't we get paid by the minute?"

"And keep your airport diagram handy," Rob advised as the pilots completed the pre-landing checks. "After we land you'll have to talk to ground control while I'm taxiing. They get upset if we take a wrong taxiway."

"Okay, Skipper."

Rob said, "Now let's stop the chatter and pay close attention to the controllers." At his request, de Gaulle tower cleared the flight for the shortened turn to base leg and to land. Cash clicked off the autopilot in order to hand-fly the aircraft. He rolled out on final centered on the glide slope, calling for flaps and gear at the proper moments, and flew a perfect approach, while Rob monitored his actions with quiet approval. Holding the left wing slightly down to compensate for the light crosswind, Cash rolled the big airliner smoothly onto the runway, then retarded the throttles, slid the reverser handles into the reverse thrust range, and gingerly applied the brakes. As they slowed to taxi speed Rob said, "I've got it. Nicely done."

Cash grinned. "Maybe it's my lucky day."

Rob steered the Starliner onto the runway turn-off and then onto the long, parallel taxiway and called for "Flaps up, After Landing checklist." Flight 810 rumbled slowly past massive, circular, glass-walled Terminal One, from which underground escalators whisked passengers to and from the half-dozen satellite terminals sprouting from the tarmac in a semicircle around the main terminal like chubby, baby mushrooms surrounding their giant parent.

Approaching Trans Globe's satellite, Rob followed the signalman's batons into the gate until waved to a stop. He parked the brakes, then gestured to Cash to finish up.

The first officer shut down the engines, turned off the various systems, then positioned switches and levers as Rob read the Secure Cockpit checklist. Rob completed and signed the logbook, and grimaced at the night's accumulation of plastic spoons, paper cups, and now superfluous paperwork. "Let's tidy up," he suggested. "The cleaners have been known to skip the cockpit, and we don't want to leave a mess for the crew that's taking this airplane on to Tel Aviv." When satisfied, Rob led Cash to Operations to turn in the flight documents and stow their flight kits.

Despite Yeganeh's cutbacks and downsizing, international flying still had certain amenities. A large highway bus—luxurious beyond comparison with the converted vans utilized in Boston and other domestic stations—with contoured reclining seats awaited the pilots when they returned from ops. Several flight attendants appeared already asleep when the two men climbed aboard. Charis caught Rob's eye as he moved down the aisle and beckoned him to the empty space beside her.

He sank heavily into the seat, weariness suddenly settling over his body. Parisian timepieces may have indicated 0800—*huit heures*—in the morning but his internal clock reflected the still wee hours in far-off New Hampshire. At this instant, he thought to himself, retirement sounded very enticing.

The bus accelerated away from Trans Globe's terminal and continued across the ramp and past the other satellites. Before exiting the airport grounds, the bus stopped at a closely guarded gate to clear customs and security. From each side of the gate, a high chain-link fence, topped with barbed wire, stretched far into the distance.

Gregory, who spoke French fluently, brought the crew list and each crew member's customs declaration form into the Bureau d'Aérogare Sécurité. This stop could be lengthy if the security officer opted to have the crew's luggage checked. Rob knew that patience and cooperation worked best. Trying to hurry the authorities usually invited a more thorough examination.

Meanwhile, two guards in combat fatigues, each with a stubby black submachine gun slung over his shoulder, boarded the bus and cross-checked each crew member's airline identification card and passport, confirming that the photographs matched the faces. Not surprisingly, the female flight attendants received meticulous scrutiny.

The guards looked concerned when they checked Cash's I.D. card. They talked to each other quietly, glancing back and forth from Cash to his photo. Then one of the guards pointed to Cash's shoulder bag on the vacant seat beside him, indicating he should open it. As he did, the guard spotted a magazine, removed it from the bag, and opened it to a fold-out, full-color picture of a naked woman, which brought laughter, groans, and various remarks from the flight attendants. Cash jumped up, yelling, "Hey, what're you doing!" The other guard fingered his weapon.

Fortunately, at that instant Gregory returned. He queried the guards, in French, about the problem. Looking somewhat indignant, the guards glared at Cash, exited the bus, and swung open the gate, allowing the bus to proceed. As it pulled away, Gregory explained why the guards had been worried. On his company I.D., Cash's hair was short, straight, and light brown; now it was longer, dark, and curly. They had been unsure that the pictures matched Cash's face, thus leading to the more thorough inspection. "And it's against their laws to bring in salacious material without a proper license," Gregory added, wagging his finger at Cash like a teacher scolding a naughty boy, "but I asked them to consider that it was your first time here."

"Thanks, Greg. Damned if I want to spend my Paris layover in some creepy dungeon."

"Changing the subject," Gregory continued, addressing the whole crew, "the security officer wanted me to remind you that Paris has a large Arab population, with thousands of immigrants from the former French colonies in Africa. There've been several anti-American incidents because of that Libyan airliner. Windows at the U.S. Tourist Agency were smashed during the night and there was a demonstration in Montmartre—people carrying placards, and so on. He suggested we stay clear of the American Embassy and other American establishments like business offices, and told me to warn everyone to be cautious."

Margot wondered aloud, "Can we still meet at the office?"

Several voices answered affirmatively, and someone suggested "Six o'clock."

Cash spouted, "Hey, I'm new here. What's the office?"

Margot informed him that the word was a euphemism for Le Café de la Belle Meunier, an unpretentious bar two blocks from the Hôtel Gallia, and gave him directions. The café served as a discreet gathering place for Trans Globe crew members, who often met there for a drink and shop talk before deciding on a restaurant for dinner.

"I'll be there," Cash announced, bringing a moan from several flight attendants.

As the bus approached the expressway on ramp, Rob mentioned to Charis that the ride to the hotel could require two hours whenever morning-commute traffic into Paris inched along bumper to bumper, but this morning, a Saturday, the traffic would be light, allowing a much quicker journey. "Thank you for volunteering to fly this trip," he said, "but you must be exhausted, living eight time zones away in California."

She nodded agreement. "How do you feel?" she asked.

"It's normal for pilots to get pumped up for the approach and landing, so right now I'm having a sinking spell."

"Close your eyes and rest. There's no need to talk."

They reclined their seats, and both dozed. Rob awakened briefly once, aware of her shoulder pressed against his arm, her soft hair brushing his cheek. He sighed contentedly, and quickly fell back asleep.

CHAPTER NINE

A RUN ALONG THE SEINE

At the Hôtel Gallia the receptionist looked up and smiled as he extended his hand. "Ah, *Capitaine* Robertson. So good to see you again."

"*Merci, Monsieur* Foret, and how are you?"

"Very well, sir. Did you have a pleasant flight?"

Rob nodded. "Yes, a routine crossing."

"Good. Now, we understand this is your last time with us. Perhaps *Madame* Robertson has accompanied you?"

"No, I am quite alone."

"Such a pity. Still, this is for you, sir. A little gift from the Gallia in recognition of your many visits. We hope you enjoy your stay." He handed Rob an envelope addressed to Capitaine Robertson, along with a smaller envelope containing the plastic magnetic card key for his room. Then, after all the crew had signed the registry, the receptionist distributed keys for their assigned rooms.

In the elevator, Rob and Charis agreed to meet after naps, at two o'clock, ready to run. When the elevator stopped at her floor, Charis said, "I'm in room eight-oh-five. Could you meet me there? I'd rather not walk into the lobby alone in my running clothes."

"I'll be there."

At room 1219, on the top floor, Rob inserted the card key into the latch and opened the door. He was surprised to discover that he had been given a spacious corner suite, not one of the much smaller rooms usually assigned to crew members. The walls, ceiling, and furniture were painted a soft linen white. Colorful drapes framed tall windows that afforded expansive views to the north and west. One window faced the Eiffel Tower, a half-mile distant, soaring majestically above the slate roofs of surrounding buildings; from the other he looked down upon the Pont de Grenelle, stretching across the Seine. A barge loaded with brand-new delivery vans, their color choices evidently limited to gray, white, and blue, plowed methodically upstream. Pedestrians walked leisurely on paths alongside the waterway.

Inside the envelope Rob found a note on the hotel's letterhead stationery. He read: Capitaine Robertson, in appreciation of your many years of patronage, this letter authorizes dinner for two as guests of the Hôtel Gallia. You may dine in the Monet Room or be served in your suite, as you choose. Bon appétit! Our staff wishes you a most fruitful retirement." It was signed C. Plubeau, Directeur.

"By golly, that's pretty nice," Rob muttered to himself, realizing that Maurice, the chief Trans Globe operations agent at Charles de Gaulle, had undoubtedly been the catalyst for this extraordinary expression of hospitality.

Determining how long to initially sleep after an all-night, five-time-zone flight had always posed a problem for Rob. Each of the crew had his or her own system for coping. The toll on an international pilot's body could be debilitating, perhaps even more so for the flight attendants, who spend more than half of each crossing on their feet. However, it was crucial for everyone to get sufficient rest during the layover, because in less than twenty-five hours, Rob and his crew would reboard the bus and return to the airport to begin preparations for the flight homeward.

The solution that Rob had evolved over the years called for permitting himself only four or five hours of sleep after arriving, forcing himself up at midday European time. With the time-zone difference, this approximated his usual New Hampshire wake-up hour, thus maintaining a semblance of his normal circadian rhythm.

(If instead of a nap, Rob succumbed to his body's plea for a full eight or more hours' slumber, the day would be gone, yet—in order to be properly rested for the return journey—a few hours later it would be time to attempt sleep again, which might not come easily if he'd slept all day.) An invigorating run would then help erase jet lag, a habit that Charis had inspired that summer long ago. Afterward, he'd still have time for sight-seeing, and dinner in the evening with other members of his crew. He sometimes attended chamber music concerts held in the church of Saint-Louis-en-l'Île, with its remarkable acoustics, and other cathedrals. As layovers were too short for adjusting to the time changes, he tried to stay on, or at least close to, his home diurnal cycle. Of course, the farther east the layover, in cities such as Tel Aviv and Cairo, and the greater the time differential from Eastern, the more difficult this routine became.

*

At precisely two o'clock in the afternoon, wearing his gray running suit over shorts and a T-shirt, Rob rapped lightly on the door of room 805.

Charis opened the door. "Good morning, or is it afternoon? Come in." She was dressed, ready to run, in modestly cut purple shorts and a white, long-sleeved cotton top, with a lavender bandanna holding her hair in place. "Care for some tomato juice before we go?"

"Sounds great," Rob replied.

She shook the can, pulled the tab from the top, poured the contents into a glass, and handed it to Rob. He waited until she had poured some for herself, then held his glass to hers and said, "Cheers." He took a sip, cleared his throat, and uttered the words he'd been thinking about since her midnight visit to the cockpit. "Cash told me . . . about your husband . . . about the crash. I'm sorry, Charis." Rob explained how he'd read about Sam's preparations for an attempt at the speed record, but hadn't known until last night that it had ended disastrously. When she did not respond, he continued, "Years before that happened, I'd figured out that you'd married. Forgive me for having been so nosy, but one day I typed your I.D. number in the FLACCS computer, just to see where you were based and what trips you were flying, and discovered that your name had changed." He didn't tell her that he'd waited exactly a year after Jane's death to make that electronic inquiry, nor about his disappointment when the screen displayed her married name, nor how, from that moment on, he had tried to banish her from his thoughts.

Charis took a deep breath. "Sam caught me on the rebound. He seemed so exciting, bursting with grandiose plans." She smiled. "I was young. Maybe I hadn't gotten over someone else." After a sip of juice, she asked, "Do you know I have a son?"

"No."

She set her glass on the dresser and removed a small photo album from her shoulder bag. "This is Danny—Daniel, after my dad. He's twelve. Just started seventh grade."

Rob examined the picture. It showed a tall, slender boy wearing a soccer outfit, with a soccer ball tucked under one arm. "He looks like a fine young man," Rob said, genuinely pleased for her. He swung an arm around her shoulder and hugged her gently. "Belated congratulations."

After Rob had skimmed through the other photos, all of Danny in action during a match, and they had finished their juice, she suggested, "Shall we be off?"

"Yep, let's go."

"Have you checked the temperature? Is it warm enough for shorts?"

Her legs were trim and well tanned—runner's legs, Rob thought. And the small poppy tattooed on her thigh brought back memories of their hike to the Acropolis, fifteen years ago. "I think so," he replied. "It should be about fifty, and the sun's shining. Heck, I'll do the same." He turned to peel off his nylon running pants. "Don't worry," he joked, "I'm wearing shorts," but he could not stop the flush of color that rose on this face.

*

As Rob and Charis stepped out the main entrance of the hotel, he said, "I have a little route mapped out, about six miles, if that's okay with you."

"I'm game. I don't know Paris, so you'll have to be my guide."

"First we'll head for the Bois de Boulogne. Mind starting a bit slowly? These old bones take longer to warm up."

"I'm no spring chicken, Robby. Haven't you noticed?" She pointed to the few strands of graying hair at her temple.

"It's quite becoming."

"I'm forty-three now."

"Forgive me if you've heard this line before, but you look closer to thirty."

"Thank you, Robby. You're such a gentleman. And you look like you've become a serious runner."

"Not sure serious is the word," he replied. "I run nearly every day, just trying to stay in shape, and it's a good way to erase the cobwebs after a long trip."

"That's true," she agreed. "Do you enter road races?"

"Local ones, occasionally. Come to think of it, in a couple of days I'll move into a different age bracket, which is about the only good thing about turning sixty."

They discussed running and compared their times for various distances. Charis admitted to being one of the top contenders in her age division; in fact, as race sponsors usually offered prize money to the top finishers, and the San Diego area afforded many events, she had found it worthwhile to remain competitive.

"How do you cope with those New England winters?" she asked.

"Some years they seem endless, but usually there are plenty of mild days, and when it's stormy or the roads are icy—or it's just too darned cold—I use a treadmill."

"Aren't those things boring?"

"Very. Listening to Mozart helps. Sometimes I envy folks in warmer climes."

"Yes, in Southern California it rains occasionally in the winter, but mostly it's quite pleasant. What about tennis?" she asked. "Remember going to Wimbledon?"

"Yes, I do," Rob replied, "but after Jane died I soured on tennis and never went back to her club."

They jogged halfway across the Pont de Grenelle and descended concrete steps near the small Statue of Liberty replica to a long, narrow island set in the middle of the Seine, and ran on the paved path along its center. Rob observed that the river was unusually high and flowing much faster than normal, and explained that the previous week there had been heavy showers in southeastern France and in the Massif Central. He commented, "Fortunately for the wine makers, the rains came after the grape harvest."

"Do you like wine?" Charis asked.

"Yes, ma'am, I do, and besides, a little red wine's supposed to be good for the heart—as well as the soul."

They chatted about wine, discovering there were several California vintages that they both had enjoyed. "Isn't today the seventeenth?" he asked.

"I think so." She glanced at him. "Why?"

"It's a significant day in France. November seventeenth is when the Beaujolais Nouveau is released to the public. Maybe we can try a bottle if you'll have dinner with me."

"I accept. Thank you."

Reaching the Pont de Bir Hakim, at the upstream end of the island, they sprinted up the steps to the street level. They continued across the bridge to the north side of the Seine, waited, along with dozens of pedestrians, for the traffic light to change, crossed the busy boulevard, and then, running silently, followed a winding, ascending street lined with multistory gray-stone apartments. Finally, both short of breath following the long uphill stretch, they reached the intersection called the Place de la Muerte, crossed another broad avenue, and via a shaded path entered the Bois de Boulogne, Paris's great park of woods and fields.

They jogged along a wide graveled track that circles two ponds, Lac Supérieur and Lac Inférieur, dodging an occasional duck searching for food scraps, kids racing by on bicycles, and young mothers pushing prams. "Charis, it's none of my business," Rob said, "and you don't have to answer, but do you have anyone now?"

"A man in my life?" Several strides later, she said, "I'm no great catch, Robby. Sure, I've dated guys, but they vanish when I tell them about my financial situation." They halted when a soccer ball bounded across the path, pursued by several boys in dark blue school uniforms. When they resumed running, she went on, "Sam left me with debts—huge debts. He was obsessed with those old fighter planes. I learned, too late, that he cared more about them than me. He certainly spent a lot more time fussing over them! And money! He poured nearly half a million dollars into that damned Sea Fury. It wasn't insured; nobody insures them for racing. Even his life insurance didn't cover that kind of flying. My whole world came tumbling down."

"I'm sorry. You don't have to tell . . ."

"No, I want you to hear this. Afterward, I sold the P-51, and his brand-new Corvette, and the house in Phoenix, but I'm still paying off the rest, a little each month. Always will be."

"I'm sorry it ended badly," Rob said. "A lot of people admired his courage."

"You're being kind, but thank you."

After several minutes he asked, "How do you manage it, you know, the flying and all?"

"It's not easy," she said. "At least I'm senior enough now to hold Honolulu turnarounds, so I have lots of time at home. Danny and I live close to my parents in a little apartment they own. They take good care of him when I'm away, but they're both getting along in years."

They jogged side by side in silence for several minutes. After they had circled the ponds, Rob announced, "Now we'll be tourists. Look ahead." They turned onto another path; in the distance stood the massive Arc de Triomphe.

"Wow!" Charis exclaimed. "It's magnificent."

The path emerged from the Bois directly onto the bustling Avenue Foch. Elegant shops packed with expensive goods lined the busy boulevard, and pedestrians jammed the broad sidewalk, forcing Rob and Charis to slow to a walk. "I feel rather naked here," she remarked, "surrounded by all these fully dressed people."

"Me too," Rob agreed, "but here's where we detour."

He steered her down a narrow side street; after a few hundred yards they sniffed the tantalizing aroma of freshly baked bread. "Shall we stop for a pastry and the best cup of coffee in Paris?" he proposed.

"How could anyone resist?" she replied, inhaling deeply. "But I didn't bring any money. Did you?"

"I always bring some francs in case I need refreshment along the way, and once I twisted an ankle and had to take a cab back to the hotel."

The compact *boulangerie* held a dozen small wooden tables, several occupied by couples chatting quietly, others by solitary men who glanced up from their book or newspaper, eyed Charis impassively—but approvingly, Rob noticed—then returned to their reading. From behind the counter, a pink-cheeked waitress greeted them with a cheerful *Bonjour*. Stacks of baguettes and other breads filled the shelves behind her.

Rob and Charis studied the tempting assortment of baked goods displayed in the glass cases, and, following his recommendation, each selected a chocolate brioche. He ordered the pastries and two cafés-au-lait in halting French, bringing a smile to the waitress's rosy face. *"Oui, monsieur,"* she replied as she placed the demitasse cups beneath the spigots and twisted handles, causing the shiny coffee machine to hiss and vent steam. "Be seated, *s'il vous plaît*. I will bring everything to the table."

Three tables were vacant; they chose one in the corner next to the lace-curtained window and sat facing each other. "How'd you ever find this place?" Charis asked.

"Easy," Rob said, smiling. "Just followed my nose one day."

After the waitress brought them the warm brioches and the hot coffee, they snacked in silence for several minutes. Then Charis said, "Can you tell me about Jane?"

Rob thought a moment, trying to decide where to begin. "Remember that last time we flew together, fifteen years ago? London, Athens, and back to London?"

"Yes. It rained, and we went shopping and to that little restaurant, and . . ."

"And it ended badly. Well, things got worse—a lot worse. The next day, after we flew back to Boston, the ops agent hailed me as I was leaving for home and handed me a message." Rob stared out the window at the quiet street. "I've never talked about this with anyone. The note said to telephone the police in Williamsport—

that's on Cape Cod, quite a distance from Deerwood, and in the opposite direction. It all seemed rather odd, but I dialed the number, and an officer said that a Jane Robertson had been killed in an automobile accident, and he wanted me to go there and positively identify the bodies."

"Bodies?"

"Yes." He faced Charis. "It turned out that the car belonged to a man from her club, Roger Henderson by name. Before I left on that trip, Jane said she might spend a couple of days with one of her sisters—her family owned a place on the Cape—but evidently she'd been there with him." Rob recalled how Jane's body had been tanned—all over. "That sister never did like me. Anyhow, I found out later that the affair had been going on for a while. It wasn't the first time they'd . . . Well, it doesn't matter now. The police said he'd been driving fast, trying to get her back before I arrived home, I suppose. Her BMW was still parked at the tennis club."

He wondered if Charis was thinking the same thing as he, that only hours after he had puritanically spurned Charis outside her hotel door in London, his wife's duplicity had made him a widower. How many times, in the fifteen lonely years since those entwined events, had he mulled over the irony that, within a span of twenty hours, he had lost them both?

He stirred his coffee, organizing his thoughts. "You know about Agent Orange, the defoliant that was used in Vietnam?"

"Isn't that what they sprayed from airplanes?" she asked. "Along roads and rivers? I saw a PBS documentary. Did you do that?"

"No, thank God. An outfit known as Ranch Hands had that nasty job. I served a tour flying C-130s, just hauling troops and cargo, but one day we carried several pallets loaded with barrels of that dreadful stuff into a place called Nhon Khe." Rob could still picture the military outpost in the Central Highlands, ringed by lush, rolling hills that looked dangerously steeper from ground level than from the air, and remembered that it had required some skill to maneuver the big Hercules onto the short airstrip. "Anyhow, as the airplane was being unloaded, the forklift punctured one of the barrels and some of the liquid spilled out. Nobody seemed concerned at the time, but since then Agent Orange has been linked to birth defects in the children of veterans, not to mention thousands of Vietnamese."

Rob's eyes fixed on a large print hanging on the white-plastered wall, a Van Gogh, of cypress trees bending in the wind and clouds drifting through an indigo sky. "After I came back from the war, Jane and I had a child. He was stillborn." If he'd lived, Rob thought silently, he'd be a grown man now. Rob looked at Charis. "But maybe it was just as well. He was malformed—spina bifida, the doctor called it. My exposure to the herbicide may have caused it."

Charis said softly, "I'm sorry."

"After that Jane said she didn't want another child, didn't want to risk the pain of disappointment. Well, like some general said, 'War sure is hell.' I'm glad for you that you have Danny."

Charis cupped her hand over his, holding it tightly. She said, "It must have been devastating for Jane."

"Things were never the same." Rob recalled how the doctor had come to the waiting room to inform him, and the moment when he'd had to tell her. "She grieved for months, and afterward she began spending more and more time at her club, and I became more involved with the pilots union." He did not explain that he'd had a vasectomy to ensure that he would not father another child. "Why am I burdening you with all this?"

"Please go on, Robby."

"We just slowly drifted apart," he continued. "After the accident, when I went through her things, I found she'd contacted a lawyer. They'd made plans to serve the divorce papers and she had arranged to move out."

Charis withdrew her hand and they both sipped their coffee.

"Don't get me wrong," Rob continued. "We had some good years. I'm not bitter. Life wasn't easy for her. She complained I was always either away on a flight or working on the Christmas trees. I don't blame her for anything." He leaned back, tilting his cup for the last swallow, then said, "Folks in Deerwood say I live the perfect life—a great job, travel to exotic places, all that. You must hear the same thing."

Charis again pressed her hand on his. "You shouldn't blame yourself," she said.

"It wasn't until I saw you last night in the briefing room that I realized . . . that you've never been out of my thoughts."

She looked down. "Nor you out of mine."

He turned his hand and gently squeezed hers. "Hope it didn't ruin your appetite but I had to get that off my chest."

"I'm glad you did."

"Shall we resume our run?"

They returned to Avenue Foch and ran on to the Place de l'É-toile, admired the Arc de Triomphe as they halted several times for traffic circling that huge wagon-wheel confluence of twelve streets, then proceeded along the broad sidewalk of the Champs Elysées, past tony shops sandwiched between touristy sidewalk cafés charging inflated prices and the ticket offices, including Trans Globe's, of a dozen international airlines. To avoid the hordes of pedestrians, Rob led Charis to a less busy road that angled toward the Grand Palais. Now able to move at a normal pace, they circled the palace, then looped around the adjacent Petit Palais, running on paths amid gardens redolent with the scent of late-blooming flowers.

Again they waited several minutes for the signal to change before crossing a busy boulevard, then descended steep granite steps to a broad quay alongside the swiftly flowing Seine. With each stride, the hectic Parisian traffic and noise gradually muted to the relative serenity of the quay. A broad, gravel-laden barge, its gunwales barely clearing the turbulent water, wallowed slowly by, straining to move upstream. On the opposite shore, four white *bateaux-mouches,* which transport tourists on sight-seeing cruises past the great cathedrals and other notable sights alongside the river, were berthed. Rob and Charis jogged past a score of low-slung houseboats of various shapes and sizes, painted in muted greens or blues, moored parallel to the quay. Most had a cabin at one end, and there might be a table and chairs set on the deck, with couples chatting over a bottle of wine. A small, colorful flower bed adorned each houseboat, and usually at least one dog tarried nearby, keeping a watchful eye on the scene.

Here, beside the Seine, they could run unimpeded by people or traffic. The air seemed cooler and less choked with exhaust fumes.

"When we get back to Boston," Rob proposed, "could you

come with me to Deerwood, to see my farm?" When she didn't respond for several seconds, he added, "There's a guest room."

"You asked me if I had someone," Charis replied, choosing her words carefully, "but what about you? Last night you said *we* will be harvesting those trees."

"Did I?" Rob laughed. "I meant Alejo Corrado. He and his wife, Isabella, work part time for me, and live next door in a little house I own. Originally, Isabella came to care for my mother and help Jane with the housework. She still cleans house and fixes me an occasional meal, and Alejo's my right-hand man around the farm. He also drives the town's school bus and in the summer operates a small fishing boat; in fact, they escaped from Cuba in a boat. Good people."

"No woman friend?"

"No. Well, there's a lady in town who was recently widowed. We were high school sweethearts, and some people seem to think we should get together again, but I've been . . . reluctant to get involved. Of course, there's Nellie."

Charis raised her eyebrows. "Oh, so you do have someone?"

He grinned. "Just teasing. Nellie's a big, very old golden retriever. She's helped me through some glum times."

Charis's tone brightened. "I bet she'll be glad to have you home for good."

"She used to run with me, but now her hips are bad and she's showing her age, like me, I guess. The Corrados' son takes care of her when I'm away. Please say you'll come. Why, Isabella even said she'd have dinner waiting. Sometimes I think she's clairvoyant."

Before Charis could respond, they both became aware of a commotion ahead. At first Rob thought a fight was in progress. Thirty or forty people jostled along the edge of the quay, some shouting, others gesticulating toward the river. The crowd seemed to weave its way downstream, matching the current. "Something's wrong!" Rob exclaimed. He and Charis rushed to the fringe of the gathering for a closer look.

Everyone in the milling throng seemed dressed for a celebration, a wedding, perhaps. Rob's eyes followed the pointing arms and frantic faces. He spotted a shape in the water, then realized it was a child, a boy, eighty feet away, his little arms thrashing in a struggle to stay afloat, being carried downstream by the rapid current. Rob hesitated, deciding on the best course of action, but before he could act Charis dived into the churning water and swam with smooth, powerful strokes straight toward the boy. She quickly reached him, wrapped an arm around him, holding his head up, and began to swim back to the quay. But stroking with only one arm, and weighted down by her running shoes, which occasionally splashed to the surface, she made little headway, and the duo continued to be swept downstream.

The crowd parted for a man running with a coil of rope. He attempted to toss an end to Charis but missed badly, and the rope sank from sight. When the man reeled it in, Rob grabbed the free end of the rope in his left hand and wound it twice around his arm. Rob ran farther along the quay to a point opposite Charis, then dived into the river. For an instant, as the cold water sapped his strength, he remembered the notoriously frigid, summertime combers of Chester Beach. He swam as fast as he could toward Charis and the child. When her tense face appeared a few yards away, he stroked harder, expending his dwindling reserves of energy to reach them. He wrapped an arm around her waist, gripped the rope more firmly with his other hand, and swung around. "PULL!" he bellowed. The rope grew taut as the threesome began to be tugged shoreward. Rob clutched Charis tightly, struggling to keep his head above water with each surge of the towrope. At last the rope took a vertical vector. His fist, then his arm and shoulder, bumped hard against the concrete quay. White hands reached down for the child, grasped his arms, lifted him, gasping and coughing, up and out of Rob's sight. Other hands groped for Charis, dangling limply as they hoisted her from the water. More hands reached down for him. Rob's legs had lost all feeling. His hand had locked, unable to unclench to release the rope; he could barely lift his other arm. His knees scraped against the quay as hands pulled him halfway out of the water, then grabbed his jacket and heaved him higher until he could roll onto the hard flat surface.

He lay there, panting, trembling with cold, slowly recovering his strength. Voices were shouting but he could not understand a word.

Gradually his hand loosened its tense grip on the rope. He sat up and looked around for Charis. She was crouched on her hands and knees, breathing deeply. She'd lost her bandanna, and water dripped from her sopping-wet hair. She looked at him and slowly smiled. He knew he would never, ever forget that smile.

The crowd had gathered around the child, everyone ignoring Charis and Rob except for one man who offered them a cigarette. Rob shook his head. Two gray-uniformed gendarmes appeared. They barked questions in French, but Rob could not comprehend a single word—that part of his brain had not come back to earth. He continued to shiver; now Charis was shivering, too. Between chattering teeth, Rob shouted to the gendarmes, "Hôtel Gallia, Hôtel Gallia, *s'il vous plaît.*"

Rob held Charis's hand as they rode silently in the backseat of the police cruiser. Her soaked cotton shirt clung to her jogging bra. When they climbed out of the cruiser, he unzipped and pulled off his nylon jacket. He twisted it to wring out the water, flapped it back into shape, then held it for her. "Why don't you put this on," he said.

"Thanks, I'll slip it over my shoulders."

She hesitated before entering the hotel, then turned to face Rob. "When I was struggling in the water I knew you'd come. Thank you for saving me—again."

"Again?"

"It's the second time. Don't you remember? In London, a long time ago. We'd been running and I looked the wrong way as we started to cross a street, and forgot that they drive on the left side of the road. I would've been hit by a car if you hadn't stopped me."

"Yes, I remember." The brief scene from that summer afternoon fifteen years ago had locked in his memory. She'd stepped off the curb, and he'd lunged to grab her just before a black limousine coming from the right swooped past, just inches away. A second later his fingertips recognized the soft, round, exquisite shape within their grasp, and he recalled, now, how his hand had lingered there an instant longer than necessary, although it had seemed an eternity. And when he'd released her, both of them shaken by the close call and thankful she hadn't been injured, he'd pretended to be oblivious of his hand's unwitting catch, but the tingling remembrance of touching her breast persisted, simmering in his subconscious, waiting to rekindle on long, lonely nights when sleep remained elusive.

Her "Why, Robby, you couldn't be blushing" roused him back to the present.

They ignored raised eyebrows and inquisitive stares from hotel lodgers and staff as they slogged hand in hand across the crowded lobby, laughed like conspirators at their sopping reflections in the mirror outside the elevator. Blood oozed from Rob's scraped knees. Their waterlogged running shoes squished on the polished floor.

As the elevator ascended, he recalled that the compact rooms assigned to flight crews usually had only a shower, no bathtub. He asked. Yes, Charis's bathroom had only the shower. "You could come up to my room," he suggested. "They gave me a fancy suite. I suspect Maurice in operations had something to do with it. It has the biggest tub I've ever seen, and you need a good hot soak right now."

"What about you?"

"I'll wait my turn."

She hesitated before answering. "Well, on one condition. No, two."

"Conditions? Okay, what are they?"

"First, no more swimming in the Seine."

He laughed. "Agreed. Next time I go for a dip, the water will be *much* warmer. And the other?"

Her eyes became serious. "A hug. A real hug. I've waited a long time."

"Can that include a real kiss?"

Rob's arms encircled her waist. Her arms slipped around his neck. Their damp bodies pressed close together. He gently kissed her lips. He stopped shivering.

CHAPTER TEN

LE RENARD ROUGE

Charis shook Rob's shoulder. "Robby, wake up! Robby!"

"Why? What is it?"

"The phone."

She switched on the lamp beside the bed. The telephone continued its insistent ringing. Rob blinked awake and fumbled for the receiver. "Hello," he mumbled.

"Skipper, it's me, Cash. I'm, uh, in a little trouble."

Rob rubbed his eyes, looked at his watch. The digital readout showed 10:05 P.M. But that was Eastern time. In Paris it would be— he had to think a second—3:05 A.M. He said into the telephone, "It's three in the morning!"

"Sorry about that, Skipper. I'm at the Renard Rouge and . . ."

"The what?"

"The Renard Rouge. You know, the Red Fox, the famous nightclub. And I don't have enough cash and, shit, my credit card won't work. Damned thing must be maxed out."

"What do you want?"

"I need some money, Skipper. To pay this goddamned bill! Don't know who else to ask. There's a couple of those French police guys here plus the manager and half the staff and either I pay up or it's off to the slammer."

"How much do you need?"

"In funny money, it's about two thousand something, whatever that is."

Rob almost blurted out, "Maybe jail would do you some good." Then he realized that there could be a heap of trouble if Cash was arrested. Their flight back to Boston would be canceled since there are no reserve first officers sitting around Paris, and it would take half the day, at the earliest, for the company to send over a replacement. Some of the passengers could be protected on the New York flight, then shuttled back to Boston. All would be unhappy. And if Rob's flight was canceled, Crew Scheduling would most likely deadhead him back on the New York flight also, because on Monday, he suddenly remembered, he'd be sixty, no more a Trans Globe captain, no longer authorized to command a flight across the Atlantic. Damn, he wanted to *work* his last crossing, to make that final landing, not *deadhead*.

Rob suspected, too, that Cash may have overindulged. It would make for a sensational story if the press learned that an airline pilot had been tossed into jail—in *Paris!*—after a night on the town. Trans Globe did not need that kind of publicity. Rob had his loyalties—despite Frank Yeganeh. "Okay," Rob said acidly. "I'll be there as soon as I can."

"Please hurry, Skipper. They're turning out the lights."

Rob replaced the telephone, then he turned to Charis and frowned. "It's Cash. He's at a fancy nightclub and can't pay the bill." Rob shrugged his shoulders. "He even said please." Rob's arm encircled her bare shoulders, and he drew her closer. He whispered, "I have to go help him." He kissed her and said, "It's been so wonderful being with you, Charis. Thank you."

He eased out of the bed and dressed quickly, then returned to Charis's side. When she sat up, the covers dropped away, revealing her small breasts, their exquisite contours silhouetted by the lamplight. He wanted urgently to caress her again; instead, he leaned over the bed, newly aware of the tiny, becoming wrinkles at the corners of her eyes. He gently kissed her lips. "Leaving you is not easy," he said softly. "I'll be back as quickly as I can."

The currency exchange window in the lobby was shuttered

closed. Rob checked his wallet and discovered he still had francs left over from his previous Paris trip that he'd expected to spend during this layover. But thanks to the hotel's generosity, he'd spent little— twenty francs at the *boulangerie* during their run and a generous tip for the room service waiter who'd brought their dinner. He found two two-hundred- and three fifty-franc notes, plus some twenties, more than enough for the round-trip cab to the nightclub. He would use his American Express card to cover Cash's bill.

A single, black taxicab sat outside the hotel. Rob tapped on the windshield to awaken the driver, who rolled down his window. When Rob said "Reynard Rouge," the driver shook his head, seemingly incredulous that anyone could possibly want a ride at such an hour. *"C'est fermé!"* he insisted, but Rob waved a two-hundred-franc note, swung open the rear door, and climbed into the backseat, nearly gagging from the odor as the cab got under way.

Rob had rarely used taxis in Paris, preferring the faster and cheaper Métro, but the ones he had ridden in were usually immaculate. The interior of this cab, a Peugeot well past its prime, reeked of stale tobacco smoke, and its atmosphere worsened when the driver lit a crinkled, brown-papered cigarette and exhaled a cloud of foul-smelling fumes. With aquiline features, olive skin, and a bushy, fierce mustache, he looked to be from North Africa, Rob thought— an Algerian or Moroccan, perhaps. He drove very fast in the light traffic, and in that curious French custom turned on only the parking lights, causing Rob to wonder about the pedestrian fatality rate. Step on the gas, jam on the brakes, speed up again—the driver made no attempt to drive smoothly, and whenever he slowed the vehicle, the front brakes squealed in distress, an indication, Rob knew, that the brake pads had reached their wear limit. It puzzled him that any taxi driver wouldn't at least *try* to give his passengers the smoothest and safest possible ride, like airline pilots do.

The driver finished his cigarette, flipped the butt out the window, and turned to look back at Rob. *"Américain, oui?"*

"Yes, *oui*," Rob replied.

"Avez-vous des cigarettes blondes—cigarettes américaines?"

"No, don't smoke." Rob fanned his hand as if to blow smoke away from his face.

Again the driver glanced at him, then waved his right arm in an undulating motion while asking, "*Aviateur, oui?*"

"Uh, yes, *oui*." Being truthful came naturally to Rob, but he felt uneasy giving the driver this information. Still, Rob rationalized, it was no secret that Trans Globe, as well as several other airlines, lodged their crews at the Gallia.

Rob's comprehension of the French language didn't extend much past greetings and deciphering menus, but the driver's French seemed coarse, difficult to understand and loaded with expletives, not the elegant Parisian accent of his language tapes and the hotel staff. Rob had to ask him to repeat the question three times when the driver asked why he wanted to go to the Renard Rouge at this hour. He replied, "Uh, *retriever mon ami.*"

"*Votre ami, un aviateur, aussi?*"

"*Oui.*" Several times during the swift ride along the Quai Branly and then the Quai D'Orsay, the driver eyed Rob in the rear-view mirror. Surely he's seen a pilot before, Rob thought, wishing the driver would keep his gaze fixed on the dimly lit streets.

They crossed the Seine, with streetlights reflecting off the churning river—and reminding Rob of the afternoon's perilous events—circled halfway around the Place de la Concorde, and continued northerly on another broad boulevard. Farther on, the somber walls of Sainte-Madeleine cathedral, bathed in soft floodlights, rose majestically out of the darkness. Then the cab plunged into a section of Paris that Rob was less familiar with, darker, more cluttered—the Montmartre. They wound past a huge railroad station, stark and strangely quiet at this unlikely hour, and continued along a narrow street. After a half-dozen blocks of shadowy, quiet tenements, the taxi emerged onto a wider avenue. On a crest in the distance, Rob recognized the ivory dome of the church of the Sacré Coeur, seeming to float above its dark surroundings like a luminous mirage. Seconds later the cab rounded a corner and screeched to a halt.

The driver had stopped in front of a building whose glass doors were flanked with huge billboards displaying colorful photographs of gorgeous, long-limbed showgirls bedecked in feathery headdresses and scanty costumes. Above the entrance, red neon spelled out LE REYNARD ROUGE and depicted, in outline, a huge fox in hot pursuit of a shapely damsel.

Rob told the driver, *"Restez ici, comprendez-vous?"* He held up a two-hundred-franc note, tore it in half, and handed one half to the driver.

The driver gave him a sour look, then his expression changed to a sardonic grin. He nodded affirmatively, raised his hand with the fingers spread, and said, *"Je rendrai—cinq minutes."*

Rob said, "Okay," certain the driver would not pass up the other half of the note, but as soon as Rob stepped out of the cab, the driver sped off in a cloud of exhaust fumes.

Although the entrance to the nightclub remained illuminated, most other lights along the front of the building had been extinguished. A polished blue taxi waited at the taxi stand, and an empty police car sat next to it. Rob tapped on the glass door to summon the doorman and explained, as best as he could in French, that he had come for his friend, who lacked money to pay his bill. The doorman disappeared inside while Rob waited, then returned a minute later with a man dressed in a shiny black suit, a pink rose in the lapel, and wearing a black bow tie.

"Ah, *Monsieur* Robertson, I believe. My name is Didier. A minor difficulty with your friend. You are so kind to come at this hour."

Didier led Rob inside, past a cloakroom, then into the foyer. Behind a low table graced with a sprawling bouquet of pink and white roses, he found Cash comfortably reposed on an elegant sofa of crimson velvet, and snuggled close beside him a stunning, black-haired woman, tightly sheathed in a strapless scarlet dress. Her lipstick matched the dress, dark eyes flashed beneath thick eyelashes, and thin eyebrows etched long, twin arcs across her pale forehead. One lovely cheek bore a beauty mark, conjuring an image of the classic femme fatale from an old movie, and an exotic scent teased Rob's nose. Cash, wearing a loud plaid sportcoat, looked like a traveling salesman, utterly comfortable but woefully out of place.

In a soft chair at one end of the table, a dour, gray-uniformed gendarme, sporting a trim mustache, sat bolt upright, but his eyes appeared fixed on the lady's ripe décolletage. Another, presumably lower-ranking gendarme, stood stiffly behind him. A second black-suited man sat at the other end of the table, while a third stood to the side of the sofa. Cash's right arm reached around the woman's bare shoulders, and he seemed to be in the middle of telling a joke. He waved a greeting and cried out, "Skipper! I told 'em you'd come."

Rob, not feeling the least bit congenial although secretly conceding that he found the scene quite intriguing, asked sternly, "Where's the bill?"

The third black-suited men handed Rob a leather-covered folder. Rob opened it and glanced at the sheet inside: *"Charge d'Entre . . . 400F, Champagne . . . 250F, Crêpes de Maison . . . 300F, Champagne . . ."* Cash said, "Don't look too close, Skipper, it's real bad. Just pay it—please! I'll make it up to you, no sweat."

Rob reached for his wallet and pulled out his American Express card. He handed it to the man, who walked hurriedly away. Everyone remained silent until the man returned minutes later with the plastic card and the receipt for Rob to sign, indicating where he could affix an additional gratuity above the already included fifteen percent *charge de service.*

Rob confronted Cash. "With the tip it'll be twenty-one hundred francs—that's over four hundred bucks. I'll pay this, but we're going straight back to the Gallia. You're not out of the woods yet as far as I'm concerned." Rob glanced at his watch and thought a moment about the time. "Our crew wake-up call's in less than five hours. You know the rules about drinking. Sure, everyone's bent the rules one time or another, but if you're not fit to do your job in the morning, you're not getting on my airplane. Period. I'll have no choice but to cancel the flight."

Cash said, "I'll be okay, I promise. But can you loan me five hundred in funny money? For my little friend here." He leaned over and kissed the woman's rouged cheek, right above the beauty mark, with a loud smack. He grinned back at Rob. "Her name's Yvonne."

Rob yanked out his wallet again and withdrew a crisp American fifty-dollar bill. "You can have this, Cash. Spend it as you like, but this is the last straw. We're leaving right now." Rob extended the note toward Cash, but before he could react Yvonne jumped up, snatched it from Rob's fingers, and in one swift motion tucked it into her enticing cleavage. She smiled sweetly and snarled, "Cheap bastard!" in Rob's face, turned to Cash, ran her fingers through his curls, murmured, *"Au revoir, cheri,"* and stepped past the now wide-eyed gendarmes. Instantly another shiny-suited man emerged from the cloakroom carrying a black fur stole and unctuously assisted in draping it across her shoulders. Then, without looking back, she walked to the door, all male eyes glued to her undulating hips. The doorman leaped to her side, bowed slightly. *"Votre taxi est ici, Mademoiselle,"* he announced, offering his arm as he escorted her out the door.

Rob, now steaming inside, growled, "At least that's settled. Let's get out of here."

Outside, the neon words LE RENARD ROUGE dimmed to a soft glow, then flickered out. As the taxicab carrying Yvonne accelerated down the empty, darkened street, Cash moaned, "Oh, man, there she goes. A million rivets in tight formation." Just as the cab's tail-lights disappeared from view, he slapped his hand against his head. "Oh shit, I forgot to get her phone number!"

When Rob, still seething, did not respond, Cash continued, "Paree may be expensive, but it sure beats Big D. Ooh-la-la, what a floor show! Those gals had the best boobs you'd ever want to see." He grinned at Rob and asked, with a trace of sarcasm in his voice, "Hey, what about you, Skipper? Did you paint the town red or just stare at your walls all day?"

"Well, I went for a run with Charis."

"Went for a run! Oh man," Cash pronounced in mock horror. "On your last trip to Paree. You really know how to live it up!" He cackled as if he couldn't believe his ears.

His patience worn thin, Rob ignored Cash's remarks and looked around for his taxi, which had not returned. He muttered "Damn!" but a moment later spotted the abused machine half a block away, racing toward the nightclub. It squealed to a stop in front of them. Cash opened the rear door and held it for Rob to enter, then followed him inside.

As soon as Cash sat down, he gagged. "Ugh! Where'd you find this one, Skipper? It stinks worse than a border-town bordello!"

"Don't complain," Rob grumbled. "We're damned lucky to

have a cab at this time of night."As it pulled away from the curb, Rob continued to fume, not becoming aware for several seconds of the presence of a second man, also with swarthy, North African features, sitting in front alongside the driver. This man and the driver conversed in low voices in an unrecognizable tongue that Rob assumed to be Arabic—in any event, it wasn't French.

Several minutes later, after the driver had changed direction several times and then turned down a narrow, dimly lit street, Rob had a second realization. They were not headed toward central Paris and the Gallia. The spotlighted dome of the Sacré Coeur occasionally peeked between buildings on his right, and when he turned to look back, he glimpsed the distant, red-beaconed tip of the Eiffel Tower. His throat suddenly dry, he leaned forward and quizzed the driver: *"Allez-vous au Hôtel Gallia?"*

The driver did not respond. Cash, his voice rising a notch in pitch, queried, "What's happening Skipper?"

Rob turned to Cash. "I don't like this. We're headed in the wrong direction." Using the sternest voice he could muster, he ordered the driver, *"Arrêtez, arrêtez!"*

The man alongside the driver swung around, his features contorted with hate. He screamed a tirade of what sounded like obscenities at Rob and Cash interspersed with *"pilotes américains"* and something like *jihad,* repeated several times. The man's right hand, clutching a dark object, slid up over the top of the seat. The glow from a streetlight glinted off the muzzle of an automatic pistol pointed squarely at Rob's nose.

Like a white blur, Cash's fist whipped out of the darkness and smashed hard into the Arab's cheek. Rob heard bones crack. The man groaned and slouched forward, clutching his hands to his face. The gun clunked onto the floor somewhere near Rob's feet. When the driver turned to see what had happened, Cash's fist flew again, smacking him in the nose. The driver keeled over, grabbing his face, gasping for air as blood spurted through his fingers. The taxi weaved erratically. Rob reached over the driver, groping for the steering wheel, but quickly realized he could not prevent a collision with a parked car. He yelled, "Duck!" seconds before the impact and reached to pull Cash down as he crouched behind the front seat.

The cab crashed into the stationary vehicle with a resounding *ca-rump!* followed by the piercing screech of ripping metal, then abruptly careened to a stop. Rob and Cash banged hard against the back side of the front seat, which helped absorb the impact for them, but the two Arabs slammed violently against the dashboard and windshield.

Rob uncoiled himself from the pretzel of his and Cash's arms and legs. The impact wrenched Rob's left shoulder, and his left wrist had whacked against something solid.

"You okay, Cash?"

"Yeah, I think so. Let's get the hell out of here."

Cash's door had jammed, but Rob opened his and clambered out, shouting, "Follow me." Side by side, they rushed pell-mell fifty yards down the gloomy street before stopping, both panting, to look back. No one emerged from the taxi. Its taillights glowed weakly. Above the crumpled front end, coolant fizzed like a geyser from the punctured radiator and formed a misty cloud as it condensed in the cool air. The taxi's front doors remained closed.

Windows in the upper floors of the tenements lining the street were illuminated, then were swung open. Heads leaned out. Voices called. Somewhere in the murky shadows a dog barked; farther away, another answered.

Almost in a whisper, Rob said, "That was mighty close."

Cash, still puffing, said, "Yeah. What do we do now?"

The high-low wail of an emergency vehicle's klaxon split the stillness, drawing nearer, louder, more shrill.

"Thank goodness it didn't catch fire," Rob said, his firefighter ethics coming to the fore. "We'd be obliged to extricate those guys, but now we probably should wait for the gendarmes." He thought a moment. "Or we could head for the hotel."

"I prefer number two," Cash said, "but how?"

"Not on the Métro—it stops running at midnight, buses, too—and it might be prudent to avoid another cab ride, even if we could find one."

"I agree," Cash said with a groan. The klaxon's blare intensified, and now a second siren could be heard as more dogs joined in the chorus. "Anyhow, sounds like the cops'll be here in a minute."

"I'd rather not get involved with the police right now; we could spend the rest of the night trying to explain this, and if things got complicated, we could be stuck here for days—or weeks."

"Not good, Skipper. I'm broke, remember?"

Rob pondered their options. "Look, Cash, it'll take forever to walk back to the hotel. Can you jog?"

"Me? You kidding?"

"It's a good time to start. Let's go." Rob led the way along the darkened streets, initially using glimpses, in the occasional gaps between buildings, of the distant Eiffel Tower to keep his bearings until they'd reached more familiar surroundings. An hour later, the first streaks of dawn washed away the night as the exhausted aviators climbed the steps of the Hôtel Gallia.

Catching his breath in the elevator, Rob said, "You throw one helluva punch, Cash. How's your hand?"

Cash, panting, his face flushed, held out his right hand. It was swollen and his knuckles were bruised and red. "It's okay. My feet are in worse shape. Hey, you weren't so bad yourself."

"No, you saved us. I won't forget that."

"Who were those guys, anyway?"

"I think we stumbled on a couple of Arab-version rednecks," Rob said. "When the driver figured out I was a pilot, he fetched his buddy while I went into the cabaret, and they took it upon themselves to be heroes by getting some revenge for that Libyan airliner."

"You can't blame 'em for trying," Cash snickered. "Doesn't Allah reward 'em with seventeen virgins when they get to heaven? Man, sure hope the supply runs out soon."

"I thought the man wielding the gun used the word *mujahidin* when he was screaming at us," Rob continued. "That means 'guerrilla' in Arabic, something like that."

"More like gorillas—as in apes—I'd call 'em. We were damned lucky, Skip. Those guys were amateurs."

"When it comes to this stuff, so am I," Rob said, "but I am concerned. In the weeks ahead there'll undoubtedly be some form of retaliation from people who do know what they're doing."

Cash grimaced. "Sometimes flying ain't all it's cracked up to be."

"That's for sure," Rob agreed as the elevator stopped at Cash's floor and the door slid open. "Look, forget what I said earlier. We may be antipodal in character, but we're both in this now."

"Anti-what?"

Rob checked his watch. The crystal had been shattered but the second digits continued silently to tick away. "Wake-up call's in three and a half hours. Sleep fast."

CHAPTER ELEVEN

THE MORNING AFTER

Charis arose before the wake-up call. She kissed Rob's cheek and whispered, "Don't get up. I'm going down to my room to pack and make myself beautiful. The hotel might be anxious if I'm not there for crew call."

He said, "Next door to the lobby, there's a small lounge reserved for crews. There'll be croissants and hot coffee. See you there?"

"Of course."

Rob dozed for half an hour, until the jangle of the telephone reawakened him. Long accustomed to this ritual, he sat up immediately and reached for the phone. "Hello," he mumbled. Sunshine streamed into the room through the large windows. He remembered last night, Charis lying beside him, admiring the lights of the city before they had drifted serenely into sleep, hours before the distress call from Cash.

"*Bonjour,* Rob, good morning. Operations calling."

Rob recognized the jovial, accented voice of Trans Globe's chief operations agent at Aéroport Charles de Gaulle. "*Bonjour,* Maurice."

"Flight eight-eleven will be routine. Would we allow it to be otherwise for your last crossing?" he said, laughing. "Routine," in

Trans Globe parlance, meant simply that no unusual circumstances existed that might affect the on-time departure and subsequent operation of the impending flight.

"Good, I'd like a nice, uneventful flight home," Rob replied. He almost said "boring" rather than "uneventful," but that would not have been truthful. He had never regarded any flight as boring.

Knowing that Maurice, to avoid being the harbinger of bad news, sometimes stretched things a bit—although always with a smile—Rob asked, "Is the inbound flight on time?"

"Ah, no, sir. Departed Cairo International Airport forty-five minutes late because of an electrical power interruption at the airport. Radar, the tower, lights in the terminal, everything out for nearly an hour." He laughed. "Don't they pay their utility bills?"

"Maybe not," Rob joked in reply, but he was thinking that, without power to the baggage X-ray machines, the Egyptian security people would have been required to physically inspect each piece of luggage and cargo. He hoped they'd been thorough.

"You're lucky today," Maurice continued. "On Thursday it was out for hours!"

"What's his ETA?"

"Eight-eleven is estimating touchdown at eleven twenty-one. Not to worry, sir. Our superb staff will perform a rapid turn-around." Again he laughed. "On-time departure guaranteed. No problem."

Rob mentally added several minutes taxi-in time and a few more minutes for the passengers and crew to disembark. That left about thirty minutes for the ground personnel to prepare the Starliner for an ocean crossing, which meant they would have to hustle. The plane would require interior cleaning and provisioning for a sizable load of passengers. It would need to be refueled, the engine oil checked, and any maintenance items corrected. Shuffling cargo and luggage into and out of the belly compartments would take the most time: inbound freight and bags would be off-loaded, while those continuing on to Boston remained on board, and then the Paris cargo and luggage added. Rob said only, "Okay."

He jotted down the details on a pad as Maurice recited, "Plane number one-five-oh-seven. Projected load, twelve in first class, two hundred twenty-four coach. Flight time to Boston, seven hours and thirty-seven minutes. Boston forecast: high overcast, visibility over five miles, temperature forty-two. You see, everything is perfect."

Crew calls within the United States had been eliminated in another of Yeganeh's cost-cutting moves, but at Trans Globe's overseas stations the operations staff still formally notified the captain of the pertinent details of his (Trans Globe still had no female captains) flight—another of the little touches that made international flying so pleasant. The ops agent would then request the hotel switchboard operator to ring the other crew members.

"Thanks, Maurice, sounds good. See you soon." Rob would use this information to brief the cabin crew in the bus while en route to the airport. He looked at his left wrist to check the time, then remembered he'd switched the watch to the other arm. The cracked crystal reminded him of the wild taxi ride; however, the watch functioned normally, displaying 04:05 Eastern. He mentally added five hours, making the local time 09:05 A.M., exactly three hours before Flight 811's scheduled departure time.

Rob stepped into the elevator twenty-five minutes later, looking alert and fresh, but harboring a sense of uneasiness about the events of the previous night. He was physically hurting, too. His neck bones creaked when he turned his head, his wrist had swollen, and his shoulder felt stiff—belated consequences of the taxi's crash into the parked car. And his knees, from being scraped against the rough concrete as he was hoisted onto the quay, looked like a cat had sharpened its claws on them. The lengthy, middle-of-the-night jog had not helped matters.

After checking out at the front desk, and thanking the concierge for the hotel's extraordinary hospitality, he stopped at the kiosk in the lobby and purchased a newspaper, *Le Journal du Matin*. In bold letters the headline blared "MONDE ARABE ENRAGÉ," and beneath it a large photograph showed hundreds of people, many in traditional Arab dress, gathered at the gates of the U.S. embassy. Some of the demonstrators flaunted pictures of Gadhafi; others carried signs bearing anti-American slogans. On the inside pages more photos showed a gang overturning a truck loaded with Coca-Cola bottles and demonstrators in Syria and Iraq burning American flags and effigies of Uncle Sam. The accompanying article reported rallies in various Middle Eastern cities. Another article, accompanied by pictures of rescue operations, confirmed that there were no survivors from the ill-fated aircraft. Rob reflected on these developments, then skimmed through the paper as quickly as his limited command of French permitted, searching for local news, but found no mention of errant taxicabs, nor of a child being rescued from the Seine.

The crew lounge accommodated a dozen small tables with white tablecloths, and featured a large coffee urn and silver trays plentifully stacked with croissants, still warm from the bakery. Rob entered the room and waved a greeting to Margot and two other flight attendants, but chose an empty table, anticipating Charis's arrival. Margot, grinning cattishly, teased, "Didn't see you at the office, Rob."

Before he fumbled an answer, Charis appeared, looking cheerful and radiant. He sprang to his feet, causing a twinge in his neck, but resisted the urge to kiss her cheek. Rob assisted with her chair. "I don't have an opportunity to serve the cabin crew very often," he said. "How do you like your coffee? But I warn you—it's high-octane stuff, not for the faint of heart."

"Make mine the same as yours, please."

"Fine. I like a little milk and sugar in my first cup of the morning, just black after that."

Other members of the crew entered the lounge and exchanged greetings as Rob doctored two white porcelain cupfuls of the rich-smelling brew, delivered them—carefully, because of his wrist—to the table, then returned for napkins and two of the warm rolls.

"Thank you, Robby," Charis said. She looked around to ensure that no one was watching, then removed a small gray bundle from her shoulder bag. "Some man left his trousers in my room. Could these be yours?" she asked, smiling innocently as she handed him his neatly folded running pants.

"Thanks," he replied sheepishly, hoping that none of the other crew had observed this exchange, and unable to prevent a blush. "I knew I'd left them in some lady's room, just couldn't remember which one."

"You're a bad influence, Captain Robertson. My first trip to

Paris, and you won't let me out of the hotel except to go for a run. I thought we'd do some sight-seeing."

"What about our little swim? How many tourists do that?"

"Oh, you win," she said, and reached across the small table to touch his hand. "How do you feel this morning?"

"Surprisingly good. My knees are a little gimpy from so much running, and my left wrist is pretty sore." He cocked his right arm. "I had to put my watch on the other wing."

She examined his injured wrist. "It's badly swollen. You may have cracked a bone."

"It's a dilemma," Rob said. "I've never tried to fly hurting like this. Pilots have a responsibility to their passengers and crew members to be one hundred percent fit, but if I called in sick now, the company would have to cancel the flight." He sipped the coffee. "A few hours ago I warned Cash that there weren't any spare first officers over here—well, there aren't any extra Starliner captains either, and we'll have a planeload of people anxious to go home."

"As soon as we board the airplane I'll prepare an ice pack."

"That'll help. I'll be okay. Besides, what else could happen on this trip?"

She smiled. "Yes, it's been an astonishing two days."

Rob bit into the buttery croissant. "Umm, these are delicious. I'll miss some things about Paris." He took another bite. "But the old hometown sounds pretty good right now; in fact, I've been thinking. You were too busy saving that boy yesterday to answer, but what would you say to visiting my farm after we get back to Boston, instead of hurrying back to San Diego?"

When Charis hesitated, he continued. "You'll like Deerwood. Colonial homes, a town hall that was built in 1778 and is still in use. There's a village green, pretty as a calendar picture, complete with bandstand and Civil War cannons, and even an old-fashioned general store with a big potbellied stove." He finished the croissant and sipped his coffee. "I hear the schools are pretty good, too."

"It sounds wonderful, but are you sure?" She reached for his right hand. "Seeing you again has been more than I bargained for. I hadn't known about Jane, of course, and really, I had just wanted to . . . to apologize, face-to-face, for . . . that we'd parted so badly in London, so long ago." Her eyes moistened. "And I wanted to be a part of your last crew, to wish you a long and happy retirement, not to rekindle . . . Please understand. I'll always cherish these few hours together, but everything's happening too fast. In some ways, it's like we've just met."

"No, Charis," he stammered. "We've known each other . . ."

"It's not so simple, Robby. Danny's involved with school and friends, and I bounce from soccer mom to swim team mom, and my parents need me, too, as much as I need them." She bowed her head. "I have obligations—that's my life now. I can't give it up. Deerwood's a long way from San Diego."

Stunned, Rob remained silent, absorbing words that stung like darts, feeling suddenly older, grayer, more aware of their age difference. He remembered a line from a poem, about how sometimes you hear the words but not the music. Finally he said, "Retirement should mean life getting less complicated, not more. I'm sorry. I was thinking only about myself."

"Wouldn't I be an intruder in your home? Wouldn't my presence infringe on your memories?" She looked at him. "Does that make sense?"

"Yes, of course."

"Wouldn't it always be Jane's house, filled with her things?"

"Some things, but not a lot, not everything," Rob replied. "Her older sister never approved of me and my country ways, and she took some of Jane's belongings, and the other sister wanted her stoneware. Her clothes went to charities. A woman from the club called and wanted her golf clubs. I donated her tennis rackets to the high school, for the team. Jane had tons of jewelry, which I parceled out to her nieces and cousins. Sounds like I was ruthless. Maybe I was. Trying to get even." Almost in a whisper he added, "I still have that opaline vase. She died just hours before I could give it to her." He looked at her hopefully. "Please say you'll come."

"My next trip isn't till Friday. I could call my parents and Danny from Boston and see how things are going. Let me think about it during the flight."

"Fine." He smiled, regaining his composure. "And don't

forget—there's a gourmet meal waiting for us in the refrigerator. Now, how about you? How are you this morning?"

"Glorious." She beamed and squeezed his hand before releasing it. "But I'm worried about you, and I'm concerned for that little boy—he swallowed so much water. And what about that awful business last night?"

"Didn't see a thing about either incident in the newspaper, which probably means that the kid's okay, and the cab episode occurred too late to make the news."

"Did you call the police?"

"There isn't time to get involved with the gendarmes right now, but I've written out a statement for the ops agent to give them. Mainly, I want to spread the word to our crews to be extra cautious on layover."

"What about Cash?"

"Well, he seemed to be okay last night, or, should I say, this morning. It's almost funny. It was his escapade that caused us to be in that darned cab in the middle of the night and nearly got us killed, but then his quick reactions saved our lives." Rob chuckled as he shook his head. "He's the most hedonistic person I've ever known, but he flies like a dream. Speaking of whom . . ." Rob checked the time on his damaged watch. He stood up and looked around the room, counting noses. Only Cash was missing. Rob said to his crew, "Well, gang, it's time to board the bus. I'll see what's keeping our first officer this time."

Rob stepped into the lobby to use the house telephone to call Cash's room. A sleepy voice grumbled, "Yeah."

"Cash, this is Rob. Didn't you get a wake-up call?"

"Damn! Must have rolled back over. What time is it, anyway?"

"It's time to leave, right now. We're all waiting. Get your butt down here right away." Rob grinned. After last night, he couldn't be angry with Cash.

*

The other members of the crew, settled into their seats in the crew bus, jeered good-naturedly when Cash finally hopped aboard, no necktie, his shirt only half tucked in, carrying his suitcase in one hand, his shoulder bag and uniform jacket slung over the other arm.

"My ex number one complained I was chronic-ologically late," he proclaimed, "so she gave me this." He grinned and raised an arm to display his enormous, multi-buttoned watch as he plunked down into a seat. "Chronic-ologically, get it?" His quip brought only a few groans as the bus eased away from the loading dock, but one of the flight attendants, Maria Gazzarelli, handed him coffee in a paper cup and a croissant. "I knew you'd be starving," she said. When he had finished eating, he tucked in his shirt, pulled a cordless electric razor from his shoulder bag, and began to look like an airline pilot, much to his crewmates' amused astonishment.

Rob and Charis sat together for the long ride to Aéroport Charles de Gaulle. Still groggy from the lack of sleep, Rob drifted off, reminiscing about the previous day . . .

In his huge, white-tiled bathroom he'd turned on the hot water for Charis and handed her a white ribbed-cotton robe with the words "Hôtel Gallia" embroidered on the chest in small blue letters. He'd closed the bathroom door behind her, and begun to dry himself in the bedroom. A few minutes later she'd called out, "This is wonderful. I'm a new woman."

"Good. Save some hot water for me," he joked.

"This tub is enormous."

"Yes, I noticed."

"Robby?"

"Yes?"

"There's room for two. You could get in, too. I don't mind."

"Are you sure?" Rob Robertson, two days shy of sixty years old, had never been stark naked with a woman—not even Jane—in broad daylight, let alone shared a bathtub. It was a paradox that he had never solved, Jane's strict rules about her privacy. She'd consented to lovemaking only in the darkened sanctity of their bedroom. And yet, right under his nose, she'd had the audacity to carry on an affair with that bastard Henderson, and, evidently, everyone had known but Rob.

"Well, you don't have to, but you should get out of those wet clothes. I won't look."

"Well, okay." He slipped out of his sopping togs, donned his robe, and gently tapped on the bathroom door.

"Come in. My eyes are closed."

Clouds of warm vapor swirled past his face when he opened the door. He stepped into the huge bathroom, slipped off the robe, and hung it on a hook beside hers. He tried to avert his gaze, but his eyes were drawn to her like to a magnet. She had slid down in the tub until the water lapped at her neck, and had raised her knees. Her wet hair clung to her scalp and neck, and the alluring sight of her smooth, tanned skin under the steamy water and glistening soap bubbles, which she had heaped strategically, stirred a warm tremor in his loins.

He maneuvered carefully into the tub and sat down in the water alongside but facing her. He elevated his knees and slithered deeper until the foamy liquid eddied around his chest, then swished some of the soapy bubbles into a mound over his lower abdomen. The heat from the water penetrated deeply through his skin, soothing and relaxing him. He sighed contentedly. "Ah, the French think of everything," he said.

"Yes. Can I open my eyes now?"

"Of course."

"Oh, look at your knees." Trickles of blood oozed where the skin had been scraped raw on the rough concrete of the quay.

"They're okay."

A few minutes later she said, "I might melt."

His Yankee reserve had thawed as well. He said, "I feel like my world is changing."

"How?"

"It's like my heart's been asleep for years, locked in the past. Charis, do you think . . ."

She held a finger to her lips. "Shh."

They lay in the great bathtub a long time without speaking, content simply to absorb the comforting warmth. Rob occasionally opened the spigot to add more hot water, maintaining the near scalding temperature. His inhibitions rinsed away by the hot water, and unable to deny his longing, he reached for her hand, gently raised it to his lips. "Will you stay with me tonight?"

She squeezed his hand while her eyes answered yes.

Rob emerged from the tub first. He wrapped one of the thick white towels around his waist, then held the other for her. She offered to dry his back and laughed. "Brace yourself! I majored in phys ed, remember?" She briskly rubbed the towel over him.

He returned the favor, starting gently with her hair and working south, past the flower tattoo. When she turned to face him, he dropped the towel, took her hand, and led her to the bedroom. He kissed her, long and tenderly. "Life is unfair," he murmured. "Why did it take fifteen years to find you again?"

Charis whispered, "It's time to make amends."

Later, Rob had called room service and they'd dined, courtesy of the hotel, in the suite, and afterward they'd reminisced about that long-ago summer. They made love again, and fell asleep in each other's arms. He'd slept deeply, contentedly—until Cash's frantic, wee-hours call.

Rob jerked awake when the bus stopped at Terminal One. Prior to 9/11, the crew bus proceeded directly to the flight line security gate, where the guards merely checked each crew member's credentials and the crew's flight orders; then the bus would continue across the ramp, straight to operations. But since that horrendous day, crews were required to pass through the metal detectors and undergo screening, the same as passengers.

After disembarking from the bus, the crew proceeded through the spacious terminal and entered the security line for flight crews. The two male personnel methodically checked passports, I.D. cards, purses, and shoulder bags. They studied Rob's flight orders, then chose Cash's suitcase for a thorough inspection. Cash groaned, "Sure wish they'd make up their minds. Yesterday they give me a hard time coming into the country, now they don't want me to leave."

Averting any appearance of sexual inequity, the guards also inspected Maria's luggage, exhibiting renowned Gallic aplomb as they poked around the woman's frilly underwear.

Once past security, Margot asked, "Rob, have we got time to hit the duty-free shops?"

He checked his watch. "Go ahead. Our plane's still twenty minutes out," he replied, and turned to Charis. "There are some terrific shops there."

"So I've heard. See you on board."

"Fine," Rob said, then beckoned to Cash. "We'd better head straight for operations."

"Yeah," Cash reluctantly agreed. "Besides, I'm flat broke."

While Gregory and the flight attendants hurried to the duty-free area, Rob and Cash stepped onto the escalator for the lengthy ride to the Trans Globe satellite. The amazing apparatus first descended underground, passed beneath the tarmac, then rose to emerge at the boarding level inside the satellite. Rob punched numbers into the combination lock on the metal door marked RESERVÉ AU PERSONNEL TRANS GLOBE, swung it open, and the two pilots descended the stairs to the operations room at the ramp level to commence preparations for the homeward journey.

CHAPTER TWELVE

HOMEWARD BOUND

In operations, Rob introduced Cash to pudgy, ruddy-faced Maurice, who looked rather like an overgrown cherub. Maurice inquired if Cash had enjoyed his first visit to Paris.

"Yeah, sort of," Cash replied, scratching his chin pensively. "It wasn't what I'd call the perfect layover."

"Perfect layover?" Maurice seemed puzzled.

"That's when the first officer gets laid and the captain gets a full night's uninterrupted sleep." Cash slapped his left hand on the counter and cackled. "Struck out on both counts! I ran out of money and had to wake up the Skipper in the middle of the night to bail me out."

Maurice, always quick to laugh, joined in. When the din had subsided, he asked, beaming like a schoolboy who had just brought home a report card of straight A's, "So, did the Gallia treat you well, *Capitaine* Rob?"

"Yes, quite nicely. Thank you, Maurice," Rob replied. "I had a feeling you orchestrated those arrangements."

"Sparky Miller sent me a teletype saying this was your, as you say, swan song, so *naturellement* I spoke to my good friend *le directeur* Plubeau. I hope it proved *convenablement*."

"Well, I don't know what that word means," Rob said, knowing that Maurice, as well as Cash, had no notion of how the hotel's hospitality had helped rekindle long-dormant yearnings, "but I think the answer is yes. Thanks again. I'm going to miss working with all you good people."

"Yeah, Skipper, but think what you won't miss," Cash interjected, "check rides and wrestling the damned simulator every six months, and physicals." He wiggled his index finger. "Having your body orifices probed, and being hooked up to the EKG that sends the trace over the phone straight to FAA headquarters in Oke City. Hell, a guy could have a heart attack right on the table."

"A few actually have," Rob commented.

"Plus random drug testing," Cash ranted on. "Last month the Feds were waiting when I landed in 'Frisco, and the whole crew had to go to a clinic and piss in bottles. Kee-riste, we get more scrutiny than the damned hijackers! Man, if doctors and lawyers and politicians got the same treatment, things'd sure be different."

"I'm sure that's true, *messieurs,* but now it's time for my speech," Maurice announced, clearing his throat as several other members of the operations staff gathered around. "Ahem. Rob, because you never give us a bad time, unlike some captains whose names I shall not mention, Paris Operations has a little memento of France for you." He reached under the counter and retrieved a package, done up nicely in Trans Globe's colors, white wrapping secured with a bright red ribbon. To polite applause from the staff, he presented the package to Rob.

Rob hefted the box inquisitively, then opened it to find a bottle of Châteauneuf-du-Pape, Domaine Verbier 1990. "*Merci beaucoup,* Maurice, everyone," Rob said, beaming. "Hmm, Châteauneuf-du-Pape, my very favorite French wine. I'll savor this. Thank you." He carefully tucked the bottle into his suitcase, then retrieved his report, handwritten on hotel stationery, regarding the taxicab incident. "Sorry to change the subject, Maurice. I'd like you to read this and pass it on to the proper authorities, and warn our crews to be extra cautious."

"*Certainement,* Rob."

Cash asked, "What's the latest on that Libyan airliner?"

"Your Navy contends they thought it was going to deliberately crash into an aircraft carrier," Maurice said. "But I checked in the International Airline Guide. It was a scheduled flight, Jedda-Benghazi-Algiers, operating on Monday, Wednesday, and Friday."

"There'll surely be retribution," Rob declared. "Who knows when it'll end. But we'd better get on with our flight planning. What's become of Pauline? I forgot about that darned storm."

Maurice had neatly arrayed the flight papers on the wide counter. The flight plan called for a standard departure to Evreux, airway Upper Red 116 to Caen, followed by Upper Green 4 to Jersey, a small British island that the Germans had occupied during World War Two, nestled close to France's Contentin Peninsula. After that, UG4 continued to an aerial intersection called LIZAD, named for the town of Lizard on the southwestern coast of England, which had been, Rob recalled, the locale of a Neville Shute novel. From LIZAD, the flight plan called for direct routing to 50 degrees north latitude, 08 degrees west longitude, then track C, utilizing the coordinates 51N/15W, 52N/20W, 54N/30W, 55N/40W, 54N/50W, to a position called CARPE. The track entry/exit points off the coast of Labrador have "seafood" designations such as SCROD, PRAWN, and OYSTR. It's not a case of bad spelling—the Air Traffic Control computers utilize pronounceable, five-letter codes for such fixes. After CARPE, the remainder of the flight to Boston would be conducted along Canadian and American high-altitude airways.

"Pauline is still a problem," Maurice explained. "Just like a woman, yes? Now she is pounding the island of Newfoundland with strong winds and heavy rain." He pointed out the storm's path on the surface analysis chart. "So tracks Alpha, Bravo, and Charlie go north to avoid her, while the others swing far to the south, too far from en route alternates for Starliner."

Rob said, "What do you think, Cash? You're getting a check ride, and you missed out on the flight planning in Boston."

"Let's see," Cash replied, glancing at the flight plan. "Maurice, did you know that flying is defined as the fastest way from the party at point A to the party at point B?" The operations agent roared as if he hadn't heard that one before.

"My rule," Rob contended, "is to get from point A to point B while breaking as few federal air regulations as possible. Now, let's be serious."

The first officer scratched his curly locks and said, "Hal says we've got Track Charlie, and our alternates are Shannon to twenty west, then Keflavik and Goose Bay."

"Shannon's clear," Rob noted. "Golly, even Keflavik's clear—that's unusual—and Pauline's keeping her distance from Goose. It's a good sign when our alternates are VFR. It seems like we only need one when the weather's lousy. We'll check on Pauline again approaching the other side of the pond, just to be sure."

"Didn't I promise you that your final crossing would be routine?" Maurice asked piously.

"Yeah, but remember that Allied Air captain who aborted the takeoff on *his* last trip," Cash bantered, "and the plane skidded off the runway, and a bunch of people were hurt during the evacuation—including his girlfriend, who was using his wife's pass."

Maurice laughed again. "Please, we'll have none of that."

"Right, let's have a smooth, uneventful flight," Rob said. "Okay, Cash, let's see what they taught you in ground school about plotting the route."

As the first officer, under his captain's watchful eye, laid out track C on the plotting chart, Maurice announced, with a devilish grin, "We have another surprise for you, gentlemen. You'll have a VIP on board."

"A VIP? Jennifer Lopez? Halle Berry? Julia Roberts?" Cash importuned hopefully.

"No, no," Maurice replied. "Today that stands for Vastly Insufferable Person. The big boss will be aboard your flight."

Rob stared at the operations agent. "Our boss?" he asked. "Frank Yeganeh?"

"Yes, the great man himself. He's in the Envoy Lounge right now. Rumor has it he's been negotiating to sell planes to an airline in the Middle East."

"How about Very Inconsiderate Prick," Cash muttered. "That skinflint sure as hell wouldn't be buying any."

"Well, that explains something," Rob remembered. "Before we left Boston, Sparky mentioned that Hollingbrooke . . ."

"Another asshole," Cash chimed in.

". . . would be meeting our flight. I thought he wanted to wish me a happy retirement." Rob chuckled and shook his head. "Should have known better."

Maurice slapped his derriere. "Soon you can tell them to kiss this area of your anatomy."

"Yep," Rob agreed. He checked the en route time on the flight plan. "In about seven hours and thirty-seven minutes they'll put me out to pasture. Well, we'll try to give Yeganeh and everybody else a smooth ride, just like always." He double-checked the route that Cash had drawn on the North Atlantic Planning Chart. "Looks okay, Cash. Let's see, any open weight? A little extra gas in the tanks beats brains any day."

Cash studied the takeoff chart. "Plenty of open weight, and we're good up to max gross on runway nine."

Rob turned to Maurice. "Make the fuel ninety-seven thousand, but first call Yeganeh and make sure he can afford it."

Maurice's laughter was drowned out by the high-pitched whines from twin Vickery engines, trumpeting the arrival of a Starliner at its parking spot outside operations. Rob glanced at the wall clock. Thirty-nine minutes to departure—not much time. With Yeganeh on board, he realized, the station manager would push the ground crew to make an on-time departure. He trusted that security would not be jeopardized. "Sounds like our bird's pulling into the gate, Cash. If you'll go kick the tires, we'll get this show on the road."

"I won't be kicking 'em too hard." He winked at Maurice. "Last night my captain made me run five miles in dress shoes. First layover where I got blisters on my toes."

Maurice roared again.

＊

To Rob's amazement—having Yeganeh aboard undoubtedly being a factor—Flight 811 pushed back from Gate 6K of the Trans Globe satellite precisely on schedule at 12:05 noon Paris time—7:05 EST on Rob's splintered watch. The familiar drill ensued: engines started during push back, brakes parked while the mechanics disconnected the tractor tow bar from the aircraft's nose-gear strut and unhooked the intercom, clearance to taxi received from de Gaulle

Ground Control. Rob returned the signalman's salute, nudged the throttles forward to coax the Starliner into movement, then eased them back to idle as it gained momentum. He steered the airplane onto the curving taxiways past the other satellites, which resembled giant mother hens with huge chicks of airliners nestled in a semicircle under their concrete bosoms. An international crayon box of colors adorned the planes' towering vertical stabilizers: the rainbow bands of an Ethiopian Airlines 767, the blue-and-yellow logo embellishing a Lufthansa A-300, a sleek Alitalia MD-80 with broad red and green stripes. Aircraft from every corner of the world—Korean Airlines, Icelandair, Aerolíneas Argentinas, Air India, Australia's Qantas, South African Airways—displayed their unique, often nationalistic color schemes.

Becoming a member of this international aviation community, achieving the privilege of flying magnificent aircraft such as the Starliner, had exceeded Rob's wildest imagination. Along the way, he had concluded that aviation may be the one human endeavor where there actually is a brotherhood of man—even the actions of terrorists would not deny that. Nationalities are not a factor when a pilot calls for landing clearance; the de Gaulle tower operator does not order a Canadian or an Iranian airliner to circle in order to give preference to Air France. Every flight, whatever its point of origin, is handled equally. Only by declaring an emergency can a pilot request priority—a status readily granted by fellow airmen, knowing that circumstances could thrust them into a similar situation.

Taxiing the Starliner proved painful for Rob, both physically and emotionally. The nose-gear steering wheel is located on the left side of the cockpit and manipulated by the captain's left hand. A stab of pain seared his wrist each time he turned the wheel, but still he savored every moment, mentally impounding the scene, knowing he would no longer be a participant in this elite, international community. He held short of runway 09 as a Japan Air Lines 747 roared by, the tires emitting a cloud of smoke as the giant plane heavily touched down; a minute later, a Saudia L-1011 repeated the vignette. Then, as the big Lockheed completed its landing roll and vacated the runway, the tower cleared Trans Globe 811 to taxi into position.

Rob said, "Notify the flight attendants." Cash picked up the public address system microphone and recited the standard announcement: "Flight attendants, be seated for takeoff."

"Before Takeoff checklist," Rob ordered as he taxied the aircraft onto the runway. When the tower advised, "Trans Globe eight-one-one, cleared for takeoff," Rob advanced the throttles, conscious that he was performing this familiar act for the very last time, locking the image into his memory. He commanded, "Trim throttles," concentrating on keeping the Starliner precisely on the runway centerline as the aircraft accelerated. Cash fine-tuned the throttles, equalizing the two engines' deafening power. At eighty knots, the speed at which the rudder becomes effective for directional control, Rob shifted his left hand from the nose-gear steering wheel to the control column, and when the airspeed indicated 156 knots, Cash called "V-rotate." Ignoring the pain in his wrist, Rob pulled back on the control column, lifting the aircraft's nose tires off the runway, and moments later the mighty Starliner thundered aloft.

Beryl Markham's words in *West with the Night* flickered across Rob's mind: "I have lifted my plane . . . for a thousand flights and I have never felt her wheels glide from the earth without knowing the uncertainty and the exhilaration of firstborn adventure."

The airplane's sophisticated Flight Management System simplified flying a complicated procedure such as the Charles de Gaulle EVX 5G Departure. In not-so-plain English, the departure instructions read: "RWY 09: Follow extended runway centerline to RSY Locator (Le Bourget 10.5 DME or Charles de Gaulle 4 DME), climb to the first FL prescribed for SID. Turn LEFT. Thence intercept Le Bourget R-052 inbound toward Le Bourget VOR/DME, at Le Bourget 5 DME fix inbound turn RIGHT, intercept Charles de Gaulle R-275 to Evreux VORTAC. Cross the Charles de Gaulle 5 DME inbound at or above FL 60, climb to FL 100, continue to FL 140 at Charles de Gaulle 14 DME fix outbound."

This complicated routing and hundreds of others were stored in the FMS's imposing memory. The pilots had only to select EVX 5G from the dozen choices on the Charles de Gaulle departure menu; the FMS then magically displayed the desired flight path as a purple line against the dark background of the liquid-crystal

Horizontal Situation Indicator (HSI) on each pilot's instrument panel. The line curved at the proper radius when the procedure required a turn. The HSI also displayed any intermediate altitude restrictions, and indicated fixes by small triangles; meanwhile, the FMS automatically tuned the navigational radios to establish the aircraft's position.

A pilot could engage the autopilot in climb and navigational modes, commanding it to follow the displayed route. Rob chose to hand-fly the aircraft—despite his wrist—savoring the feel of the controls in his hands. Roll smoothly into turns, keep the airspeed needle glued to the proper climb speed, precisely track the purple line on the nav display but don't fixate on any one instrument, integrate other clues to maintain positional awareness, anticipate intermediate level-offs, make easy power changes—these techniques had become as instinctive to him as walking. But any pilot can become absorbed in the fancy instrumentation, and Rob reminded himself to get his head "out of the cockpit." European skies were less crowded than those over the United States, but vigilance was still necessary. He recalled from his copilot days a veteran captain's admonition: "Keep your head on a swivel, Robertson. One little midair collision can ruin your whole day."

The Paris environs dropped away as the aircraft soared ever higher over textured fields of wheat and maize; farther west, vineyards became quilted patterns of gold, yellow, and brown as the aircraft continued its climb. Trans Globe 811 approached the ancient city of Evreux at Flight Level 240—24,000 feet—then received clearance to FL 390. Passing south of the D-Day beaches of Normandy, Rob again remembered his uncle James, who had flown interdiction missions in an A-20 Havoc that fateful day. Rob used the public address to point out the historic area to the passengers, then gave the usual spiel describing the route and flight conditions. He concluded: "And if you've heard about Hurricane Pauline, don't be concerned. Our routing takes us well clear of the storm, and in Boston it's a fine autumn day."

An airplane flight is like a novel, Rob thought. Each has a beginning, interesting things happen along the way, and then comes an ending. A book may conclude happily or not as the author chooses.

Each airline flight, being a finite event limited in endurance by fuel, must terminate as well. These lofty journeys almost always end without incident, with loved ones happily reunited, vacations begun, business deals completed. Rarely, an unforeseen catastrophe brings a tragic finale. But today he anticipated no change in the familiar plot, not in this final chapter of the book that would complete his aeronautical library, this last crossing.

Two knocks on the cockpit door interrupted Rob's reverie. Margot entered with two cups of coffee. "I hear you boys didn't get much sleep last night," she teased. "Better have some coffee before you both fall asleep!"

"Just in the nick of time," Rob joked. "Thanks, Margot."

She asked, "How come you didn't warn us about that turbulence ten minutes ago?"

"What turbulence?" Rob replied, slightly annoyed. "It's been smooth as glass."

She winked at Rob as she said in mock sincerity, "Well, it made Maria accidentally dump a cup of coffee down the front of that man sitting across from Mr. Yeganeh. They're working out some sort of business deal."

"Okay, Margot. Why'd she do something like that?"

"The jerk offered her a thousand dollars to spend the night with him in Boston. That's when we hit the turbulence."

"Well, if you have to make a report," Rob pondered, "yes, I guess there was a little unanticipated rough air about then."

"Thanks." She leaned forward and put her hand on Cash's shoulder. "You wouldn't believe the young lady who's with Mr. Yeganeh. A real knockout."

"Really? That old fart's got a trophy girlfriend? I've gotta see that. Mind if I take a look, Skipper?"

"No, go ahead," Rob replied. He donned his oxygen mask as Cash quickly slid out of his seat and left the cockpit following Margot.

Cash returned a few minutes later. "Beautiful, yes," he said, "and about twelve years old." He grabbed his shoulder bag from the bin, and set it beside his seat before strapping in. "Margot says she's his granddaughter. Kee-riste, that kid acts like she adores the bastard."

"She might be the only person on this airplane who does," Rob said.

"Yeah. Well, I guess it's back to gazing at pictures for me," Cash remarked as he pulled the contentious girlie magazine from the bag and began to thumb through the pages, accompanying himself with low whistles of approval.

Rob tolerated this blatant breach of directives for less than a minute, then, reluctantly, admonished him. "C'mon, Cash, you know the rules. No reading in the cockpit except for material that pertains to the operation."

"Dammit, Skipper, there's nothing but ocean and sky to look at for the next five hours, and besides, it's your last flight. Relax a little."

"I'm plenty relaxed, but until we're at the gate in Boston and I've set the parking brake and shut down the engines, we follow regulations."

Cash groaned, but returned the magazine to his shoulder bag.

Trans Globe Flight 811 passed LIZAD, with Land's End, the southwestern tip of Great Britain, glowing green in the distance. Leveling at FL390, nearly seven and a half miles above the earth's surface, with clearance received to proceed along track C, Rob engaged the autopilot. He selected NAV and ALT HLD modes, engaged the autothrottles to maintain the assigned Mach cruise speed, and made sure that the aircraft responded properly to the automatic functions. He said, "Cash, you've got the airplane. I'm going back to the cabin to welcome Yeganeh and his granddaughter to our flight. Much as I detest his guts, it's the courteous thing to do."

"Give him my warmest regards," Cash muttered before donning his oxygen mask.

Rob removed his reading glasses, unstrapped his seat belt, and maneuvered himself out of his seat. He refastened the top button of his shirt, tightened his necktie, and slipped on his jacket. Usually he did not wear his captain's hat with its "scrambled eggs" visor when he visited the cabin, figuring that the four gold stripes on his sleeves and the metal wings pinned above the jacket's breast pocket sufficiently denoted his command position. And he hadn't forgotten that his parents had taught him to remove his cap indoors. But in this instance he would look as professional and authoritative as possible. He donned his hat and set it at a somewhat jaunty angle. Then he turned to Cash. "Can I bring you anything from the galley on my way back?"

"Yeah, Skipper," he moaned, "a couple of more aspirins."

CHAPTER THIRTEEN

FRANK YEGANEH

Rob stepped out of the cockpit, firmly closed the door, and took a moment to survey the Starliner's utilitarian interior that he knew so well. Aft of the cockpit, the forward lavatory and a coat rack occupied opposite sides of the center aisle. A small closet above the coat rack contained a first-aid kit and portable oxygen bottles. Next came two rear-facing folding seats for flight attendants, located adjacent to the L-1 main boarding door. The R-1 galley service door, which rendered double duty as the R-1 emergency exit, was on the opposite side, flanked by the galley counters, ovens, and storage compartments. A divider, adorned with a mural stylishly depicting Trans Globe's routes, separated the first-class passenger compartment from the boarding area and galley.

Rob looked back into the cabin and immediately recognized Yeganeh, sitting in the aisle seat in the first row past the divider. The front pair of seats are reserved for VIPs or celebrities, if any happen to be aboard; they afford a degree of privacy—such as it is in an airliner—from other passengers and, being close to the galley, their occupants are served first by the flight attendants. Yeganeh wore a tailored gray suit, a pale blue shirt, and a gaudy, flowery silk tie. A cocktail glass, empty except for an olive, perched on the tray between the armrests.

A young girl, her hair a mass of dark curls, sprawled sideways across the adjacent seat, her head propped against Yeganeh's arm, a pillow under her back. A jade green stone sparkled on one of her fingers. She wore jeans and a maroon long-sleeved sweater with big letters on the front, and held a book, open to a colorful map, in her lap. Pausing in her reading, she looked up at Rob and smiled, displaying silver braces on her teeth. Her eyes shone large and round beneath surprisingly long dark eyebrows, reminding Rob of the stylized depictions of princesses in Old Kingdom wall paintings from ancient Egypt.

Rob extended his hand to the haughty owner of Trans Globe Airlines. "Good afternoon, Mr. Yeganeh. I'm Captain Robertson. I hope you're enjoying the flight."

Yeganeh looked up and fingered his goatee, eyeing Rob coldly. Ignoring Rob's outstretched hand, he said, "Roberts. Yeah, I remember you." That screechy voice struck a discordant note in Rob's memory. A smirk crossed Yeganeh's face, which Rob interpreted as, "And I stuck it to you and your damned union, right?"

Rob retracted his hand, suddenly aware of an odor not unlike the musky scent left behind by the mink that skulked around the stream at the farm. Even the rapid air exchange provided by the Starliner's efficient ventilation system could not diffuse the pervasive smell. Replacing politeness with the most caustic intonation he could muster, Rob said, "We should be landing in Boston right on schedule."

"That's exactly what I pay you to do," Yeganeh snarled, baring his teeth in a fiendish grin.

The girl tugged at Yeganeh's sleeve. "Grandpa, what's the highest capital city in the world?"

"Denver. Don't interrupt, sweetie."

"No, not a state, a country!"

"Then Switzerland, probably—Geneva."

"Wrong, Grandpa." She looked inquiringly at Rob. "I'll bet you know."

"I believe it's La Paz, Bolivia," Rob answered. "Over twelve thousand feet in elevation. I landed there once in a C-130." A memory flickered across his mind of bronze-skinned people wrapped in

colorful, woven blankets, both men and women wearing old-fashioned black derbies, who had somberly regarded his Air Force crew
as if they were visitors from another planet.

"Who asked you, Roberts?" Yeganeh snarled.

"He's right, Grandpa." She grinned at Rob. "Grandpa took me
up the Eiffel Tower."

"Did you enjoy that?" Rob asked.

"Uh-huh. And he bought me a pony last week."

"How nice. Yes, I've heard that your grandfather has taken an
interest in horses."

"I named him Sandy because that's what color he is."

Yeganeh continued to scowl. "Look, flyboy, stop bothering us.
Just make sure you get me to Boston on time." He tugged at his
sleeve, tapped on a gold Rolex with his finger. "I have an important
meeting at . . ."

"Well, sir, I hope it's not about shrinking this airline any further," Rob snapped, aware that he was out of line now, and beyond
caring.

Yeganeh glared at Rob, then turned to grin conspiratorially at
the passenger in the opposite aisle seat, a corpulent, olive-skinned
man with shirt sleeves rolled up over short flabby arms. A large
brown stain smeared the front of his white shirt. Beads of sweat,
reflecting the overhead lights, sparkled like miniature bulbs on his
huge bald head. The man looked up at Rob with disgust, then continued to shuffle through a folder of documents while a cup, half full
of coffee, balanced precariously at the edge of his tray.

"Listen, Roberts," Yeganeh said. "Passenger loads are down.
Haven't you heard? The airlines are in trouble."

"Is this airline in trouble?"

"It's losing money, but I'm not in as much trouble as you are.
I've had it up to here"—he swept his hand across his throat—"with
you glorified bus drivers. Tomorrow I'm going to demand an immediate twenty percent pay cut from every employee, and if you and
the mechanics and the other goddamned unions don't go along, I'm
ready to sell every damned one of these Starbirds—in fact, they're
worth more now than when they were new. So why don't you just
get your ass back to the cockpit, and on your way, tell her," he

gestured toward Margot, who was serving passengers several rows back, "to bring me another drink."

"The name's Robertson, sir. These airplanes are called Star*liners,* and about the beverage service—you know I can't do that." Rob tapped the tiny gold Trans Globe Pilots Association pin in his lapel. "Union rules." He nodded to the little girl, turned on his heels, and strode back to the galley. He found a packet of aspirins for Cash, then poured himself a cup of coffee. He looked back and matched Yeganeh's angry stare. The girl smiled sweetly at Rob before returning to her reading.

As Rob rapped twice on the cockpit door, it occurred to him that retirement had suddenly become a far more attractive proposition.

CHAPTER FOURTEEN

REVENGE?

Three hours and fifty-two minutes into the Boston-bound flight, Cash waited for a break in the radio traffic, then called, "Gander, Trans Globe eight-one-one, position. Over."

"Trans Globe eight-one-one, Gander. Go ahead."

Although modern equipment had simplified and greatly improved air-to-ground communications for aircraft crossing the oceans and other remote regions, eliminating the requirement for a specialized radio operator, communications could still occasionally be a problem. Unlike the VHF radios (118–136 Megahertz) employed for air-to-ground discourse on domestic routes, which are limited to line-of-sight range—about two hundred miles between a ground station and an aircraft at cruising altitude—the HF (3–30 MHz) sets used on transoceanic flights have unlimited range, as these wavelengths do not escape into space, but instead are reflected back by ionized layers in the stratosphere. Occasionally, however, interference from atmospheric conditions such as solar flares incite considerable static. For this reason aircraft flight numbers, call signs, and other data are reported in single digits. More than once on long ocean crossings, Rob had wished that someone like Sparky was on board to handle the tedious communication chores.

"Trans Globe eight-one-one, five-five north, four-zero west at one-four-five-seven, flight level three-niner-zero, estimating five-four north, five-zero west at one-five-four-one, CARPE next, Mach decimal eight zero, fuel remaining five-eight decimal zero. Over."

Gander Radio confirmed the numbers, then advised, "Report fifty west."

Rob said, "You're getting the hang of this international routine, Cash."

"It's like teaching a dog to dance, Skip. You have to be patient."

"You did a good job on the flight plan, too."

"Hey, we make a pretty good team." Cash grinned as he held up his swollen right hand.

"Maybe we should keep quiet about last night," Rob advised, adjusting the ice pack on his wrist. "Might be hard to explain to the chief pilot what we were doing at the Renard Rouge at that time of night. This is my last flight,, but you have a long career ahead."

"Right, Skipper. I don't need any trouble with the head honchos. And look, I'm right sorry about reporting late to Beantown. I was in the condo in Houston, ready to catch the nine o'clock through K.C. It was already about eighty degrees and I looked out at the swimming pool and there was this red-haired dolly squeezed into a tiny bikini, sitting there all alone in the morning sun." He rolled his eyes. "Man, built like a brick outhouse! I *had* to check her out and," he grinned lecherously, "well, you know."

Rob chuckled. "That's understandable, but there'd have been hell to pay if you'd arrived any later. Anyhow, you've demonstrated that you can fly the airplane, and you know the procedures satisfactorily. After we land I'll sign off on your international qualification."

"Thanks, Skipper."

"The one bit of advice I give young pilots," Rob continued, "is always to have a backup plan—a heading, altitude, and airspeed—if you get in a bind. These modern airplanes may be very reliable but things happen, usually when you're least prepared."

"I know what you mean. Say, mind if I take a whiff of O-two? My head's a little fuzzy."

"No, go ahead." The cockpit oxygen system, completely separate from that of the passenger compartment, utilized high-pressure steel bottles to store three hours' supply of oxygen, which provided for emergency scenarios such as smoke or fumes in the cockpit, or prolonged unpressurized flight at altitudes above ten thousand feet. In addition, at higher altitudes, if one pilot stepped out of the cockpit, federal regulations required that the other pilot don his or her oxygen mask as a safeguard against possible hypoxia, which can induce a subliminal state of mind and ultimately incapacitate an unsuspecting victim. More important, having the mask in place meant one less task for the lone pilot in case of a sudden loss of pressurization.

Of course, pilots had long ago discovered that a good dose of pure oxygen provides temporary relief from headaches and hangovers.

While Cash unlatched his oxygen mask from the quick-release hanger above his right shoulder and held it to his face, Rob remarked, "That right engine's burning a tad more gas than the left. I'll balance the tanks." He reached up to the overhead panel and turned the rotary fuel cross-feed switch. He noted that the valve in-transit light illuminated briefly, indicating that the cross-feed valve had opened. He next turned off one of the two boost pumps in the right fuel tank, which enabled the now higher pressure from the left-tank pumps to supply both engines.

After taking several deep breaths from his oxygen mask and returning it to the hanger, Cash checked the INS distance readouts. "Goose Bay's our closest alternate now," he said. Surveying the seemingly endless expanse of ocean below, he added, "Sure be glad when we're back over solid ground. I feel less comfortable flying over the briny deep."

"You'll get used to it," Rob commented, while observing that the sea, which had appeared quite tranquil earlier in the flight, had taken on an angry note. Miles beneath Trans Globe 811, huge, sullen swells roiled the gray-green surface, the effect of Pauline's strong winds, although the waning storm lay hundreds of miles to the west, now thrashing the island of Newfoundland. But it doesn't look very inviting today, he thought, reminded of that swim in the Seine. He gingerly raised the locking lever on the left side of his seat, slid the seat one notch rearward in its track, then propped a polished black shoe on the footrest bar at the base of his instrument panel. "Three hours and forty-five minutes to go—we're halfway home. I say that calls for another cup of Frank Yeganeh's fine coffee. How about you?" He reached up to press the call button.

Kerpow! Before Cash could reply, a muffled explosion jolted the airplane. "What was that?" the pilots exclaimed in unison, instantly startled into full alertness. The blast quickly faded, replaced by the *whoosh* of pressurized air being sucked from the cockpit.

Choo-choo! Choo-choo! Sounding like an old-fashioned steam locomotive, the right engine compressor stalled, causing the airplane to lurch abruptly to starboard. *Choo-choo!* The right engine N_1 and N_2 tachometers spun down while the exhaust gas temperature soared into the red band. The autopilot strained to hold the aircraft on course as the airspeed began to unwind, reflecting the loss of power.

Rob dropped the ice pack as he grabbed the control wheel with his left hand, thumbed the yoke-mounted autopilot disconnect button, and leveled the wings with aileron input while shoving on the left rudder pedal to counteract the yaw. His other hand gripped the right throttle and retarded it to idle, reducing the severity of the compressor stalls.

The aircraft shuddered like a giant frightened beast. Images of the Lockerbie disaster raced through Rob's mind. An acrid odor, demanding urgency, suddenly permeated the cockpit. One side of his brain tried to deny the unfolding calamity; the other clamored, "This plane's in trouble and you'd better deal with it—fast!" He glanced at Cash, who seemed momentarily paralyzed.

"Crew on oxygen and interphone," Rob ordered. In synchronized, reflexive motion, each pilot yanked his quick-donning oxygen mask from its quick-release hanger and in one sweeping motion slipped it over his head and into place, covering his nose and mouth—the initial, Pavlovian response in the loss of pressurization procedure, drilled into every airline pilot's cranium twice a year in the nonthreatening environment of an earthbound flight simulator.

"F/O checking in," Cash's voice crackled from the overhead speaker, all signs of paralysis vanished. With his oxygen mask snugly in place, each pilot communicated with the other by interphone, using the mask's built-in microphone.

Rob quickly scanned the pressurization controls on the overhead panel. The cabin rate-of-change needle had pegged at the maximum climb index; the outflow valve, which controls pressurization by modulating the volume of air exiting the aircraft's interior, indicated fully closed, automatically striving to contain the pressurized air.

A blaring *beep-beep-beep* alerted the pilots that the cabin "altitude" had surpassed ten thousand feet. Normally, with the aircraft at cruising altitude, seven or more miles above the earth's surface, the system maintained the cabin at a pressure equivalent to seven thousand feet. "Silence the horn," Rob commanded. Remembering his passengers and cabin crew, he pressed a switch that instantly deployed the oxygen masks stowed in compartments above each row of passenger and flight attendant seats and in the lavatories, and signaled canisters at each location to chemically generate oxygen. The cabin oxygen system, once activated, could not be discontinued. This switch also illuminated the FASTEN SEAT BELT signs and initiated a recorded announcement, first in English, then in French, instructing the passengers to be seated with seat belts fastened, and to use the emergency oxygen masks until further advised by the captain.

A vision of Jane, the terror she must have known that instant before Henderson's Corvette slammed into the bridge abutment, flashed across Rob's mind. For the first time in his career, he considered his own mortality. If this was the end, two hundred and thirty-six passengers and ten crew would perish with him. Headlines would blare "ANOTHER JETLINER LOST AT SEA—NO SURVIVORS," and the storyline might hint at a bomb, revenge for the Libyan airliner.

"We're lit up like a Christmas tree," Cash blurted out, gaping at the numerous warning lights that had suddenly become illuminated, indicating multiple malfunctions.

His heart pounding, yet surprising himself with his composure, Rob said, "We'll handle 'em one at a time, but we've gotta descend—right now! Transmit in the blind on one twenty-one point five, give our position, and say we're leaving three-nine-oh, starting an emergency descent to ten thousand, and turning north off Track Charlie." Because all transoceanic aircraft routinely monitor 121.5 MHz, the international distress frequency, this message would warn nearby flights of their intentions. Pilots hearing it would understand that the crew of Trans Globe 811 was too busy to watch for traffic. And by vacating Charlie during its descent, 811 should remain clear of any lower-altitude aircraft assigned this track.

Charis—was she okay? Rob wondered. Then he remembered her selfless dive into the Seine, and decided she could handle any situation. He resolved not to let her down.

He gingerly rolled the Starliner into a right turn, simultaneously lowering the nose of the aircraft to ten degrees below the horizon, heartened that the flight controls responded normally. If they had been severed, all the years of training would not prevent Trans Globe 811 from succumbing uncontrollably to gravity's embrace. He retarded the left throttle to the idle stop, then gripped the speed brake/spoiler lever and pulled it smoothly aft. This raised the spoilers on the top surface of the wings, disrupting lift and increasing aerodynamic drag. The aircraft's rate of descent increased rapidly until it stabilized at six thousand feet per minute.

The cabin emergency oxygen system dispensed its crucial sustenance for just six minutes, barely time for the pilots to execute what the flight manual sanguinely termed a "rapid descent" from cruising altitude to one with sustainable air, a race against time before the passengers and cabin crew exhausted their limited oxygen supply and became hypoxic. Another phrase sprang into Rob's mind: "If structural damage is suspected, descend at turbulence penetration speed." He eased back on the control column until the indicated Mach/airspeed stabilized at the stipulated speed, putting less stress on the airframe while decreasing slightly the rate of descent.

Completing the radio call, Cash aimed a finger at the center panel. An amber light flashed FWD CARGO, signifying that the forward cargo door, on the right side of the fuselage, had unlatched—or been blown away. Above it, a red light blinked intermittently, indicating excessive heat in the forward cargo compartment; another light signaled that the CO_2 extinguishing agent had automatically discharged. "We're on fire!" Cash bellowed, sweat shrouding his forehead.

"We'll be okay," Rob avowed, not convinced but aware that the cargo compartment, in addition to its fire detection and suppression devices, had a fireproof lining. "Loss of Cabin Pressure checklist," he commanded.

Cash pulled the red-bordered checklist from its holder on the center console and began reading, adjusting each switch as required: "Oxygen mask and interphone on. Begin rapid descent. Select manual pressurization . . . manual selected. Toggle outflow valve closed—it shows closed. Engine bleed valves, open. Pneumatic crossfeed's closed. Seat belt sign's on. Deploy passenger oxygen masks—they're deployed. Complete, and we're passing through thirty-five thousand."

"Rapid Descent checklist," Rob ordered as he leveled the wings on a heading ninety degrees from the track course.

"Autopilot and auto-throttles off," Cash recited. "Throttles closed. Speed brakes extended. Do not use high indicated airspeed if structural damage suspected."

"I'm at two-eighty."

"Checklist complete, out of thirty thou."

Rob checked the engine instruments, verifying the engine failure. "Shut down the right engine," he said. "Engine Failure checklist." In addition to losing half of the available thrust, shutting down the engine meant the loss of the right alternating-current (AC) generator, the right engine-driven hydraulic pump, and engine bleed air for heating and ventilation.

"Throttle closed," Cash intoned. "Fuel control—confirm I have the correct switch." Per Trans Globe's procedure, Cash needed Rob's concurrence that fuel to the failed engine was being shut off. In the long history of multiengine airplanes, more than one pilot, in the heat of an emergency, had mistakenly cut the good engine.

"That's it." Rob made a mental note to compliment Cash—later—for his coolheadedness.

"Right fuel control's off, and we're leaving two-five-oh."

"Okay."

"Hydraulic panel checked," Cash continued. "Standby pumps armed. Air-conditioning panel checked. Fuel panel checked, boost pumps on, cross-feed valve . . . Skipper! Look! We're losing the right hydraulic system. Low pressure light's on and the reservoir's going down fast."

"Turn off the right standby pump and close the fluid shutoff," Rob commanded, noting thankfully that both the left and center hydraulic systems still functioned. With no hydraulic pressure to the flight controls, the aircraft would become uncontrollable, its tragic destiny sealed.

"Off and closed," Cash responded. "We're passing twenty—oh shit! There go my flight instruments!" He reached for the bus-tie switch.

"Wait!" Rob ordered. The Starliner had a split AC electrical system, each bus powered by an engine-driven generator. If one generator failed, its bus should be powered automatically by the operating generator or the auxiliary power unit, or the buses may be tied together manually by an override switch. He scanned the overhead panel, where a number of warning lights continued to glow. "We'll have to leave right AC unpowered," he advised Cash. "We've got a ground-fault light." This indicated the system had locked out due to a short circuit; because of the danger of igniting a fire in the electrical bay, it must not be repowered. "Right AC Inoperative checklist."

The loss of the right alternating-current electrical system meant the loss of all flight instruments on Cash's side of the cockpit, the #2 INS, all #2 radios and navigational receivers, one of the two boost pumps in each of the two fuel tanks, the right hydraulic standby pump, and less crucial components such as certain cabin lights and the aft galley power. Cash completed this and the Engine Failure checklists. "Start the APU?" he asked.

Rob nodded. The auxiliary power unit's generator would back up the left AC system. Suddenly he felt pressure against his eardrums and realized that the rapidly rising cabin "altitude" had ascended to the actual altitude of the swiftly descending airplane, so that now the interior altitude would plummet at the same rapid rate as the aircraft itself—for the passengers, a physiological sensation similar to being on a rapidly rising, high-speed elevator that suddenly reverses direction. Rob eased back on the yoke to decrease the dive angle and slowly retracted the speed brakes to maintain speed. "Hope I didn't bust anybody's eardrums," he groaned. "Okay, Cash, what's left?"

"Just the Hydraulic Fluid Loss checklist. Right engine-driven pump off. Standby pump off. Fluid shutoff closed. Review effect of inoperative system."

"That can wait," Rob decided. "Call Gander on HF. Tell them we're declaring an emergency, and that we've turned north off Track Charlie, descending to ten thousand, and request clearance direct to Goose. Ask them to alert air-sea rescue—maybe they'll send an escort. And, just in case, request the locations of any ships between here and the coast."

While Cash radioed Gander, Rob turned left to parallel track C and proceed toward Goose Bay. He set the transponder to code 7700, the emergency squawk, enabling the aircraft to be readily identifiable when within range of coastal radar stations. Meanwhile, he had noted that the #1 INS responded erratically—his heading indication wandered and the mileage readout had frozen. He swallowed hard. More complications.

As the aircraft descended through fifteen thousand feet, Rob observed that the cargo overheat light had gone out, and he suddenly felt less daunted by the combination of problems. He waited a moment for Cash to finish the radio call, then said, "Look, Cash. The extinguishing system worked as advertised. Things are looking up."

"Yeah," Cash agreed, cupping his hand on his chest. "My heart's beating again."

Gander called with a revised clearance. "Trans Globe eight-one-one, cleared direct SCROD, direct Goose Bay. Maintain one zero thousand. Altimeter three zero zero two. Forward SCROD and Goose Bay estimates when available. Over."

Rob gripped Cash's arm before he could reply. "No, tell them we're going *direct* to Goose—as best we can." He explained, "Looks like our inertial's gone haywire."

After Cash relayed this information to Gander, the operator responded, "Sorry, Trans Globe. Cleared as requested, and be advised air-sea rescue has been notified, but is unable to dispatch an escort aircraft from Gander at this time due to severe weather. Your company has been advised of your intentions."

Cash replied, "Roger, Trans Globe eight-one-one."

With the instruments and FMS on his side of the cockpit inoperative, Cash reached across the center console and selected the

Single-engine Cruise page on the left FMS, displaying the optimum power setting and resulting speed for that altitude. He advised, "One point eighty-five EPR on the good engine, should give us two hundred forty-eight knots indicated, about three-oh-five true."

"If we're lucky," Rob said. "There'll be more drag if there's nothing but a big hole where that cargo door should be."

Passing twelve thousand feet, Rob shallowed the descent rate. He advanced the left throttle to the cruise setting as he leveled the aircraft at ten thousand feet. The indicated airspeed slowly bled off to two hundred forty knots, resulting in a true airspeed of two hundred ninety. He retrimmed the rudder, set course direct toward Goose, and engaged the autopilot. "Cash, you're the guinea pig," Rob said. "Sniff the air to make sure there are no toxic fumes—who knows what precipitated that cargo overheat?"

Cash tilted his oxygen mask away from his face. He inhaled deeply and gave a thumbs-up to indicate that the air was safely breathable.

Both pilots removed their oxygen masks and stowed them on the hangers. Rob wiped sweat from his forehead with the back of his hand, trying to visualize the situation in the cabin. The meal service had been completed and the in-flight movies playing when the explosion and decompression occurred, so most passengers would have been seated. When the oxygen masks deployed, he knew that the flight attendants, after quickly assisting any passenger having difficulty with his or her mask, were trained to sit in the nearest available seat and, like the passengers, breath the emergency oxygen until he instructed them otherwise.

Rob reached for the public address system handset. "Ladies and gentlemen, this is the captain. You may discontinue use of the oxygen. Flight attendants, check our passengers." He took a moment to collect his thoughts before continuing. "Here's what happened. It appears there was an explosion in the cargo bay, which caused the aircraft to lose pressurization, forcing us to descend as quickly as possible to a lower altitude. In addition, we've had to shut down the right engine, and some electrical circuits have failed, which is why the movies stopped and some cabin lights are inoperative. However, we have the situation under control, and have set course for Goose

Bay, Labrador. I will keep you informed of our progress. Service manager, please report to the cockpit."

These few minutes had been the most hectic of Rob's life. He had momentarily forgotten his fear, but now his throat felt dry. He relaxed his tense grip on the control wheel, and whispered a silent thank you to Trans Globe's training department for imbuing him with the confidence, discipline, and knowledge to respond decisively to the crisis.

"I like a little excitement in my life," Cash said, sighing, "but that's enough for one day."

"Agreed." Rob retrieved the ice pack from the floor and held it over his wrist as fleeting images—the afternoon run with Charis, lying beside her in his bed in the Gallia, Cash and his red-frocked friend at the Renard Rouge, the wild cab ride—swept in succession across his mind.

Cash continued, "For a while there I thought my future love life looked pretty bleak. Man, this is the most fucked-up airplane I've ever seen—no pressurization, an engine out, fire, all my instruments shot, hydraulic and electrical failures. What else could go wrong?" He threaded his fingers together as if in prayer and looked reverently toward the heavens. "Please, God, just get me through this one and I promise I'll never screw up again."

Rob breathed deeply, remembering the softness of Charis's skin. He must not lose her now, not be denied this rekindling of love. He again considered his own mortality. He had willed the farm to the Corrados, but now realized that he had no close relatives—only his former in-laws and their grown children, plus three rarely seen cousins and their offspring—to claim his investments and life insurance. He vowed to make major changes in those arrangements tomorrow . . . if that *left* engine kept running.

When Gregory came to the cockpit, Rob expounded on their situation and asked how the passengers were coping.

"At first there was pandemonium," the service manager replied. "We yelled to them to sit down, and then the oxygen masks deployed. They handled the masks and the dive very well, and now everyone's quiet. Some couples are holding hands and several people have a death grip on their armrests."

"And the crew?" Rob asked.

Gregory smiled nervously. "If we weren't so busy, we'd be scared, too. None of us had ever been through an emergency descent before, but we have confidence in you guys."

"Thanks," Rob replied. "Neither had we. First time for everything, I guess. Now, let's take stock of our situation. I mentioned on the P.A. that we've shut down the right engine."

"Yes, I was going to tell you that it's damaged—some passengers noticed it."

"That's what we suspected," Rob said. "Let's see, we're nearly seven hundred miles from Goose—that's about two hours and twenty minutes . . . on one engine." The "two-hour rule" was based on a "drift-down" descent from cruise altitude to optimum single-engine cruise altitude, Rob knew, but clearly the Feds hadn't contemplated this predicament—heading for an alternate at ten thousand feet following an emergency descent. "We've also lost the right electrical system, which means the right AC and DC, all the number two radios, GPS, and the number two INS. Also, the right hydraulic system failed, but otherwise we're okay. We're still flying, and the weather at Goose is good." He paused, looked first at Cash, then at Gregory. "However, if that left engine quits, this airplane just becomes a big expensive glider, and in five minutes we'll be in the drink, ready or not. Take a look at the ocean."

"I've been looking at it!" Cash piped in. "Kee-riste, is it too late to bid domestic?"

On prior Atlantic crossings, Rob had often marveled at how the sea, when seen from cruising altitude, could sometimes appear as invitingly blue as a swimming pool, and at other times a subdued bluish green that stretched to the far horizon like an endless, undulating carpet. But now, from ten thousand feet, with the horrifying possibility of confronting it, the ocean loomed dark and foreboding, seething with huge, angry swells erupting into long, silvery, wind-blown spumes of spray. Rob knew that their chances of surviving even a smooth touchdown in that frigid, furious sea would be slim at best. And the thought of ditching this stricken airplane seemed sadly ironic now, when just hours before he had held Charis in his arms, the prospect of a sublime future dancing in his head. "You gents ever heard of Bret Harte?" he asked.

"Wasn't she in an old movie about bullfights in Spain?" Cash offered. "Saw it on the movie channel."

"No, he was a writer," Rob explained. "He wrote a poem called 'Fate' that goes like this: 'The sky is clouded, the rocks are bare, / The spray of the tempest is white in the air, / The winds are out with the waves at play, / And I shall not tempt the sea to-day.' Now, let's hope that includes us. Nobody's ever made an open-sea ditching in one of these crates and we don't want to be the first, but if it must be, there'll be little time to prepare. So, Greg, you and the flight attendants get the cabin ready: Brief the passengers, life vests on, everything, as a precaution. I'll make another announcement explaining why we need to be ready for the worst. Cash and I will review our procedures, too, because we'll be all rear ends and elbows if that engine quits."

"Makes sense to me, Captain. We'll be ready."

"By the way, what does Yeganeh think about all this?"

"He's mad as hell. Says he has to be in Boston at five o'clock. I think he crapped in his pants, or does he always smell that bad?" The three men chuckled despite their tension.

After Gregory returned to the cabin, Rob again addressed the passengers. "Ladies and gentlemen, this is the captain. As I said before, we are proceeding to Goose Bay, Labrador. We should be landing there in approximately two hours. I apologize for this disruption to your plans. We have not had time to communicate with the company yet; however, I anticipate a replacement aircraft will be dispatched to Goose Bay as soon as possible to enable you to continue your journey to Boston. We do not foresee any further problems, but as a precautionary measure I have instructed the service manager to prepare the cabin for a water landing. Thank you."

"Water landing?" Cash queried skeptically.

"It's a euphemism for ditching, but that's the term on those plastic cards in the seat pockets. Sounds less terrifying, I guess. Well, if we smack into the face of one of those big swells, it won't matter what it's called. It'll be like running headfirst into a brick wall at about a hundred and thirty knots. But let's be ready."

The two pilots donned their life vests and reviewed the ditching procedure in the flight manual—admonitions to stow loose equipment, secure seat belts and shoulder harnesses, broadcast a Mayday with their position. In addition, the manual gave advice on choosing a ditching heading. Ideally, one would ditch into the wind and parallel to the swell, but when the surface winds were strong, as they appeared to be—and growing stronger as Trans Globe 811 proceeded westward—the swell could be at right angles to the wind, and a compromise heading must be determined. The manual called for ditching with the landing gear up, of course, and flaps down, and recommended a power-on approach with a shallow sink rate of two hundred feet per minute. But if their left engine failed, demanding an incontrovertible, immediate confrontation with the sea, such an ideal scenario would be unattainable.

When, as innocuously expressed in the flight manual, the aircraft "came to rest," the first officer was instructed to assist in the aft cabin while the captain directed the evacuation at the forward exits. "Fat chance of getting back there with the aisles full of people," Cash muttered.

"Be the first one down the aisle or scramble over the seat backs," Rob advised.

Each of the six, forty-person (if squeezed closely together) life rafts, which performed double-duty during land evacuations as escape slides, was mounted on the inside of an exit door, and, when armed, inflated automatically when the door was opened. In addition, there were two overwing exits that utilized smaller, sixteen-person rafts. All cockpit and cabin crew had practiced deploying and boarding rafts in the tepid waters of the indoor swimming pool at the Sunshine Motel, adjacent to Trans Globe's Kansas City training center. Rob recalled how he had enjoyed those annual drills. In addition to meaningful training, they provided a splendid opportunity to observe the latest feminine swimwear. Now, however, he could not dispel grave doubts about successfully evacuating two hundred and thirty-six untrained passengers of differing physical capabilities; with this raging sea, even the crew would have difficulty.

And should they ditch, he realized, he and Charis would man separate rafts. She would deploy the raft at the L-2 door, aft of the wing, in accordance with the assigned crew ditching stations, while the manual stated that the captain should board the L-1 raft. The aircraft could not be expected to stay afloat for more than a minute.

The rafts would drift apart. He might not know if she escaped from the aircraft.

Two loud knocks resounded on the cockpit door, interrupting his thoughts. Rob pushed the door-release button and Margot immediately burst into the cockpit, her face flushed. "Rob, Mr. Yeganeh's collapsed!" She took a deep breath. "Could be a heart attack."

"Is he breathing?" Rob asked.

"Just barely. We're giving him oxygen from a portable, but he looks bad."

"Want me to ask on the P.A. if there's a doctor aboard?"

"Gregory already did. No doctors, nurses, not even a veterinarian—can you believe it?"

Rob said, "Keep a close watch on him. We'll make sure an ambulance is waiting at Goose. Any other problems? Any suspicious-looking passengers?"

She relaxed a little. "No, no one like that, and all the other passengers seem to be all right. Most of them look scared. Some are praying. A few may have wet their britches."

"Can't say I blame them. Okay, Margot, keep me informed."

When she returned to the cabin, Cash radioed Gander to request that medics and an ambulance be standing by for their arrival at Goose Bay. Gander responded, "Roger, Trans Globe eight-one-one, and be advised we have just been notified by the Royal Police that an unidentified Middle Eastern terrorist organization claims to have planted a bomb on an airliner. Over."

"Roger," Cash replied, "but the warning's a little late. Looks like we're it." Then to Rob, he groaned, "In the simulator it's one problem at a time, none of these multiple emergencies. Even if you crash, the instructor pushes a button and you're right back in business."

"Our training saved us," Rob said. "A bomb. Frankly, I'm amazed this airplane's still in one piece." He shook his head in disbelief. "We were on the cusp of extinction."

Cash nodded. "Yeah, for the second time today! Man, wouldn't this make a great movie. Maybe they'll pay us royalties and we'll be rich." He grinned at Rob. "Say, you ready for that cup of coffee?"

"Yes, please, but first stroll back in the cabin and look at that right engine." Because of the Starliner's swept-back wings, the engines were not visible from the cockpit. "The passengers will pump you with questions. Act confident, and tell them not to worry, but don't linger!"

"Okay, Skipper. Be right back. Black, right?"

CHAPTER FIFTEEN

DECISIONS

"Are we there yet?" Cash joked when he returned to the cockpit.

"Don't I wish," Rob replied.

Cash handed Rob a paper cup of hot coffee. "The front galley works okay but Greg says the one in coach is inop," he reported.

"It's powered by the right AC, so it should be," Rob commented. "Thanks for the coffee. What about that engine?"

"It's a mess. Some suitcases got sucked right into the intake."

"That explains the compressor stalls and engine failure."

"The cowling's got a big dent, right on the inboard lip," Cash added, "and a section of the pylon fairing is crumpled. Looks like the cargo door slammed right into it."

"That door may weigh a thousand pounds and it's over five foot square," Rob said. "Probably nothing but a gaping hole there now, and maybe some structural damage. Did you go back to coach to look at the engine from that angle?"

"No way," Cash replied. "Folks in first class peppered me with so many questions I figured if I went back into coach, I'd never get out."

Rob said, "We're mighty lucky the door didn't wrap itself

around the horizontal stabilizer." He made a looping motion with his hand. "We might've gone right into the drink."

Cash stared down at the sea, which was churning and ominously growing darker. "No thanks."

"What about the passengers?"

"Some are scared shitless, but most of 'em just look worried. A little old lady asked me if she'd miss her connection to Poughkeepsie, and a guy with a long beard said God was making us pay for our sins." Cash snickered nervously. "Do you suppose he meant me?"

Rob asked, "How's our crew coming with ditching preparations?"

"The cabin's ready," Cash replied. "Man, I give 'em credit—they really show their stuff when the chips are down. But it sure looks weird back there, with the oxygen masks dangling from the overheads and everybody wearing Mae Wests." He shook his head. "Oh, it looks like the floor bulges a little right above where the cargo door is—or was."

Rob thought for a moment. "That definitely points to an explosion in the forward cargo bay, and that may explain the problems with the number one INS. My attitude indicator seems to be okay and the autopilot works in attitude mode, but the directional information's useless, and the distance readout has frozen."

"Could the blast have jarred the gyros?" Cash asked.

"Quite likely," Rob acknowledged. "On preflight, when the INSs are initializing, the airplane can't be moved. In fact, if it receives a sharp jolt, like a bump from a commissary truck, you have to restart the procedure."

"But shouldn't the comparator light be on?"

"Only if the two systems disagreed. But with no power to the right INS, there's nothing for the left one to disagree with."

"Designed by geniuses to be operated by idiots!" Cash said with a groan. "No power to the GPS and the number two INS, and the number one's useless. Do I dare to ask where we are and how you're navigating?"

"I estimate we're about six hundred miles from Goose Bay," Rob replied. "About three hundred and fifty from the coastline." He didn't add: that's two hours of flying on one engine, most of it over cold, hostile ocean. "Right now I'm using the mag compass to fly the course on the flight plan, with the wind from the ten-thousand-foot weather chart mentally factored in. It's all we can do for the moment. When we get closer to the coast, ATC will pick us up on radar and vector us to Goose. We should be okay."

"So we're back to the basics," Cash muttered. "Like you said, they don't teach us everything in ground school."

The magnetic compass is the most basic instrument in the cockpit, a simple, magnetized sphere, calibrated in ten-degree increments, and requiring no electrical power. It bobs freely in a clear liquid within a small transparent receptacle; thus aviators have long referred to it as the "whiskey compass." A similar device has been fitted to nearly every flying machine ever built. Along with ever-increasing aircraft technology, compass systems became more accurate when engineers learned how to combine magnetic information with gyro stabilization. Inertial systems carried the art one step further, eliminating any need for magnetic input.

Pilots of modern airplanes rarely have cause to refer to the magnetic compass, on the Starliner located ignominiously on the center windshield frame to prevent its polarized inclinations from being swayed by electrical currents to the flight instruments. No checklist stipulated its use.

"Oh, I forgot to mention," Cash said, "there were funny-looking chunks of white stuff stuck in the front of that engine, too."

Rob said, "Let me see that cargo manifest." He studied it briefly. "A crate of alabaster vases was loaded in Cairo. Might have made a handy hiding place for a bomb, and there's an explosive called *semtex* that can be molded into odd shapes. Who'd have thought to open that crate and check?" He looked at Cash. "Here's my hypothesis. Somebody planted that stuff in a vase, with a timing device set to go off when they figured we'd be in mid-Atlantic, and maybe running an hour late. Maurice mentioned that the power was out briefly at the Cairo airport, rendering the X-ray machines inop. The crate was packed into a baggage container—luckily, the last one to be loaded, adjacent to the cargo door. Any other location, and we'd be another statistic."

Cash said, "I noticed during the walk-around that the baggage smashers were cramming suitcases into the containers. That may have absorbed some of the blast."

"Sure, like the way bomb squads pack mattresses around a suspicious object before detonating it. Yep, Cash, this must be our lucky day."

"Yeah, Skipper, *real* lucky."

Rob asked, "What about Yeganeh?"

"He was looking blue in the face. Margot's giving him oxygen from a portable."

"And his granddaughter?"

"She's being brave, but . . ."

The chime of the interphone interrupted Cash. Rob picked up the handset. "Captain speaking."

"Robby, this is Charis. From the windows at row twenty-six I can see vapor coming from under the right wing. Did you know about that?"

"No, we didn't. Thanks." Both pilots' eyes darted to the fuel gauges on the overhead panel. Rob pointed to the right fuel tank quantity indicator. He expected the digital readout to show approximately 28,000 pounds remaining, but instead the numbers displayed only 7,800 pounds. The tank had lost fuel. A lot of fuel.

The Starliner had what pilots called a "wet wing." Outboard of the engines, a huge fuel tank resided within each wing, sandwiched between the upper and lower aluminum surfaces, enclosed on each end by ribs and framed fore-and-aft by the two wing spars. The forward spar separated the tank from the leading edge slats, pneumatic ducts, electrical wires, and anti-icing tubes, while the rear spar isolated it from the control cables, hydraulic lines, flaps, spoilers, and ailerons. Each tank had a maximum capacity of 10,448 gallons—70,000 pounds—of jet fuel.

"Holy shit!" Cash exclaimed. "Is the gauge bad or do we have one helluva leak?"

"I don't think it's the gauge, not with that vapor trail," Rob said. "Let's see. The right engine fuel shutoff valve indicates closed. Hmm. . . . The fuel line upstream of the shut-off may have been severed—you said the pylon was damaged—or the cargo door may have punctured the wing tank. There's a huge leak somewhere." He received another shock when he checked the left tank indicator. "Damn! Look at this." That gauge showed 24,600 pounds of fuel.

Cash grimaced. "Shit, are we losing gas out of that tank, too?"

"The cross-feed must be open. I thought you closed it."

"I did, Skipper. See, the switch's in the closed position."

"Did you check the in-transit light?" Rob reached up and turned the rotary switch that controls the fuel cross-feed valve. When the valve in-transit light did not illuminate, he pushed the light-test button. Along with other warning lights, the blue in-transit light glowed brightly during the test, but when he cycled the switch, the light remained unlit. "The valve's stuck open," Rob said. "Check the circuit breaker. It's on the E-4 panel, row seven."

"How'd you know that?"

"It's in the book."

Cash twisted around in his seat, checked the orderly array of several score, similar-looking circuit breakers, and located the proper one. "Yeah, it's popped."

"Reset it."

"It popped again. Won't stay in."

"The manual allows only one reset attempt," Rob said. "A short circuit could overheat and start a fire in the electrical bay." Rob scrutinized the fuel panel, then tapped the left fuel tank quantity indicator with his finger. "We've got two more problems: a bad fuel leak and a cross-feed valve stuck open, not a good combination." It jarred his pride that he hadn't noticed the alarming loss of fuel sooner; his spirits wilted under the lash of those sardonic words from his dream: *You're too goddamned old!*"

"Been sitting here with my brain up and locked, expecting you to do all the thinking," Cash grumbled. "I should've been watching that damned light when I turned the switch."

"It wouldn't have made any difference; the valve won't budge."

"Well, I should've kept an eye on the gas, too."

"I should have noticed the imbalance. It's my responsibility," Rob said. "With everything else that's happened, who'd have thought a fuel leak would be added to the stew." Regaining his composure, he mentally traced the physical locations of the fuel lines, valves, and associated plumbing that constituted the Starliner's intricate fuel system. "The cross-feed valve is mounted on the forward bulkhead of the main gear wheel well, just aft of the front cargo compartment. Maybe the electrical wires that control it were severed, or the valve could've jammed if the explosion deformed that bulkhead."

"And if the right tank's punctured or there's a busted fuel line," Cash broached cautiously, not wanting to believe his words, "fuel from both tanks is being dumped overboard."

"Yes, and the airflow around that damaged pylon might create a venturi effect, sucking it out faster."

Cash swallowed hard, studying the fuel gauges. "A couple of minutes ago I thought we had it made. Now we might not have enough gas to reach Goose."

"We can't stop the loss of fuel from the right tank, but we can utilize what's remaining," Rob said, switching on a pump in the right tank and turning off the operative pump in the left tank. "With just a right pump on we'll burn fuel out of that tank first."

"Good idea, Skipper. Like they say—use it or lose it, and it sure looks like we're gonna need every drop. What about the APU? Want me to shut it down? That'll save a little."

Rob nodded in agreement. Fifteen minutes later the right tank showed nearly empty. "That's close enough," Rob decided, turning the left pump back on and the right one off. After waiting a few seconds to ascertain that the left engine continued to run smoothly, he said, "Now, this isn't in the book. Let's see if that left engine will run without the boost pump. The fuel should gravity-feed from the left tank, but there'll be no pressure in the cross-feed line, which should reduce the amount of fuel being siphoned out the right side."

"Sounds good," Cash agreed.

As a precaution, Rob activated the engine-start ignition, then switched off the left pump, ready to turn it back on if the left engine hiccuped. As he'd anticipated, the big Vickery continued to purr smoothly while both pilots monitored the fuel level in the left tank. The quantity continued to drop, but more slowly.

Rob set the ice pack into the plastic bowl, sipped his coffee, and returned the cup to the holder. He reached into his flight kit to retrieve a small calculator. "Let's figure this out. The left engine fuel flow reads seventy-five hundred pounds per hour." He punched numbers into the calculator. "So in five minutes it should burn six hundred and twenty-five pounds. Now we'll determine how much the quantity actually decreases in five minutes. Get ready to start your fancy stopwatch, Cash. When the left tank shows exactly twenty-four thousand pounds, start timing."

A few seconds later, Cash started the timer on his watch. The minutes slowly ticked away. Finally, he said, "Hack."

"Okay," Rob said. "Now that tank reads twenty-two thousand, nine hundred and sixty pounds, so the fuel quantity dropped one thousand forty pounds in five minutes. That's, let's see," he mulled aloud, inserting these numbers into his calculator, "twelve thousand five hundred pounds per hour." His hands became clammy, a vise tightened slowly around his chest. His words came out slowly, reluctantly. "You're right again. We can't reach Goose."

The two pilots stared at the fuel panel in disbelief as an aura of gloom pervaded the cockpit. To Rob's recollection, nothing like this had ever happened before. He tapped the indicator again, knowing that fuel gauges occasionally fluctuate; perhaps the readings would oscillate upward. He waited, hopefully, for this to happen, but in vain. The cavernous right tank showed empty; the left tank fuel level continued its relentless decline.

"Will we have to ditch this bastard?" Cash asked. "Holy shit!" He stared down at the increasingly agitated sea. "We'll die, and I didn't even get laid last night."

"Ditching wasn't on my agenda either," Rob allowed, wondering how Cash could joke at a time like this. "Not with that sea, and a big hole in the fuselage." He scratched his head in thought. "Ever hear that line, 'Situation desperate but not hopeless'? Maybe we can do *something*." No Trans Globe captain had ever lost a plane or a passenger on the North Atlantic run, and by God, Rob silently vowed, he wasn't going to be the first. He reached again into his flight kit, and this time pulled out a dog-eared *National Geographic* map titled *Quebec and Newfoundland*. "There used to be a Canadian air force base right on the easternmost tip of Labrador; that'd be two hundred and fifty miles closer than Goose. Sparky, the

Boston ops agent, was based there." Rob carefully unfolded the tat-tered map. "The base was deactivated years ago, but this map's probably old enough to . . . yep, here it is." He held the map for Cash. "See? On this little peninsula that juts out into the Atlantic? Fortune Bay RCAFB."

Cash's eyes followed the direction of Rob's index finger. "Nice name, Skipper, but what good is it, even if we could make it?" Cash looked at the fuel gauges. "The field's closed, right? So no radar there, right? And no approach charts for a place that ain't even an airfield anymore. And shit, Skipper, what about that goddamned hurricane!"

"We do have a choice," Rob said. "One, we should know soon if there's a ship in our vicinity. We could ditch alongside, if we could find it, in which case our safest bet would be to do so while we still have enough fuel to make a gradual, power-on descent to the water."

"Plan A doesn't exactly turn me on."

"The other option is this, and it's not in the book, either. We head straight for Fortune Bay, the closest point of land. We climb back up to, say, eighteen thousand feet, the best we can do on one engine. We'll burn more fuel in the climb, but once at eighteen we'll get better miles per gallon."

"Sounds okay, but what about the passengers?" Cash asked. "We can't pressurize, and the cabin oxygen system has already shot its wad."

"That's true," Rob agreed. "Without oxygen, that altitude will be tough on the passengers, but not fatal. Lots of people climb Denali—Mount McKinley—every year, and it's over twenty thousand."

"What about Yeganeh?"

"We'll have to wait and see how he does," Rob replied, know-ing that a man experiencing a heart attack would have difficulty in the thin air of eighteen thousand feet. Would he sacrifice the impe-rious owner of Trans Globe Airlines in order to save everyone else on board? "When we reach eighteen, we'll recheck the fuel con-sumption. If it looks like we can make Fortune Bay, we'll continue toward it; if not, we'd better hope there's a ship nearby. What do you think?"

"I think. . . . Ah, shit, it's up to you, Skipper. But how can we possibly shoot an approach to that place?"

"I'll explain that later. Call Gander again. Tell them we've got a fuel problem and need to head for the closest field. Maybe they can suggest someplace better, but in the meantime we're going direct to Fortune Bay to attempt a landing on the old military airstrip. And beginning a slow climb to eighteen thousand." Rob pulled the reference card from his shirt pocket. "And tell them I want a phone patch to Boston Operations. Here's the number."

While Cash radioed Gander, Rob, after ascertaining Fortune Bay's approximate coordinates from his *National Geographic* map, marked its position on the plotting chart and verified the location by comparing coastline features of the two maps. Then, using his Scripto pencil and the straight edge of his plastic plotter, he drew a line from the aircraft's estimated position to Fortune Bay and determined the new course. He advanced the left throttle to climb power, retrimmed the rudder, and turned the aircraft to the new heading as it began to climb.

Two minutes later, Gander called back with the locations of two vessels, one a Japanese fishing trawler about one hundred miles south, the other a Greek container ship one hundred and thirty miles southeast, both reporting heavy seas. But there were no known ships between Trans Globe 811's present position and the coast of Labrador. "No one on the day shift's ever heard of Fortune Bay," the operator said. "Must've been before our time. What about St. Anthony? Over."

Rob advised Cash, "I checked. It's too far. Tell them we can't make it." Cash relayed this information to Gander.

"Roger, Trans Globe eight-one-one," Gander responded. "Cleared as requested. Air-sea rescue has been notified of your intentions. Boston Operations is on the line. All other traffic on this frequency switch to eighty-seven thirty-six. Go ahead, eight-one-one."

Rob said, "I'll talk to ops." He picked up his microphone. "Boston, this is Trans Globe eight-one-one. Is Sparky on duty? Over."

"Speaking. That you, Rob?"

"Yes. Listen, hold the bubbly. We've got problems, can't explain it all now. We may have to ditch this crate, but we're trying to reach the coast of Labrador. Tell me everything you can about Fortune Bay, because it's the only airfield we can reach. Over."

"Fortune Bay? That's my old stomping ground. We used it as a forward operating base for our Northstars sometimes, and occasionally we dropped in to refuel," Sparky responded. "We called it Misfortune Bay, it was so darned bleak and isolated. But it's closed now, Rob, has been for years. Stand by a sec, got a Canadian Airport Directory here someplace. Knew it'd come in handy someday." A long second later, Sparky continued, "Let's see. . . . Well, how about that! Fortune Bay's not even listed. Sorry, Rob. Over."

"What about a nondirectional beacon? How'd you find the field when you returned from a patrol if there were low ceilings and poor visibility? Over."

"There was a beacon, but it's not listed either. Must have been shut down. Let me think. Yeah, there was a radio station in Saint Josephine, a little fishing village north of the field. Played Franco-American music and broadcast weather reports so the local fishermen would know when to head for port. Might still be on the air. See, if the beacon was down, which wasn't unusual, we'd just home in on the radio station and use it for a makeshift ADF approach to the field. Over."

"Can you recall its frequency, and the bearing and distance to the field? Over."

"Now you're really testing my memory," Sparky answered. "Let's see. Around fourteen hundred, maybe fourteen-fifty, kilocycles rings a bell. Yeah, and the field was due south of the station—a hundred eighty degrees magnetic for six miles put us right over the runway. Over."

"Roger," Rob replied, aware that the variation may have changed a few degrees since then—but not enough to matter, he hoped. "What do you remember about the runway orientation and length? And the elevation? Over."

"It's coming back now. Elevation one hundred and twenty feet. Just one runway, number one three landing toward the ocean. Saved our hides so many times we called it Lucky Thirteen. About five thousand feet long. But it's dangerous, Rob. A couple of hundred yards beyond the southeast end of the runway it drops off, all one hundred and twenty feet, right down to the sea. Be mighty careful. Over."

"I see what you mean. What about the outlying terrain? Over."

"To the west, three or four miles away, there're some low hills, maybe three to four hundred feet in elevation, but farther west it gets higher. Listen, Rob, it was different then. We knew the terrain like the back of our hand, every little stream and bend in the road. Wouldn't consider shooting that approach unless we had a fifteen-hundred-foot ceiling and a couple of miles vis. It was one thing to swan about down low in a Northstar, but in a Starliner? Over."

"You're right, Sparky, but it looks like our only choice. Now, if we're able to land there, we're going to need help—a doctor, an ambulance, and some way to get everyone off the airplane. Over."

"There're only a few hundred people in St. Joe, but the fishermen won't be out in that storm. I'll handle it, Rob. I have friends there, and the town has some fire-fighting equipment. Let's see, the closest weather I can give you is for Gander. Want that? Over."

"Yes, go ahead. Over."

"Three hundred broken, eight hundred overcast, one-half mile vis, wind zero-seven-zero degrees at forty-seven gusting to sixty, altimeter two-niner point three-five. Heavy rain. Should be a little better at Fortune Bay. On the latest surface chart the eye of the storm is still down over Torbay and heading east. Over."

"Good. Got it all. Over."

"What's your ETA? Over."

"We'll be there in about one hour, Sparky. Either that or in the drink. Over."

"Air-sea rescue been alerted? Over."

"Affirmative."

"Did you receive the message about the bomb threat? Over."

"Affirmative, but a little late. Looks like we were it. Over."

"Roger. Anything else I can do? Over"

"Negative, that's about it. Thanks a lot, Sparky. Over."

"Good luck, old friend. Boston ops clear."

Cash groaned. "Seventy minutes! That's a long time to think about dying."

"Let's not worry about that just yet," Rob said. Again using the tattered map, he roughed out the coordinates for the fishing village and transferred them to the plotting chart, determined the new heading, and altered course slightly. "Here's my plan. This heading should bring us close enough to Saint Josephine to pick up that radio station, if it's still on the air. From there, we'll attempt Sparky's ADF to Fortune Bay. What do you think, Cash?"

"Sounds okay to me. We're running out of choices fast."

Rob made another P.A. announcement. "Ladies and gentlemen, this is the captain. In order to use less fuel, we are climbing to a higher altitude. This may make breathing more difficult, as we are unable to pressurize the aircraft. Advise a flight attendant if you have problems. Service manager to the cockpit, please."

When Gregory reported to the cockpit, Rob explained his plan to attempt a landing at Fortune Bay, and instructed him to prepare the passengers for a rough landing—one that might require an evacuation. He also told the service manager to continue readiness for a possible ditching, then asked, "How's everyone doing?"

"They're holding up pretty well," Gregory replied. "We've gone around and talked to each passenger individually, and picked out some able-bodied men to help with the slide-rafts and assist a handicapped woman. There are four children in coach but all have parents to help. We've briefed the passengers and rehearsed our procedures twice. Everyone's wearing a life vest, so they'll be ready to head for the exits and jump into the rafts."

"Sounds like you're all doing a good job."

"To tell you the truth, Captain, we're too busy to be scared."

"Gregory, we're climbing up to eighteen thousand to save fuel. The air will be thin. I want you and the flight attendants to come up here one or two at a time and use the oxygen mask at the jump seat—we can't have any of you becoming hypoxic." The cockpit oxygen system still held several hours' supply, and Rob wanted to ensure that each crew member functioned flawlessly, especially during the final, critical moments. "And try not to overexert yourselves."

"Okay, Captain."

"You might want to stow the passengers' masks back into the compartments to get them out of the way. They're of no use to anyone now."

"We've already started, but there's something else you should know," Gregory replied. "Yeganeh stopped breathing. Charis is doing mouth-to-mouth CPR on him, and Margot and I are taking turns with the chest compressions."

"When did that happen?"

"Just a few minutes ago."

"Is he responding?"

"Not yet."

"What irony," Rob said, shaking his head. "The FAA has mandated that by January air carriers must install cardiac kits with defibrillators as part of their emergency equipment, and most airlines already have—but not Trans Globe."

"Yeah," Cash agreed, "because that bastard's too cheap to spend money until he has to."

"Okay, keep me informed of his condition," Rob said, suddenly realizing that in the thin air of eighteen thousand feet it would be impossible for anyone to perform the deep breaths required for CPR. After a moment's reconsideration of the overall situation, he advised Cash, "I've changed my mind. Tell Gander we're going back down to ten thousand."

"What about fuel?" Cash asked, dubiously eyeing the dwindling quantity.

"It'll be tight," Rob acknowledged, "but there's an old aeronautical saying that you start with a bag full of luck and an empty one of experience, and the trick is to fill up on experience before using up all your luck. After today, I think my bag of experience is darned near full, so let's hope my luck bag isn't empty—yet."

Minutes later, Rob again leveled the Starliner at ten thousand feet, reset the power for maximum single-engine range, and applied the ice pack to his wrist. He had been distracted from the pain. "Cash, I want to know what you think," he said, looking his copilot in the eye. "Do we head for that trawler or press on for Fortune Bay?"

Cash peered down at the sea. Huge sheets of spindrift scudded across its foreboding surface, torn from the crashing wave tops by an increasingly furious wind. "Ah . . . I say we press on."

"Good," Rob said. "That makes it unanimous."

CHAPTER SIXTEEN

COMMITTED

The first bumps of turbulence from the fringes of the storm called Pauline, now thousands of miles from its birthplace over tranquil, tropical waters, buffeted the Starliner as Trans Globe 811 irreversibly advanced toward whatever fate awaited its crew and passengers.

The pilots established VHF contact with Moncton Control as their aircraft came within range of Air Traffic Control radar; however, Moncton reported that, because the former Canadian air base at Fortune Bay was not displayed on ATC's radar screens, no assistance could be offered in locating it. Nevertheless, Rob felt a tiny measure of assurance knowing that, should they be compelled to ditch, the radar might be able to pinpoint their position.

In the cockpit of the stricken airliner, Rob said to his copilot, "That means we'll have to find the field on our own. Sparky said it was due south of the radio station in Saint Josephine. Our present heading should bring us close enough for us to pick up the station, assuming it's still on the air, so here's my plan." Rob turned over the weather chart to the blank side and sketched a small circle. "That's the Saint Joe radio." Using the straight edge of his plotter, he traced a six-inch line below it and drew a narrow rectangle. "And here's the

Fortune Bay airfield, six miles on a bearing of one hundred and eighty degrees. I'm using a scale of one inch equals one mile."

Cash muttered, "Okay, I'm with you."

"Now, Sparky said they flew straight for the field and circled to the runway when they broke out, which sounds reasonable for a Northstar, but that would be impossible in this airplane, especially now, considering the weather, an engine out, and the various malfunctions. He called it runway one-three, so let's assume a runway heading of one hundred thirty degrees. Rob sketched in the runway and continued the line on the reciprocal of the runway heading toward the northwest. He marked this line with a tick one and a half inches away from the runway, equaling one and a half miles, and drew another line from the radio station to the tick, then determined the bearing and distance. "From Saint Joe it's five and a quarter miles on a course of one hundred ninety-five degrees." He marked off one-mile intervals from the station, and at the five-inches-equals-five-miles mark drew an X. "Let's call that the TP—turning point. If we start our turn to final there, at the five-mile mark, we should roll out lined up for runway one-three, one mile from touchdown. What do you think?" He handed the sketch to Cash.

"Looks feasible," Cash acknowledged. "Lucky thirteen, huh? I like that. What about altitudes?"

"We'll ask ATC to advise us when we're twenty miles from the coastline, then begin descending so as to initially pass over Saint Joe at four thousand. I'll make a procedure turn by flying north for a minute. We'll burn a little more fuel, but after turning back toward the station, I should have time to nail the wind drift. I'll cross the station the second time at two thousand and descend to six hundred approaching the TP."

"So after you turn to line up with the runway," Cash said, nodding his head, "we should be in a perfect slot—one mile out, five hundred feet above the touchdown zone, like on a normal approach." He shrugged. "It should work, Skipper, if there's still a runway, and if we break out!"

"Yep, those are mighty big ifs," Rob conceded, stowing his reading glasses in his flight kit. "Guess I won't need these with this chart," he joked.

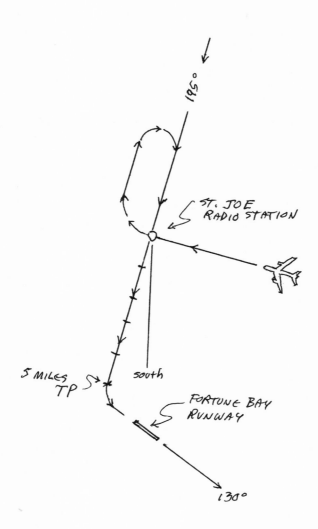

195°

ST. JOE
RADIO STATION

5 MILES
TP

south

FORTUNE BAY
RUNWAY

130°

Rob's sketch

"What about those hills? A buddy of mine tried boring a hole in a mountain with a corporate jet. The mountain won."

"There should be adequate terrain clearance," Rob said, "but with just the mag compass for heading information, and a low-power AM radio station, and that crosswind, it'll be tricky." He paused, then looked at Cash. "If we can't immediately spot the runway after completing the turn to final, or some terra firma flat enough to set this crate down on, there'll be insufficient fuel to go back for another try. We'll have to proceed straight ahead, back over the ocean, and ditch."

"Some choice," Cash said. "In the movies an Air Force tanker would slide in front of us, and the hero would shinny down the refueling hose and figure out some way to pump in some gas. Damn. How much longer to Saint Joe?"

"I estimate about twenty minutes." Rob rechecked the fuel burn with his hand calculator. "We'll have about five thousand pounds over the station. You know, since I've been flying Starliners, I've never blocked in with less than nine thousand in the tanks."

Cash glanced up at the fuel indicators. "It's sure disappearing fast." He peered warily at the storm-tossed sea through a break in the clouds. "We'd better find that runway. Makes my stomach churn just to look down. The condo swimming pool's more my style."

Rob tried dialing in the radio station, but only static emanated from the speakers. "Nothing yet, but at least we should have a tailwind now, thanks to Pauline."

"Yeah, they mentioned that in ground school—how winds rotate counterclockwise around hurricanes. You banked on that, right? And that extra gas you ordered is all that's keeping us aloft." Cash extended his bruised hand to Rob. "Whether we make it or not, Skipper, you're one helluva pilot." Each man gripped the other's hand tightly.

"Thanks, Cash," Rob replied. "You've done a darned good job today."

"Hope I made up for the way this trip began. Look, I won't forget that godawful tab from the Renard Rouge, plus the fifty bucks you gave my friend Yvonne." He grimaced and slapped his thigh. "Damn! How could I forget to get her phone number?"

Rob remembered the torn one-hundred-franc note, fished it out of his wallet, and handed it to Cash. "Next time you're in Paris, would you look up a certain cab driver? Dark complexion, big mustache, smells bad. Maybe he'll return the other half."

"I never want to see those hombres again, but if I was you . . ." Cash gestured toward the cabin, ". . . I sure wouldn't let that nice lady get away."

"I don't intend to," Rob said. "You've got the airplane. I'll be right back. Keep trying that radio station—we should be coming into range."

Rob set down the ice pack and hoisted himself out of the left seat. He did not remove his life vest nor don his hat before leaving the cockpit. Glancing down the aisle, he observed Yeganeh lying flat on the carpeted floor, with Charis, Margot, and Gregory hovering over him. Rob stopped first at the lavatory to drain his bladder, remembering that in the final seconds before an impending airplane or automobile crash, people sometimes did precisely that—involuntarily.

He washed and dried his hands. The mirror reflected a face that looked older, fatigued, and creased with wrinkles that he did not recognize. Was this the face of a man committing ten members of his crew and two hundred and thirty-six hapless men, women, and children to their untimely deaths, or one whom they might everlastingly bless for prolonging their existence? He felt humbled by the awesome task that had been thrust upon him, yet somehow calm.

Rob stepped back into the cabin, conscious that the passengers scrutinized his every move, searching for some signal of deliverance from an uncertain and frightful destiny. Two well-dressed, middle-aged women in the third row clutched rosary beads. Farther back, several couples held hands, and the cheeks of many passengers revealed a trail of tears. The sparse air of ten thousand feet had not dulled anyone's senses, Rob saw. He tried to allay their fears by acting confident and composed.

Between the first row of seats, the three crew members performed cardiopulmonary resuscitation on the lifeless, prostrate owner of Trans Globe Airlines. Yeganeh's pricey shirt had been ripped open and his undershirt pulled up, exposing a sallow chest beneath a sparse veil of scraggly black hair. Charis crouched on her knees beside Yeganeh's head, propping his chin in the "tilt-lift" technique with one hand, pinching closed the nostrils of his beak nose with the other. As if locked in a rhythmic embrace, at intervals she cupped her mouth over Yeganeh's thin lips and forcefully expelled air from her lungs into his. Gregory knelt on the opposite side, with his arms extended vertically downward and his fingers interlocked on Yeganeh's chest. The chest rose as Charis's exhalations filled Yeganeh's lungs; when it deflated, Gregory methodically executed five chest compressions, coercing the inert heart to circulate blood. With each downward thrust of Gregory's hands, a tinge of pink infused Yeganeh's ghastly countenance, then quickly faded as the service manager relaxed pressure. Margot crouched on the opposite side, ready to spell Gregory, while the tyrant's devoted granddaughter perched at the edge of her seat, legs doubled beneath her, hands clenched, her dark eyes damp with tears, observing the tense proceedings.

Rob leaned close to Charis and asked softly, "Any response?"

Gregory halted the compressions while Charis pressed two fingers against the side of Yeganeh's Adam's apple, palpating his carotid artery, probing for the faintest sign of life. After a moment she shook her head. "Still no pulse," she said cheerlessly.

"We're exhausted," Margot said. "How long must we keep this up? Can't someone tell us to stop?"

"That's my job," Rob responded grimly, realizing that he must not allow his personal feelings, his loathing of the man lying helpless on the floor of this airplane, to blur his judgment. But he understood his duty. He knew, from Deerwood Volunteer Fire Department training, that CPR protocol obliges rescuers to continue the procedure as long as they are physically able, until properly relieved, or until a doctor or person of appropriate authority commands them to desist. As captain of this aircraft, he had that authority; he alone had to make the decision best for all. "Stop the CPR," he ordered. "We have to let him go. You've done your best. Now we must concentrate on the other passengers and our own survival." Rob looked at the little girl. "I'm sorry," he said simply.

"What'll we do with him?" Gregory asked.

"We'll need the aisle clear if we have to evacuate," Rob answered. "Let's prop him in a seat and strap him down." He crouched beside the lifeless body, preparing to help Gregory lift it into an empty seat.

Margot directed the fat man, whose shirt collar was drenched with sweat, to move to the seat beside Yeganeh's granddaughter, but before he had budged Charis shouted, "Wait! I'm getting a pulse!"

The crew stopped, transfixed. Above the hum of the aircraft ventilation system and the distant growl of the left engine, an electric silence charged the front cabin.

Charis leaned forward, placing her ear close to Yeganeh's mouth. "He's breathing! He's alive!" She looked at Rob. "He'll need oxygen—we've used up all the portable bottles."

"Let's drag him into the cockpit," Rob ordered, slipping his arms under Yeganeh's armpits. "I'll hook him up to the crew oxygen system." He smiled at Yeganeh's granddaughter and said reassuringly, "Your grandpa's going to be all right." She brightened and began wiping away tears with the back of her hand.

"Cash, how'd you like some company?" Rob shouted as he inched backward into the cockpit, tugging the listless body. While Rob laid the comatose tycoon on the floor, Charis arranged pillows to elevate Yeganeh's feet and slipped another under his head to cushion it. She checked his pulse and breathing and nodded affirmatively to Rob. Margot snatched a red and white blanket, adorned with the Trans Globe logo, from a cabin overhead bin and carefully tucked it around him. Rob checked the crew oxygen quantity indicator. He turned on the regulator adjacent to the jump seat and selected 100 percent flow. Placing the mask—identical to the pilots'—over Yeganeh's nose and mouth, he snugged the size adjustments.

"His color's improved already," Charis observed.

Rob asked Margot to monitor Yeganeh for a minute. Then he took Charis's hand, led her back to the galley, and slid the blue curtain across the opening. Her lips were puffy from the CPR. He removed a paper cup from the dispenser, filled it with water from the tap, and handed it to her. She rinsed her mouth and spat into the trash bin, then she took another sip and tossed the cup into the bin.

When the airplane rocked in turbulence, Rob grabbed the counter with his right hand and slipped the other around her waist. "You're amazing," he said.

Charis sighed, exhausted from the strenuous rescue effort in the thin air. "I was a lifeguard in college—I've done it before. Even took a refresher class when Danny came along, in case he swallowed something he shouldn't." She gripped his arm tightly. "Are we going to make it, Robby? I've been too busy to think."

He hesitated. "Yes. Well, it's going to be close. We've worked out an approach. In fifteen minutes we'll be on the ground . . . or in the sea." He wondered again what the headlines would proclaim. "This may be our good-bye."

She managed a thin smile. "Such a brief romance."

He embraced her, their life preservers forming a barrier as he drew her close, wondering if last night would be their only night of love. "No, not really. For me it began fifteen years ago, in London, the day we went to . . ."

"Wimbledon. Yes, I remember."

"I resisted falling in love with you then, but I can't deny it now. I love you, Charis." He bowed his head. "I'm sorry it's come down to this. I don't know how it will end."

She leaned back to look directly into his eyes. "You've saved my life twice—you can't stop now. You'll find a way." Her arms slid around his neck.

"Charis, if . . . I realize I'm a lot older."

"And I'm no teenager, Robby, but I'd have to talk things over with Danny. He's never had to share me with anyone." She pulled back slightly, still in his grasp. "What am I saying? This is crazy. Everything's a blur."

"I have no heirs, Charis, no one. I want to devote my life, everything, to you and your son." He smiled. "Besides, Nellie's great with kids."

"I . . . I can't think right now." She clutched his arm. "Tell me. Will I see him again?"

"You will, and I'd better get back up front to make sure you do." He kissed her, gently, then slowly released her. "So, would you like to visit a place called Fortune Bay?"

She smiled again. "Yes. Very much."

Back in the cockpit, Charis appraised Yeganeh's condition. He was still unconscious but breathing rhythmically, and his complexion had lost its pallor. "Margot, what if you and Charis switch positions," Rob proposed. "She should stay here in the cockpit to monitor our illustrious patient. She can cover L-1 from here, and you take L-2. Okay with you?"

"Sure," Margot agreed. "Besides, she knows how to care for him better than I do."

Rob noticed Margot's array of gold bracelets and dangly earrings. "Did you remind the passengers to remove and stow their jewelry?" he asked, patting her wrist. "You wouldn't want to get snagged on something if we have to evacuate."

"I'm not me without my jewelry, Rob." She shrugged. "Okay, I'll stow them. Sorry."

"Now, this isn't in the book, either," Rob declared after Margot exited the cockpit, "but let's make sure we're not trapped in here by a jammed cockpit door." He swung open the door, stretched a luggage tie-down strap around the doorknob, and tightened it securely. Then he climbed into the left seat, fastened his seat belt, and turned to Cash. "Any luck with that radio station?"

"Not yet. Nothing but static since we got in the soup."

"Keep trying—it should be coming in." The aircraft bounced in and out of the ragged cloud tops, and sheets of rain within each cloud peppered the windshield. Rob picked up the P.A. handset. "Ladies and gentlemen, this is Captain Robertson. You have shown great fortitude under these difficult conditions. Now I must ask you to be brave a little longer. In a few minutes, we'll begin our descent. The turbulence will get worse, but don't be afraid. This airplane is very sturdy, and we will not be out of control." He took a deep breath. "We will attempt to land on a small, isolated airfield. If we're unable, we'll have no option but to ditch in the ocean. That's why the flight attendants have prepared the cabin for both contingencies. Please follow their instructions. Again, I thank you for remaining calm, and for your courage."

Rob sighed. "That may not have reassured the passengers, but at least I feel better."

"I will, too, if I make one last pit stop," Cash joked. Then he scowled. "Did I say *last?* Let's hope not." He unbuckled, stepped over Yeganeh, and hurried out of the cockpit.

Rob said to Charis. "When we left Boston I thought Cash would drive me nuts, but now we're friends."

"I'm glad," she said. "I think he means well."

And as Cash had said, this trip would make lively Hollywood fare, Rob mused, if we locate the Saint Joe radio station. He suddenly realized that, just as the airfield and beacon had been abandoned, the radio station may have been deactivated as well. Sparky may have friends in Fortune Bay, but how long since he'd actually been there? Maybe there was no way in hell to make an instrument approach, no choice but to ditch. Cautiously, he raised the switch on his interphone panel that enabled the audio signal from the ADF receiver to be broadcast over the speakers.

Normally, the ADF receiver is used to tune in a nondirectional radio beacon located in conjunction with an instrument landing system; however, it is also capable of being tuned to AM commercial radio broadcasts. A needle in an instrument on the pilots' panels shows the direction to the station in relation to the longitudinal axis of the aircraft; thus if the needle points to three o'clock, the station is directly abeam the right wing, and so on. Rob slowly rotated the tuning knob, searching for the station, but only scratchy squeals emanated from the speakers.

What if severe turbulence within Pauline's murky, tempestuous vapors waited to pummel their aircraft? The Starliner was a sturdy machine, but with its wounded, weakened airframe, anything could happen. And what dreadful irony if Charis's fate, and his, was to brutally imitate her husband's violent demise, to perish as this airplane disintegrated. Or were they, like Jane, to die in a wrenching confrontation with an immovable object, a stony ridge, perhaps, that lay hidden, obscured by the dense clouds.

Cash returned to the cockpit saying. "I talked to Yeganeh's granddaughter. Her name's Suzy. What a sweetie! Now we've gotta make it."

"Sounds like you're gunning for chief pilot," Rob chided as he continued adjusting the tuning knob. Gradually, the static gave way to music, a bouncy tune with a woman's voice singing in French. "I think that's our station," he announced, feeling a glimmer of optimism. "Our odds just improved a notch." The ADF needle swung around slowly, but rather than pointing straight ahead as Rob desired, it oscillated erratically between the top of the instrument and twenty degrees to the right. He felt certain—*almost* certain— that it would settle down as the aircraft drew closer to the station.

"Catchy tune," Cash joked, increasing the volume on his overhead speaker and snapping his fingers in time with the music.

"Yep, but I don't like where the needle's pointing. I'd hoped it'd be right on the nose."

"How far are we off?"

"Not far, I think, but we've probably picked up more crosswind," Rob replied. "This wind analysis chart is six hours old now. Let's see. The heading we've been flying could be several degrees off, and we've covered nearly four hundred miles since the explosion and emergency descent. That could put us . . . about twenty miles off course, either way."

"Add a few more minutes of flying time," Cash moaned, "and a little less gas."

Rob banked the aircraft to home in on the station while exhorting himself to concentrate on the known problems, to keep superfluous thoughts from interfering with the task at hand. But doubts filled his mind. He recalled the oft-repeated aviation axiom: *The superior pilot avoids situations where he must demonstrate his superior piloting skills.* Yes, he had carefully avoided trouble throughout his airline career, but was he *too* cautious? Charis had plunged first into the Seine; Cash had reacted instantly with his fist in the taxi. And today he'd been slow to recognize the fuel loss. Maybe he *was* too damned old. In Vietnam, as a young Air Force pilot, he had felt supremely confident of his abilities. He remembered landing his battle-damaged C-130 during a heavy downpour. Did he still have the mettle to see things through? The skill? Would it matter? Face it, he told himself. The only hope for a successful landing in Fortune Bay, for not brutally, prematurely extinguishing the lives of innocent passengers and crew, and his own, lay in shooting a perfect approach, finding sufficient ceiling and visibility, and locating that long-abandoned runway.

Rob silently considered this paradox. He'd always prided himself on flying by the book, yet now, at the most critical juncture in his career, the hefty flight manual, which he knew so well, and those hundreds of approach charts, which he'd fastidiously revised hundreds of times, were useless. Instead, he must entrust this crippled aircraft and its captive occupants to an operations agent's distant memories and to seat-of-the-pants flying from an aviator being put out to pasture.

"Are you religious, Skipper?" Cash asked, interrupting Rob's thoughts.

"What?"

"I noticed a lot of people in the cabin were praying, even a couple of guys wearing turbans and some other guys with funny-looking black hats. Do you think their prayers will save us?"

"I don't know, but let's hope so," Rob replied. "Flights come to our Paris hub from Israel, Saudi Arabia, even India. The Bushmen of the Kalahari have a saying: It's all the same God; it's just that everyone talks to him in different ways." But Rob was certain of one thing—he was not ready to die, not now. He needed time with Charis, time to fill the void of the past fifteen years, time to live. But whatever was to happen, for better or for worse, he knew he must lead by example, he must appear confident of success. I can do it, he vowed. I must.

Rob said, "Let's compute the time and distance to the TP. As we approach the station after completing the racetrack, I'll slow to one-sixty, and with that east wind we'll have a direct crosswind, maybe a little tailwind, so let's figure a ground speed of one seventy." Rob reached into his flight kit and pulled out his well-used E6B computer. This was not a modern electronic marvel with push buttons and digital readouts, but rather a simple mechanical device with two superimposed circular slide rules. He rotated the inner dial, lining up the numbers. "Five miles at a hundred and seventy knots gives us one minute and forty-six seconds to the TP. So, Cash, at station passage, start your stopwatch."

Cash held up his wrist, adjusting his oversize watch. "Will do, Skipper, but first, tell me the truth. On a scale of one to ten, what're our chances?"

Before Rob could answer, the song ringing from the overhead speakers ended, and a female voice announced, first in French, then in English, "That was Josée LaBonte singing the title song from her album *Avec Moi*, and this is station CNSJ, 1460 on your dial, with news and weather every hour, and the music you love all day long."

"That's it, Cash!" Rob exulted. "S-J stands for Saint Josephine, and the station's coming in strong. Means we can attempt an approach. I'd say our odds are looking a lot better."

"Me too, Skipper. Ready to review the Loss of Right Hydraulics procedure?"

"Go ahead," Rob replied, glad to have been reminded.

"Right thrust reverser inop," Cash recited from the checklist. "Flaps and slats operate at reduced speed, outboard spoilers inop, increased effort required for flight controls."

The Starliner's sizable ailerons, spoilers, elevators, and rudder were positioned by three independent hydraulic systems, working in parallel. Triple redundancy provided a safety feature. Any one system enabled the pilots to maneuver the airplane. Turning the control wheel or pushing on the rudder pedals moved control cables that repositioned valves, allowing hydraulic fluid at 3,000 psi to course into actuators that deflected the control surfaces. The loss of any one system, however, meant less assist. That reminder intensified the pain in Rob's wrist, but he said only, "Anything else?"

"Use manual gear extension—gear will freefall into place but take longer to extend. And maintain at least 135 knots on final approach."

"If I forget anything, let me know."

"I will," Cash said. "You know, I've been thinking about Shelley, my number one ex." His eyes fixed in a faraway look. "Maybe we can get back together, me and her and the kids. Can't blame her for ditching me—caught me in bed with her best friend."

"She might forgive you," Charis said, "if you promise to mend your ways."

"I will, honest, if we make it."

"We'll make it," Rob insisted, then turned to Charis. "How's your patient?"

"He's still unconscious, but his pulse and breathing are stronger. What about your wrist?"

"I'm okay. Charis, you'd better strap in now, here in the jump seat."

The left fuel gauge indicated forty-four hundred pounds of fuel remaining. Both pilots attached their shoulder harnesses and cinched their seat belts tighter. When Moncton Control advised that Trans Globe 811 was twenty miles from the coastline, they completed the Descent checklist, then Rob clicked off the auto-pilot and retarded the left throttle to idle, retrimming the control surfaces as he gently lowered the nose of the aircraft to begin the descent. "Tell Moncton we're leaving ten," he said, "and request the closest altimeter setting."

Moncton replied, "The latest altimeter setting at Gander International is two nine point three seven, at Goose Bay it's three zero point zero three. Since you're about halfway between, our meteorologist estimates two nine point six seven at Fortune Bay with wind from ninety degrees at thirty-five knots gusting to fifty. Also be advised that air-sea rescue will launch helicopters as soon as weather conditions improve." Moncton advised Trans Globe 811 to reestablish contact with Gander Radio on HF, as radar contact and VHF communications would be lost when the aircraft descended. The controller added, "And your vice president for operations is standing by for a phone patch. Over."

"That must be Hollinbrooke," Rob said, "worried that his boss will miss the meeting. Tell Moncton we're too busy to chat."

"Roger, Moncton," Cash radioed. "Can't talk right now. We'll call Gander when and if we're on the ground. If nobody hears from us in ten minutes, it means we're in the drink. Over."

"Roger. Good luck, Trans Globe 811. Sorry we can't be more useful. Moncton's standing by."

CHAPTER SEVENTEEN

FORTUNE BAY

"This turbulence is impressive," Rob joked apprehensively as the aircraft descended into the ragged cloud tops, obscuring any further view of the earth's surface. The vertical speed and airspeed indicators on his instrument panel bounced erratically when each cloud-shrouded gust rocked the aircraft, sending a tremor through the control wheel that his wrist painfully absorbed as he attempted to soften the jolts. The aircraft's weather radar would have been helpful in avoiding areas of heavy precipitation and associated turbulence, and, more important, in displaying the silhouettes of Fortune Bay and the peninsula on which Sparky's old airfield presumably lay, but it remained inoperative, another casualty of the failed AC system.

"Who turned out the lights?" Cash groused as the thickening vapors enveloped Trans Globe 811 like a dusky cloak, transforming the opaque afternoon sky into somber murkiness. Rain pelted the windshield and skimmed past the side windows. Rob swallowed hard, suddenly perceiving that spotting an unlit airstrip in this muck would be difficult, if not impossible. Why hadn't he foreseen this complication before he committed his crew and passengers to this perilous plan?

But committed they were, and Rob knew he had to direct his focus on the approach. He lifted the public address handset from its cradle, swung around, and handed it to Charis. "We'll have our hands full from here on. You can help by giving the thirty-second warning for the passengers to assume the crash-landing position."

"Just tell me when," she replied, sounding remarkably composed.

The darkening conditions made the small numbers on the magnetic compass difficult for Rob to read. He said, "Got another job for you, Charis. Cash, give her your flashlight."

The first officer rummaged in his flight kit, found the light, and pressed the switch to test it, but it failed to illuminate. "Damn, I meant to change the batteries," Cash said. "Does it mean I flunked my checkout?" he joked nervously.

"Maybe," Rob replied, equally tense. "Use mine," he said, reaching for the flashlight in his flight kit. He pointed to the compass. "Shine it right there, please."

The aircraft's occupants endured continuous, unsettling turbulence as they descended into the thickening gloom, and the precipitation beat more heavily on the cockpit windscreen. "The needle's holding real steady," Cash shouted above the din. "Looks like we're getting close to Saint Joe."

Rob prepared to increase power on the good engine to level off as the aircraft approached four thousand feet. As if deliberating its cooperation, the ADF needle swayed briefly in each direction, then abruptly swung around to the tail of the instrument. "There's station passage," Rob said. "Flaps ten, time us for one minute." He banked the Starliner to the right and began slowing to 180 knots as Cash pushed the elapsed-time start button on his wristwatch.

Approaching the desired heading of 015 degrees, Rob leveled the wings. He waited a moment for the magnetic compass to settle down in order to determine its exact indication, which wasn't easy with an instrument calibrated in ten-degree increments that, because of the turbulence, bobbed around in its liquid-filled receptacle like a rowboat adrift on a stormy sea. And the rarely needed instrument had other aberrations. In right turns the compass "led" the actual heading; when turning left, it "lagged"—or was it the other way around? He'd had no cause to recall its idiosyncrasies in years. No matter; the compass wobbled around so much he had to mentally average the readings.

Except for the racket from the pounding torrent, Trans Globe 811's descent seemed eerily quiet—no crisp instructions from air traffic control, no curt pilot banter in reply. Rob agonized for his passengers. Scared, trembling, strapped to their seats in the cabin awaiting an unknown fate, their precious lives entrusted to two anonymous pilots—fallible human beings like themselves. His own skin prickled at the thought.

Rob continued descending the aircraft to three thousand feet on the northerly heading until Cash said, "Minute's up, Skipper," whereupon Rob ordered "Flaps twenty" and began a right turn to intercept the inbound, 195-degree course to the station, the ADF needle likewise pivoting around to continue pointing toward the station. When established on course, he further descended to two thousand feet. Reaching that altitude, he called "Flaps thirty" while slowing to 160 knots.

The seconds ticked away slowly as the aircraft again approached the station. Rob silently considered his dilemma. The key to a successful landing depended on breaking out of the clouds and finding enough visibility to spot the runway, and with sufficient altitude and space to maneuver to the touchdown point. Being too high would cause an overshoot; too low increased the danger of confronting a hilltop concealed in the clouds. The relentless turbulence and gale-force winds further complicated matters. The ADF needle wavered, then swung around as the aircraft again flew over CNSJ's transmitting tower. "Station passage," Rob called out. "Start timing again."

Cash responded, "Out of two thousand, a minute and forty-six seconds to the TP."

Rob established the aircraft in a gradual descent and corrected the heading to adjust for drift, attempting to maintain the desired 195-degree track from the radio station as the powerful east wind vied to heave the aircraft off course. The meteorological commotion complicated the painful task of controlling the aircraft, while the mag compass's erratic oscillations made determining an exact heading impossible. Rob struggled to average the extremes. Each brutal gust shook the Starliner as if it were being disciplined by a Dickensian schoolmaster.

Two miles deeper into the maelstrom, Cash reported, "One minute to go, Skipper, leaving fifteen hundred."

"How much gas?" Rob asked.

"Twenty-five hundred pounds."

Rain rattled hard against the windscreen. The windshield, layers of Plexiglas sandwiched between thick slabs of tempered glass, should withstand the bruising deluge, Rob knew, but the hairs at the back of his neck tingled at the notion that it, like other man-made components, could fail.

"Thirty seconds to the TP," Cash barked. "Man, it's worse than a West Texas gully-scrubber! Sure glad that Vickery runs under water."

Rob continued battling the meteorological conspiracy as the Starliner descended through one thousand feet, still engulfed in clouds and rain. Within minutes, he realized, he must land this airplane, someplace, somehow. Would it be safely on a runway, he wondered, or would they smash into a rocky slope? Or would the mangled hulk of Trans Globe 811 disappear into the raging sea? One thing was for certain: He, Cash, and Charis would be the first to know.

As the aircraft approached six hundred feet, Rob advanced the left throttle to maintain that altitude, and the instant Cash bellowed "Time's up," he banked the aircraft to the left, beginning the turn toward the final approach course. "I'll stay glued to the gauges," Rob shouted over the racket as he muscled the controls, sending another shot of searing pain into his wrist. "Keep your eyes peeled for that runway,"

"I'm looking," Cash hollered. "Nothing yet."

When would they break out of this stuff, Rob wondered. Would they find sufficient daylight and visibility to spot the runway? Was there still a runway? And maneuvering space to align with that coveted sanctuary and set the airplane down safely? Or worse, Rob suddenly realized, what if Sparky had the numbers all wrong? Even if they were correct, Sparky may have figured the mileage from the station to the field in statute miles, not nautical! In those days, weren't distances calculated in statute miles and airspeed indicators calibrated in miles per hour, not nautical miles and knots like now? Using nautical miles, which are eight hundred feet longer than statute, might mean they had badly overshot the turning point. Had he made the right decision? Doubts swept across his mind like the rain streaking past the windshield. His heartbeats throbbed in his ears. The rain intensified, clattered more viciously against the thick glass. "Wipers on," Rob ordered.

"Coming on," Cash replied. "Damn, why's it so dark!"

"The thick clouds, I guess. Gear down."

"Wait till we see something, Skipper. With no right hydraulics, we can't raise the gear back up if we have to ditch."

"You're right." Damn, he was losing it! Sweat rolled down Rob's forehead into his eyes but he dared not take his hands from the controls to wipe it away. Ordinarily, he'd have worked the yoke with his left hand and the throttle with his right, but because of the turbulence, and his wrist, he needed both hands on the control wheel, and each movement brought another stab of pain. "Cash, work the throttle for me," he commanded.

"Okay, call out the power setting you want."

Rob was glad his hands were busy. Cash—this brash, brave man who may have just saved his hide yet again—couldn't see how tightly they clenched the control wheel.

"I'll inch her down to four hundred," Rob said, "but that's as low as we go. If we don't spot the field, there's enough fuel to get over the water before we meet an immovable object."

A few seconds later the aircraft began breaking out of the gray broth, and the rain and din abruptly subsided. Cash yelled, "Skipper, check one o'clock."

Rob stole a glance outside. Ahead, the clouds seemed aglow with a white luminescence and pulsated with flashes of crimson, reminding him of the aurora borealis that had flooded the northern sky, heralding the awakening of long-dormant feelings. A moment later, as the Starliner skimmed through the bottom of the clouds, the visibility instantly improved. "Look! Lights!" Cash exclaimed.

A half-mile ahead, but offset far to the right, Rob spied two parallel files of double lights—headlights, serving as widely spaced runway lights, a dozen vehicles in each row. The flashing red lights of emergency vehicles marked the runway threshold. Sparky's doing.

"We can't make it!" Cash yelled. "We're too far left."

"We'll make it," Rob said. "Give me max power!" He felt a reassuring shove in his backside as Cash jammed the left throttle forward and the trusty Vickery responded with a mighty surge of thrust, which Rob countered with aggressive pressure on the left rudder pedal. "Call out the numbers."

"Speed one-fifty, sink rate three hundred," Cash shouted. "We're damn near scraping the treetops!"

"Gear down, landing lights on," Rob ordered. Cash pulled the uplock release handle and switched on the lights as Rob cranked the Starliner into a steep bank, hearing the *whoosh* of air as the nose-gear doors opened, silently pleading for enough time for gravity alone to draw down all three landing gear. "Charis, tell 'em to brace for impact."

No time to be smooth now. The luminous twin columns defining the runway looked short, impossibly deficient for landing and stopping the Starliner. Not an inch of runway could be wasted. Rob remembered Sparky's warning, that past the end of the runway, the ground fell away into tumbling space, then into the sea. This landing, this final act of Rob's Trans Globe Airlines career, demanded his supreme moment.

"Flaps forty," Rob commanded as he felt the reassuring *clunk* of the main landing gear dropping into place. He glanced at the center instrument panel to observe the green gear lights, but only the main gear indicated down and locked. If need be, he would land on just the mains, he quickly decided, although directional control could be a problem as the aircraft skidded on its nose, posing a further risk to his aircraft and passengers, and to the parked vehicles and their occupants as well. "Eighty percent power and complete the checklist."

Cash eased the throttle back and reported, "Main gear down and locked, nose still in transit, flaps forty, speed one-forty."

"Come on, nose gear," Rob pleaded as the airplane approached alignment between the two glistening strings of headlights a quarter-mile ahead. He rolled the aircraft sharply to the left, called "Flaps fifty," and a moment later "Close the throttle." Rob lowered the left wing while pushing top rudder, sideslipping the huge Starliner toward the end of the runway as if it were the little T-34 trainer he'd soloed in at primary flight school thirty-seven years ago.

"Speed one thirty-five, but the nose gear's still . . . it's down and locked!" Cash yelled as it finally plunked into place.

Rob finessed the rudder and leveled the wings just as the Starliner thumped down on the runway. He tromped down hard on the foot brakes, simultaneously deploying the spoilers/speed brakes, and called, "Max reverse!"

Cash lifted the left throttle past the lockout and yanked it back to the maximum reverse stop as Rob fought the resulting yaw with rudder, straining to hold the aircraft centered on the rough, narrow surface. He caught fleeting glimpses of pickups and automobiles whose headlights blurred rapidly past the cockpit side windows. The end of the runway loomed ahead, approaching rapidly, and now visible beyond it, the angry sea. Rob continued firm pressure on the brakes; the antiskid system cycled repeatedly as the tires groped for traction through windblown sheets of water. The mighty Starliner slowed . . . slowed more . . . then reluctantly, like a proud stallion yielding to the bronc buster, shuddered to a stop.

Cash eased the throttle into the idle notch. Rob, his legs quivering, pressed down hard on the foot brakes as he engaged the brake locking handle. The aircraft had come to rest on the few remaining inches of pavement; a hundred yards ahead, the rough ground dropped from sight. Below the cliff, huge swells crashed into jagged rocks lining the shore, whipping up vast gray-green spumes of spray.

Both pilots sat motionless for what seemed an eternity, overwhelmed by their accomplishment, mesmerized by the tempestuous scene as gusts of wind lashed the cockpit.

Gradually at first, then rising in crescendo, a torrent of applause and cheering erupted from the passenger cabin and cascaded into the cockpit through the open door.

Cash, wiping sweat from his brow, spoke first. "Sure glad we didn't ditch this bastard."

Rob stared ahead at the roiling sea, but he was remembering the good years, and home, with Nellie waiting by the driveway, and thinking about renewed life and the woman whose warm, slender arms reached over his shoulders, embracing him. "Me, too," he said.